OWL OUT OF MAGIC

OWL STAR WITCH MYSTERIES BOOK 14

LEANNE LEEDS

Owl Out of Magic
ISBN: 978-1-950505-91-3
Published by Badchen Publishing
14125 W State Highway 29
Suite B-203 119
Liberty Hill, TX 78642 USA

For permissions contact: info@badchenpublishing.com

CONTENTS

Chapter 1   1
Chapter 2   21
Chapter 3   39
Chapter 4   59
Chapter 5   79
Chapter 6   97
Chapter 7   117
Chapter 8   135
Chapter 9   153
Chapter 10   171
Chapter 11   191
Chapter 12   207
Chapter 13   229
Chapter 14   249
Chapter 15   265
Chapter 16   283
Chapter 17   299
Chapter 18   317
Chapter 19   337
Chapter 20   355
Chapter 21   367

KEEP UP WITH LEANNE LEEDS   375
Find a typo? Let us know!   377
Artificial Intelligence Statement   379

OWL OUT OF MAGIC

CHAPTER ONE

The back of my neck was damp with sweat as I carried another heavy box of Halloween decorations out of the U-Haul truck. The mid-morning Florida sun already beat down relentlessly, turning the truck into an oven. I hoisted the box onto the grass in front of city hall, wiping my brow with the back of my hand.

"Remind me again how we got roped into this?" my sister Ami asked, setting her own box down with a huff.

Before I could respond, the front door of city hall flew open and Councilman Marcus Clinton came bounding down the steps.

"Good morning! Well, if it isn't my favorite Arden sisters!" he bellowed, spreading his arms wide. His voice sounded like a foghorn cutting through the humid air.

I suppressed an eye roll. Marcus had all the subtlety of a rampaging elephant. And about as much charm.

"Mr. Clinton, I doubt you could pick us out of a crowd," I pointed out dryly.

Marcus waved a hand. "Details. What are there, three of you? Five of you? Anyway, I knew Forkbridge could count on its resident witches to whip up a Halloween celebration to remember!" He then thumped his chest, his pale blue button-down straining against his ample belly. "Those weirdos over in Cassandra think they have the market cornered on spooky, but they don't have what we've got!"

He reminded me of an overeager circus ringmaster, with his bombastic voice and exaggerated mannerisms. I had to resist the urge to shake my head in exasperation at his inflated sense of self-importance.

Marcus clearly fancied himself the head honcho of Forkbridge, the big man in charge. But to me, he seemed more like a puffed up rooster, crowing loudly to compensate for his lack of any proper authority. His insistence on throwing the biggest, best Halloween bash was nothing more than an ego-driven power play.

I shifted the box in my arms. "Oh? What don't they have that our town does have?"

"Witches!" Marcus roared, like it was obvious. "I mean, they have ghosts, but we have witches and people can actually see our witches, so we should be able to put on a much better festival than they do..." Marcus paused for breath in his lengthy monologue, as if expecting me to applaud his grand plans for Forkbridge. "I would think, anyway."

"You do realize there's only five of us, right?" I asked.

In all fairness, Forkbridge had a lot more than just witches, not that Marcus would know. As a member of the town council, he was woefully uninformed about the supernatural community taking up residence in the area.

As it should be.

"Councilman, we're excited to showcase everything that makes Forkbridge special," my sister told him earnestly (though I could hear the strain in her voice after lugging heavy decorations in the sweltering heat.) "It's warmer than we expected, and we assumed there would be a bigger budget to hire extra help."

At my sister's words of "bigger budget," the man's eyes widened like saucers, his face morphing into a caricature of shock and indignation. Marcus swelled up like an irritated blowfish, no doubt ready to launch into a lengthy tirade about fiscal responsibility and budgetary constraints.

But then Marcus let out a sharp, sarcastic bark of laughter that made me flinch.

"I figured you two could just wave your little magic wands and make everything appear." He chuckled at his own joke. "Besides, budgets are tight right now. The council can't justify spending taxpayer money on frivolities like paid labor, you know."

I bit my tongue before a snarky retort could slip out.

Ami smiled tensely. "Don't worry, we'll get everything done in time. It's going to be an outstanding event."

"You bet your broomsticks it will be," Marcus said, slapping her on the back.

Ami winced.

"I expect the whole place decorated by nightfall. Cobwebs, zombies, gravestones—the works! We'll show those Cassandra freaks who really knows how to do Halloween!" He checked his watch. "Better hop to it, ladies. The undead wait for no witch!" Chuckling, he turned and lumbered back into the air-conditioned city hall, the door slamming behind him.

I scowled at his retreating back. "Charming as always," I muttered.

Ami sighed, tucking a piece of hair behind her ear. "Well, to be fair, he's under a lot of pressure. The council wants this to be an enormous boost to tourism."

"Doesn't give him an excuse to be a jerk," I grumbled, setting down another box. I swiped my hand across my forehead again. My t-shirt clung to my back unpleasantly.

"No, it doesn't," Ami agreed quietly. She surveyed the boxes remaining in the truck, shoulders drooping. "It's not that much more, though."

I blew out a long breath, gearing myself up.

We had a lot of work ahead of us. And though I'd never give Marcus the satisfaction of knowing, I really could've used a little magic to speed this process along. My psychometry powers (the ability to get visions and emotions from objects and people by touching them) weren't exactly useful for manual labor.

It seemed we had a long, sweltering,

completely unenchanted day of physical grunt work ahead of us. I glanced up at the cloudless blue sky, the sun glaring down like a silent tormentor.

"All right," I said with determination. "Let's do this."

Ami offered me a tired smile.

Over the next few hours, we worked steadily to transform the grounds around city hall into a Halloween wonderland. Arms aching, we strung up orange lights, arranged carved jack-o-lanterns, and hung hand-painted banners with ghosts and bats.

As we laid cobwebs over bushes and arranged fake graves around the perimeter, I had to concede the decor was looking pretty good.

By early afternoon, we had most the decor in place. I stood back, hands on my hips, surveying our handiwork.

"Not too shabby," I remarked.

Ami nodded, gazing around appreciatively. "It's really coming together."

I wiped my hands on my pants, glancing toward the parking lot. "Let's get the coffin set up and then take a lunch break. I'm starving."

We located the collapsible coffin prop leaned up against the side of the U-Haul. With some effort, Ami and I wrestled it onto a rolling cart and pushed it toward the front steps of city hall.

"Here?" Ami asked as we positioned it on the walkway leading up to the entrance.

"Looks good to me," I confirmed. I flipped the lid open, admiring the velvet lining inside. "Very classy. I wouldn't mind taking a nap in this, actually. Get out of this heat."

Ami laughed and fanned herself. "You'd suffocate and bake in the thing, Astra. It's basically a lined oven. Let's close it up for now. We can put whatever goes in there in later. I can't lug another thing."

We stepped back to survey our handiwork, admiring the grounds now thoroughly decorated with a spooky, festive flair. Cobwebs blanketed the trees like eerie lace while hand-carved jack-o-lanterns lined the paths. Their flickering candles would create an inviting, amber glow come nightfall.

"I think we did good," I said, putting an arm around Ami.

She smiled. "We make a pretty talented team."

My stomach rumbled loudly just then, and we both laughed.

"Come on, let's go get some food," I said. "We can tackle the rest after lunch."

We locked up the truck, grabbed our things and headed out in my Jeep, ready for a break and meal. I had to admit, Marcus and the heat aside, it felt good to be working on something fun for the town for a change.

* * *

As soon as Ami and I walked into the Spice Fusion Shack, the scents of exotic spices and sizzling meats enveloped us, causing my mouth to water as the rich aromas of garlic, ginger, and cinnamon teased my nose. The restaurant pulsed with energy—servers expertly balancing loaded trays, customers chatting and laughing between bites. Ami's eyes widened at the sight of the sizzling plates zipping past, no doubt already planning her order.

Behind the counter, the staff stirred aromatic curries in woks, flipped naan and roti on the grills, and assembled colorful dishes. My eyes roved over the globally inspired menu boards overhead.

"I'm feeling those Korean barbecue tacos," I remarked to Ami.

She nodded. "Ooh yes, and I'm absolutely craving some mango lassi right now."

When it was our turn, we placed our orders—tacos and an iced tea for me, vegetable biryani and lassi for Ami. The cashier rang us up, and we grabbed the last little table by the front window, the sun-warmed red vinyl seats creaking as we slid in.

I leaned back in my chair, rolling my shoulders to relieve some soreness. "That was quite the workout this morning."

Ami rotated her own shoulders with a wince. "No kidding. My arms will be feeling it tomorrow."

"At least Forkbridge will have one killer Halloween celebration thanks to us," I said.

Ami smiled. "Very true. Like I said, we make a good team."

Our food arrived shortly after, my tacos overflowing with tender bulgogi beef, crunchy kimchi, cool lime crema, and fiery gochujang sauce. The flavors exploded in my mouth with the first bite—the sweet and smoky beef contrasting the salty tang of kimchi, rounded out by the cooling crema and spike of spicy sauce.

Ami hummed appreciatively as she dug into her biryani. "So delicious. I'm so glad we're getting little gems like this in Forkbridge."

We ate in contented silence for a few minutes,

focused on replenishing calories while enjoying the air conditioning. As we neared the finish line of our meals, Ami gave me a sly look over her glass.

"Sooo... how's the situation between you and Lothian?"

I slowed my chewing, cocking an eyebrow at her. "Subtle segue, sis."

She laughed. "Come on, give me the scoop! I want details."

I wiped my mouth with a napkin, buying time to gather my thoughts.

Lothian and I had been engaged in a will they/won't they romantic dance for months now. I was surprised to find the tough werewolf had a soft side to him. He wooed me with long walks on the beach, cozy dinners by candlelight, and stolen kisses on the shadowed patio behind the Spellbound Emporium. It had been wonderful in its own way, but very... undefined.

"We're still figuring things out, I guess," I said finally. "But it's good. He challenges me, keeps me on my toes. Keeps life interesting."

Ami smiled. "I'm happy for you, Astra. I'm glad you're moving on from your situation with Jason. He's found happiness and love in the underworld. You deserve an amazing guy up here."

"And you've heard Lothian is an amazing guy, huh?" I cleared my throat, redirecting. "I take it you heard it from Wyatt?" My sister was only in her early twenties, whereas Wyatt was nearer to my midthirties age. I didn't have any right to forbid my sister from dating whomever she wished, but seeing her with a werewolf so much older definitely concerned me. "What about you and Wyatt? How are things going with the old codger, anyway?"

A faint blush colored Ami's cheeks. "Don't be mean." She was clearly smitten by the older, protective werewolf. "Really great," she said softly. Then she quirked an eyebrow. "At least he pays attention to me. That's more than I can say for Hermes."

Ami's father was Hermes, the elusive messenger god.

My own father Apollo, along with Althea's father Poseidon and Ayla's father Hades, had all reached out to some degree after our mother's scandalous history of divine affairs came to light.

But Hermes?

He hadn't even sent a simple letter Ami's way. I found that strange considering he was literally the god of communication and travelers—you'd think he'd at least try to get in touch with the daughter he never knew.

But nope.

With an inward sigh, I made a mental note to do something extra nice for Ami later. She hid her hurt well, but I knew her well enough to see it in her eyes.

The Olympians hadn't exactly won any Parent of the Year awards in their dealings with us half-mortal witch daughters.

"I'm sorry, Ami. I really am. You don't deserve the way he's treating you. At least we have each other," I said finally. I gave her hand a squeeze across the table. She smiled gratefully.

"I know. It's just..."

She was clearly bothered that Hermes hadn't reached out, but she couldn't bring herself to say it out loud. I wished I could shake Hermes by the shoulders and force him to speak with Ami.

She deserved that much from him.

We finished our meals, then bused our dishes. Back outside, the afternoon sun still blazed high overhead. "Ugh. This heat."

Ami bumped me with her hip. "Come on. Let's get home and see what Ayla and Althea are up to." She paused. "There's air conditioning there, and I don't want to finish in this heat. We can go back tonight after the sun goes down and finish. There are lots of lights around there."

I intertwined my arm with hers. "I'm right behind you."

* * *

AFTER A QUICK STOP in the house to scrub off the layer of grime that had accumulated on me during the morning's work (and change into fresh clothes that didn't smell like a high school locker room) we were ready to lend our younger sisters a hand in the cozy converted-garage storefront.

The bell above the door let out an overly cheerful jingle as Ami and I entered our family's magic shop, Spellbound Emporium, through the side entrance that led to the house. I wondered why we didn't have something more mystical, like wind chimes or a gong. Nothing ruined the mysterious vibe of a magic shop faster than a peppy bell that sounded like it belonged on Santa's sleigh.

I breathed in the comforting scents of dried herbs, melted candles, and nag champa incense as we stepped inside. Spellbound was a treasure trove of wonders—shelves bursting with crystals catching the light, leather-bound spell books packed with mysteries, charms dangling from the ceiling, and other magical wares. Our youngest sister, Ayla, stood behind the glass counter, her bracelets jingling as she rang up a customer's purchase.

Across the room, Althea was advising a woman on love potions, gesturing so animatedly she looked like she was directing air traffic. But when she spotted us, her eyes narrowed into serpentine slits.

"Well, look who's back," Thea said, excusing herself from the customer and making a beeline over. "Have fun playing manual laborer for the city?"

Althea greeted us with all the warmth of an iceberg, and I held up a hand before she could really get going. "Pull your claws in, Thea. We're too tired for a lecture."

"Astra's right." Ami gave her a pleading look. "Please don't start. We're just doing our part for the local festival."

Thea crossed her arms, scowling. But seeing our exhausted faces, she backed down. "Fine. But don't think I'm happy about you two being volunteered without discussion, and with Mom gone, I'd hoped we could stay out of town politics for a chance. Trying to do anything good for this town with those crooks is like swimming through peanut butter—it's slow, sticky, and likely to get stuck to your hands." She turned back to the customer. Is this something you want or not? If you had this much trouble deciding on a course of action with your girlfriend, it's no wonder she left you."

The customer looked at Althea with an expression of total bewilderment, as if she had just spoken to him in clicks and whistles instead of plain English.

Althea cocked her head to the side, sighing in exasperation. "I'm speaking English here, buddy. Plain old English, nothing fancy. So what's it gonna be? Do you want this potion to help you win back your ex or not?" She tapped her foot impatiently on the shop's creaky wooden floorboards.

The poor customer just stared at her, eyes bulging like he'd seen a ghost.

Then, without warning, he bolted for the door as if the hounds of hell were on his heels, nearly taking out a display of crystal balls in his panicked rush to escape.

"Can't say I'm surprised. The guy looked like

he couldn't pick a coffee order, let alone get an ex back. I mean, my potions are good, but they aren't bottled miracles."

"Your salesmanship is incredibly impressive," I said sarcastically.

"He didn't need a potion. He needed a therapist."

From his perch behind the counter, Archie gave an emphatic hoot of agreement. I stepped up to give his feathers an affectionate ruffle, and he leaned into my hand, nipping my fingers affectionately.

"His good mood? Yeah, that's because he stole the bacon off my plate this morning," Ayla commented.

Just then, a customer wandered over from a shelf of tarot card boxes.

"Wow, a real live owl!" the woman exclaimed, her eyes lighting up like a kid on Christmas morning. Without thinking, she went to boop Archie's dagger-like beak, seemingly unaware he wasn't a fluffy petting zoo creature.

"Aren't you just the handsomest fella-" she cooed.

Every feather on his body went rigid, giving him the appearance of an electrocuted cotton ball as I quickly caught the woman's wrist with a seeker's reflexes, pushing her eager hand back from becoming bird food. "I wouldn't do that if I were you," I warned. "He may look cute, but this bird could snap those fingers off like peppermint sticks. That's why we have the sign." I pointed to the sign that said DO NOT TOUCH THE OWL in all caps. "It's for your protection and his."

The woman paled, jerking her hand back. "Jeesh, sorry. You don't have to be so rude." She turned and hurried away. "Why have him in here if no one can pet him?"

I rolled my eyes and gave Archie a conciliatory scratch under his chin. "Don't take it personally. Some people have no common sense."

"I expect more bacon for putting up with that," he grumbled.

The front door bell rang out gleefully as more and more buyers continued swarming through the shop. Spellbound hummed along with its customary Halloween crowd of normal and mystical visitors as Ami and I snapped into retail autopilot, taking care of customers like a perfectly calibrated set of gears.

Ami arranged a crystal ball display, then retrieved some herbs for a regular customer, Mrs. Foster. The poor elderly woman was convinced her neighbor, Councilman Marcus Clinton, was hexing her azaleas again.

"Here's some protective basil and rue, plus a vial of uncrossing oil," Ami said gently, handing the bundles to Mrs. Foster. "Use them to make sachets and sprinkle around the garden. That should undo any curses regardless of who cast them."

I watched Ami interact with Mrs. Foster, a soft smile on my face. Even after all these years, Ami's inherent kindness never failed to warm my heart. Mrs. Foster looked relieved as she took the herbs, like a weight had been lifted from her shoulders.

"Bless you, dear." Mrs. Foster patted Ami's hand gratefully. "You've always been so good to me. And to my garden."

The steady stream of customers kept us occupied over the entire afternoon. As closing time neared, the shop finally emptied out. I stretched my back with a satisfied groan, the muscles pleasantly sore after a long day on my feet. It had been nonstop helping customers for hours, but I didn't mind.

"What a day," I muttered. "Halloween is always so crazy."

Archie blinked golden eyes at me, giving a soft hoot.

Ami finished wiping down the display cases, then tossed the rag under the counter. "At least helping out here was a nice break from slaving away outside. And if we hadn't come back, Ayla and Althea would have been slammed."

I nodded wryly. "No kidding."

Thea shut the register, eyeing us sympathetically. "You two look dead on your feet. Why don't you go put them up for a bit? We can handle closing duties tonight."

Ami tried to protest, but I hooked my arm through hers. "Don't argue with the offer of a break. Let's leave them to it." Leaning over, I offered my shoulder to Archie. The owl's claws pricked through my shirt as he landed, and I steered us toward the front door and flipped the "Closed" sign.

I had a feeling we hadn't seen the last of chaotic days with Halloween approaching. But tonight, rest and recovery and dinner were in order before anything else. As we exited the busy shop below for the peace of home, I breathed a contented sigh.

It wasn't a perfect life, but it was ours.

CHAPTER TWO

The mouthwatering aroma of Aunt Gwennie's famous enchiladas wafted through the air as Ami and I entered the cozy farmhouse kitchen. My stomach let out an eager rumble—Aunt Gwennie's cooking was legendary.

Archie swooped in ahead of me, landing on his perch and eyeing the steaming platters hungrily, his feathers puffed up in anticipation.

I chuckled, giving him an affectionate scratch.

"Smells amazing, Aunt Gwennie!" I said, breathing in the rich scents of cheese, peppers, and spiced meat. Ami hummed in agreement, a small smile quirking her lips.

Aunt Gwennie beamed, gesturing us toward the table proudly set with vibrant clay plates and woven napkins. "There are my hardworking girls!" Aunt Gwennie said warmly, drying her hands on a dish towel. "Come sit, eat. You must be starving after decorating all day."

I was almost forty.

I was not a girl.

But I let it pass.

Ami and I quickly grabbed generous portions of the cheesy enchiladas, rice, and beans. The spicy, cheesy blend of flavors did not disappoint.

As we dug in, Althea and Ayla filtered into the kitchen, followed closely by Althea's crow Lily and Ayla's enormous hellhound Cerberus.

The animals wasted no time in surrounding the table, gazing longingly and lovingly at us with big, manipulative eyes and parted mouths. They knew we couldn't resist slipping them bits of buttery tortillas under the table.

"So, how are the festival preparations coming along?" Aunt Gwennie asked.

I swallowed a mouthful of enchilada. "Good. The grounds are pretty much decorated. Just have to add some finishing touches later on tonight after dinner."

"It was really hot, and it will be nice to check it at night with the sun down and the lights on,"

Ami added. "But there's not that much more to do."

"That's nice. I'm sure it will look lovely," Aunt Gwennie said, her smile not quite reaching her eyes. She spoke in a low voice, leaning closer. "Although your Aunt Gertie told me earlier that she's detecting some problematic juju surrounding this event. It has her quite unsettled."

My Aunt Gertie is a ghost, so only Ayla can see her. The rest of us, including Aunt Gwennie, can talk to her using some fancy magic mirror cleaner Althea whipped up that let's us talk to folks in the underworld, but I tend not to use that.

Too high a chance my mother will show up.

Some doors were better left closed.

Ami paused, fork hovering halfway to her mouth. "Aunt Gertie is probably just sensing Marcus Clinton," she said after swallowing. "He came out while we were working and if he didn't say 'witch' five times during a two-minute conversation, I'd be surprised. He just has weird vibes."

"Ugh, that guy." Ayla rolled her eyes, shaking her head. "Imagine if he knew what witches were instead of thinking we're basically cosplayers that play pretend to make our shop more authentic."

"Let's not tell him," I said.

Althea shot me a sharp look, her eyes narrowing.

"What?"

"Just lighten up, Astra. She wasn't suggesting that."

"Lighten up? I just made a comment." I stared at Althea, eyebrows raised. Her usual demeanor tended toward the serious, but the brooding glare was new. "What crawled up your butt today?" I asked bluntly.

The moment I spoke, I wished I had been more careful with my words. Althea's scowl deepened, and she crossed her arms defensively.

Clearly something was bothering her, and my flippant question hadn't helped.

I softened my tone. "Hey, seriously though— Thea, you okay? I'm getting grumpy-hippo vibes over here. Did I do something?"

At the affectionate nickname, Althea's expression finally cracked a bit, the corners of her mouth twitching. She sighed, dropping her arms. "Yeah, sorry. Just woke up on the wrong side of the bed today, I guess. Didn't mean to bite your head off."

I gave her a sympathetic smile, making a mental note to check in with her later. Sometimes, just an ear to listen was exactly what Althea needed when she was in one of her moods.

Aunt Gwennie pursed her lips and redirected the conversation back to Aunt Gertie's sense of incoming doom. "Yes, well...I suppose we'll see what comes of it. I do hope she's just being paranoid."

"She's probably just sensing the whole thing." Althea let out an exasperated huff. "I mean, of course there's terrible energy. This whole festival is a stupid rip-off of Cassandra's legacy. It's intended to steal their festival."

Lily cawed in agreement from her perch on Althea's shoulder.

"It's tacky, and it's wrong," Althea continued heatedly. "Forkbridge should work with Cassandra, not try to undermine them."

Ayla chimed in next. "You know, Melvin said the same thing. His dad is really worried their gas station in Cassandra could go under because of the loss of Halloween business thanks to Forkbridge."

I sat back in my chair, frowning.

"Maybe you all are right," I acknowledged. "But the council isn't likely to cancel the entire event now. And I don't disagree with you that there are some political issues here. I just think our energy is better directed elsewhere. The politics between Cassandra and Forkbridge? Not our problem."

Aunt Gwennie gave an approving nod. "Wise words, Astra. Your mother always—"

"Mom's not here anymore. We need to navigate the town politics in our own way." I offered her a small smile before continuing. "Has Gertie sensed any specifics we should be worried about?"

Aunt Gwennie's brow furrowed in thought. "No, just a general feeling of foreboding. But you know how she gets this time of year. All the spirits passing through and showing up unsettle her."

"We'll keep an eye out for anything suspicious," I assured her. To Ami, I added, "Maybe you can do a reading, see if your cards pick up on any threats?"

Ami nodded. "Good idea. I'll do it tonight. After we finish."

The conversation lulled then as we all focused on eating. Cerberus finished the last scraps from his bowl, then plopped his massive head in Ayla's lap. She scratched behind his ear absently.

After a few moments, Ami spoke up hesitantly. "I was thinking...maybe we should extend an olive branch to Cassandra. Let them know Forkbridge intends no ill will or disrespect."

I considered her suggestion. It wasn't a bad idea.

"What if they do, though?" Althea asked. "We don't know they don't."

"That, and Lillian Thornton would never accept it," I said.

Ami gave me a sad, knowing look. We both knew Lillian, the mayor of Cassandra, blamed the entire town for her son Jason's death—and she blamed me most of all. It was a wound that ran deep for her.

An uncomfortable silence settled around the table. I cleared my throat.

"Look, it can't hurt to try mending fences," I said finally. "I'll talk to Emma, too, to see if she has any ideas. She's probably more familiar with the politics than we are."

As we all finished up our meals, my thoughts turned to Aunt Gertie's ominous warnings. If there really was trouble brewing around this festival, I hoped it was just politics as usual and not something more ominous.

* * *

THE LAST FADING rays of daylight cast an amber glow as Ami, Ayla and I drove back to city hall to put the finishing touches on the decorations. Althea had opted to stay home, insisting someone needed to "hold down the fort" while the rest of us were out.

"More like hold down the couch for nonstop Netflix binging," Ayla joked from the backseat.

We all laughed, the mood in the car light despite the lingering heat.

"She really has been so grumpy lately," Ami said, turning down the radio.

"Seriously." Ayla leaned forward between the seats. "This morning I asked if she wanted pancakes and she practically bit my head off about how she 'doesn't want my lumpy pancake failure.'"

I shook my head, turning onto the main street that went through town. The orange sky made me narrow my eyes. "She even snapped at me yesterday for buying the wrong brand of ice cream. And what's with the constant baking? I'm about ready to ban her from the kitchen."

"Oh no, don't do that," Ami said. "You know how she stress bakes. I'm certainly not one to encourage anyone's anxiety, but as long as she's going through a bad patch, let her bake. I love her pies."

Well, I suppose it's better than potion experiments that blow up the house.

I sighed.

Althea's mood had been stormier than the autumn skies lately, and I wasn't used to that. Her usual serious but witty disposition had clouded over, replaced by brooding silences and snappish outbursts.

She was clearly wrestling with something internally, I thought as we arrived. I wished more than ever that she would open up and let us help shoulder the burden, but Althea had always been more of a closed book than the rest of us in many ways.

"Oh, that's pretty," Ayla murmured as we parked.

I was pleased to see the pumpkins and lights now cast a properly spooky, inviting glow as dusk settled over the grounds.

A few townspeople out for evening strolls admired our work. Mrs. Foster waved merrily from across the street. "You girls did a splendid job!" she called as we walked toward the display.

"It looks perfectly horrid! I mean that as a compliment, dears."

I waved back with a smile.

Maybe this festival wouldn't be a total disaster after all.

"So, what's left to do?" Ayla asked, surveying the area.

I glanced around, hands on hips. "Just need to get that fake body in the coffin, I think, and double-check all the lights are working. Then we can set the timers for the light displays, and we're done."

After retrieving the heavy zombie-fied mannequin from the truck, we dragged it up the brick path to the steps of city hall. Its limbs bounced limply over the pavers.

"Ready for your creepy undead closeup?" I muttered, heaving the dummy up the stairs by its rigid waist. Its lolling head stared blankly ahead through peeling face paint.

Ami staggered up the steps behind me, face flushed. "It looks great," she admired, a little out of breath. "I don't get why it has to be so heavy, though."

"So no one will steal it, maybe?" Ayla guessed from the bottom, her brow furrowed as she lifted the mannequin's legs. They jostled in her grip.

I paused to catch my breath once we reached the top, the dummy slumped between us. "Well, it'll definitely deter any would-be thieves. I feel like I just lifted a sack of bricks. We should have gotten a potion from Althea." I massaged my sore arms and eyed our zombie's crooked leer. "Let's get this beast in place before my spine gives out."

The hinges creaked as I opened the display coffin.

As we turned to heave the dummy, an ear-piercing scream ripped through the cool night air.

Whirling back around, we saw a woman pointing a trembling finger at the coffin, her face drained of color. She choked out panicked, incoherent words before dissolving into hysterical sobs.

My stomach dropped.

This was no frightened reaction to a fake prop.

Exchanging alarmed looks with Ami and Ayla, I stepped around the coffin and looked in.

Inside, dressed in a tailored suit and tie, lay the very real, very dead body of Councilman Marcus Clinton. His vacant eyes stared up at the starry sky, cloudy and unseeing. They seemed to look right through me.

"Oh goddess," Ami whispered, hand to her mouth.

I shook off my shock and quickly checked for a pulse—more out of fruitless habit than any genuine hope. As expected, there was none.

Straightening slowly, I met Ami's wide, frightened gaze. She looked like she might be sick, one hand clasped over her mouth.

"Ayla, call 911," I instructed, forcing my voice to remain steady. I turned to Ami, speaking more gently. "Hey, you okay?"

She nodded mutely, face still drained of color. I squeezed her hand before moving to intercept the panicked woman who had found the body.

Ayla already had her phone to her ear, answering the dispatcher's urgent questions. Her eyes darted between me and the gruesome scene.

As a daughter of Hades, Ayla had no problem with death.

Aunt Gwennie's ominous words echoed in my mind: *Aunt Gertie says she senses some dangerous energy around this event. It has her quite unsettled.*

I found it all right, I thought grimly, staring at Marcus's lifeless body.

Dangerous energy indeed.

* * *

THE WAIL of sirens cut through the night as a brigade of police vehicles descended on city hall. Chief Daniel Harmon barreled out of the first cruiser, face like a thundercloud.

Great.

Just who I didn't want to deal with right now.

"What the hell happened here?" he barked at the officers securing the scene. His flinty gaze landed on me, eyes narrowed. "Arden. Can't say I'm surprised to find you here."

I bristled at the implication in his tone. I briefly considered some sarcastic retort, but managed to rein in the impulse. Mouthing off would only make things worse. "My sisters and I were only finishing the decorations, Chief. We just found the body. Not my fault someone stashed him in a decorative coffin."

He scowled, glancing over at the open coffin where forensics techs were now photographing and processing the scene. "I want full statements from all of you. Now."

I ground my teeth, biting back another retort. Harmon and I had history—namely him firing me from my consultant role with the department at the insistence of the mother of my deceased ex-boyfriend/his girlfriend, Cassandra Mayor Lillian Thornton.

Needless to say, things had been strained ever since.

My sisters and I recounted everything leading up to the gruesome discovery, answering questions from the officers taking our statements. It was tedious going over the details again and again, but we cooperated fully. The sooner we got through this, the sooner we could go home.

When we'd finished, I noticed a familiar face approaching through the chaos of red and blue flashing lights. Vince Briggs, a patrolman who now, apparently, worked homicide.

"Vince! You're a detective now?"

Officer—oops, Detective Vince Briggs cracked a smile beneath his bushy gray mustache.

"Yup. When Emma left, they were short on folks and I applied. Heard the call come in and wanted to help." His expression turned sober. "This is a damn shame. Marcus could be obtuse, but he didn't deserve this."

I frowned.

I didn't know Emma had left. I thought she was just on maternity leave.

I shook my head. "No kidding." I hesitated and looked at my watch. It was almost nine at night.

"We saw him at about nine in the morning. He had to have been killed inside city hall, right?"

"I hope you're wrong." Vince sighed wearily as he jotted down what I said. "A city hall murder. This should be fun." He nodded before moving off to consult with the forensics team.

I turned to Ami, who was hovering nearby, arms wrapped around herself. She still looked pretty shaken.

"You doing okay?" I asked gently.

She nodded, biting her lip.

"How about you?" I asked, turning to Ayla.

She leaned in and lowered her voice. "I didn't want to say anything with the cops around, but...I can see Marcus's ghost. He's here, and he is seriously mad."

My eyes widened slightly. Having a deathspeaker for a sister came in handy at times. "Can you tell if he knows who killed him?"

Ayla shook her head regretfully. "No. Right now, he is excessively irate and perplexed. He needs some time to process." She glanced around. "But he's here, no doubt about that. And he doesn't look like he's leaving any time soon."

"Gotcha." The ghost of Marcus Clinton could prove useful, if we could get him to focus long enough to communicate. "You think you could call him to our house?"

She shrugged. "Maybe."

I walked back over to Vince, the rookie detective who had taken my statement. "Any chance we can get out of here soon?" I asked, nodding toward where Ami stood hugging herself, eyes fixed on the black body bag being wheeled toward the coroner's van.

Vince grimaced sympathetically. "Yeah, I think you three can go." He lowered his voice and stepped closer. "Between you and me, Chief Harmon seems a little suspicious that you and Ami were the only ones who saw Councilman Clinton today."

"What?" I blurted, incredulous. "How could he possibly know that already? You guys have been here all of five minutes!"

"Hey, I'm just the messenger," Vince said, holding up his hands. "But the chief's real fast at leaping to assumptions."

I crossed my arms, heat rising to my face. "Well, he can take his conclusions and shove them right up his—"

I caught myself and took a breath.

No point taking this out on Vince.

But if Harmon wanted to turn his suspicions

on me or Ami, he had forgotten who he was dealing with.

I met Vince's eye, feeling a swell of frustration. "For the record, there's no way I had anything to do with...this." I gestured sharply at the body bag, unable to keep the bitterness from my tone.

Vince just nodded, looking uncomfortable at being caught between me and the chief's potential conflict. "Let's just worry about getting all the facts first," he said diplomatically.

I swallowed back a retort, not wanting to drag Vince any further into this. "Yep."

I stomped off toward Ami and Ayla, emotions churning. As much as I tried not to let it show, the chief's suspicion cut. I'd worked with him. He knew what and who I was. I'd trusted him with paranormal knowledge he—as a human— shouldn't have.

Now I wondered if that had been a mistake.

As we turned to leave, I cast one last look at the decorative coffin that had become a makeshift morgue. We were just days away from Forkbridge's biggest event of the year.

And now it was the backdrop for murder.

CHAPTER THREE

I let out a weary sigh as I trudged up the front steps of the house, the events of the evening bearing down on my mind. I could still picture his vacant eyes staring out from that open coffin.

Inside, I poured myself a warm mug of herbal tea and sank onto the plush brown couch, resting my hand on my face as I tried to process everything that had happened. The minty aroma of the tea wafted up and soothed my nerves somewhat, but my mind still swirled with unanswered questions.

Who could have plotted to eliminate Marcus? He wasn't exactly well-liked in the community, but I had no idea what could have motivated such a public end.

And how on earth did the killer manage to strike him down right in front of everyone and drag him to the front of city hall without being seen?

There were so many puzzling details about the brazen murder that just didn't make sense to me.

Ami came over and sat down next to me on the couch, tucking her feet underneath her as she settled in. "Some night, huh?" she mumbled, her voice tinged with both exhaustion and disbelief.

I nodded, taking a bracing sip. "No kidding. Finding a town councilman murdered and stashed in a display is definitely a new one, even for us."

She leaned her head against the back of the couch, her usually sparkling green eyes now dimmed by what took place tonight. We sat in silence for a few moments before Ami spoke again. "Do you really think Chief Harmon suspects us?"

"I don't know." I stared broodingly into my glass. "Wouldn't be the first time he's blamed me for something going wrong in this town."

Ami picked at a thread on the cushion

absently. "I know you two have history, but he can't possibly think we had anything to do with this."

What's possible and what isn't possible isn't always obvious, I thought.

"Like I said, I don't know. But let's hope not." I drained the rest of my drink and stood. "I'm going to call Emma. She apparently quit the force and forgot to mention it to me. Maybe that's why Harmon's gone so sour on me."

Ami was taken aback and her eyes widened. "What? Really?"

I nodded, a flare of irritation rising at Emma's lack of communication. She was my closest friend—we told each other everything. If she had left the police force, why wouldn't she have told me? According to what I was told. According to Vince Briggs, he got promoted to detective to fill her spot."

I grabbed my phone and headed to the porch for some privacy, dialing Emma's number. She picked up after a few rings.

"Astra! Hey, I've been meaning to call you..."

I cut right to the chase. "Yeah, funny how I had to hear from someone else that you quit the department. What's going on?"

Emma sighed heavily on the other end. "I

know, I'm sorry. It was a last-minute decision. I was reluctant to go back to the politics and garbage that the police department entails after the wedding. I'm happy being home with Hunter." In the background, I could hear the sounds of the baby fussing.

"And the chaos of five werewolves," I added wryly.

"Six, if you count Hunter." She laughed. "That too. It's a zoo around here, really. But a good zoo. I didn't really quit formally, Astra. I just didn't come back once my leave was over." Her tone grew more serious then. "I heard about Marcus Clinton. How are you holding up?"

"How'd you hear about that so fast?"

"I still have a police scanner."

"Right." I leaned against the porch railing, glancing up at the inky night sky. "Honestly? It shook Ami up a bit, I think. What's got me annoyed is that Harmon apparently thinks Ami and I are suspects since we saw Marcus this morning."

"Oh, he does not."

"Vince Briggs—your replacement, by the way —says he's a bit suspicious."

"What?" Emma sounded outraged on my behalf. "That's absurd."

"That Vince Briggs is your replacement, or that Harmon is suspicious of us?"

"The latter. There's no way either of you were involved."

"I know, but try telling Harmon that. Anyway, I don't know what's going to happen now. I find it hard to believe Forkbridge is going to cancel this festival." I quickly filled her in on everything else, including Aunt Gertie's premonition.

Emma made a thoughtful noise. "With a warning like that, something wicked could definitely be brewing in Forkbridge. By the way, I assume you didn't touch the coffin and get any info on who could have done it?"

"I did not." I frowned. "I did touch him to see if I could feel a pulse, but I saw nothing. I didn't realize that until just now."

"Is that unusual?"

Was it unusual that I hadn't tried to glean any information from Marcus's corpse?

In most murder cases, I would be laser-focused on examining the body for magical clues that could point to the killer. But with Emma on leave from the police force, investigating crimes hadn't been at the forefront of my mind lately.

Not only had I been preoccupied with running the Spellbound Emporium lately instead of sleuthing, but I had received no mystical signs or messages from Athena urging me to investigate anything, either. As someone who had been unwillingly gifted a lightning bolt justice power from the Greek goddess, she would occasionally send me urgent assignments demanding I step in and prevent untimely deaths.

But... not recently.

Huh.

In fact, now that I thought about it, I realized I had received no communiqués from Athena since my mother died. Was this why I had thrown myself so fully into my shop? Because subconsciously I felt rudderless and—

"Astra?"

I refocused on Emma. "Sorry. I was just distracted. Back at city hall, too. Ami was a little green, and I was worried about her."

We chatted a few more minutes before I headed back inside and found Ayla sitting at the table, deep in concentration as she, presumably, communicated her invitation to Marcus's recently deceased spirit.

"Any luck?" I asked, taking the seat across from her.

She shook her head with a frustrated huff, her dark hair swinging like an irritated horse's tail.

"He's too angry and confused right now to respond, I think. You know something?"

"I know lots of things," I replied breezily. "I'm like a walking encyclopedia of weird trivia and random facts."

Ayla glared at me like I'd just told a terrible dad joke. "You'd think, as the daughter of Hades, when I tell a ghost to snap to it and get over here, they'd listen and come running. But apparently it doesn't work like that." She snapped her fingers for emphasis.

"Sorry communing with the dead isn't as easy as ordering a pizza delivery for you," I said. "Have you tried shouting out at the universe 'Do you know who I am?! I'm the daughter of Hades!' and then mic dropping like a boss? Maybe that will help."

Ayla shook her head, but I caught the corner of her mouth twitching in a suppressed smile. "You're ridiculous, you know that?"

"Maybe, but I also got you to crack a smile, so I'm counting this as a win."

"You do win." She sighed. "And I get your point. I'll keep trying."

With a nod, I headed off to bed, hoping things would be clearer in the morning.

But as I lay there staring up at the ceiling,

sleep remained elusive. My mind spun round and round like clothes in a washing machine, full of unanswered questions about who could've wanted Marcus dead, how Emma could have quit a job she loved, and how my relationship with Harmon had deteriorated so much that he thought I might be a murderer.

* * *

I AWOKE to dazzling sunlight spilling across my face, the attic bedroom immersed in a warm golden glow. A gentle breeze drifted in through the open window, carrying the faintest hint of salt and seaweed from the ocean miles away. I inhaled, letting the invigorating air fill my lungs.

Stretching my arms over my head, I stifled a yawn as my joints popped. The white linen sheets rustled around me as I sat up, rubbing the last remnants of sleep from my eyes.

Archie became agitated and flapped his wings. He turned his sharp gaze on me, clacking his beak. "Well, it's about time you joined the living," he snapped. "Some of us have been waiting all morning to discuss the sordid details of last night's murder."

"Good morning to you, too," I muttered,

getting out of bed. "It's always nice to wake up to your judgment and sarcasm." I crossed to the window overlooking the backyard. The sun had fully risen above the treetops now, promising another scorcher of a late October day.

I leaned on the window frame, gazing out. The sun beat down, warm on my skin, at odds with the Halloween decorations adorning the houses in our neighborhood. Palm trees swayed under an azure sky, and birds twittered from their branches.

In the yard next door, Mr. Jenkins spotted me in the window. He wiped his brow with a handkerchief after hanging fake cobwebs on the bushes, sweat beading at his temples. "Some weather we're having," he called over with a chuckle. "Feels more like the Fourth of July out here than Halloween, huh?"

I smiled. "It is warmer than usual, Mr. Jenkins."

Even with Halloween fast approaching, there was no hint of autumn in this persistent Florida warmth. It was hard to get into the spooky spirit when it felt like the peak of summer.

"I think he's disappointed every time he looks up and doesn't see you naked in the bay window," Archie cracked.

"Mr. Jenkins is a nice old man, and you're wrong," I remarked. Then I sighed. "I still can't believe Marcus Clinton is dead and someone dropped him in the middle of our display. This whole nasty affair is shaping up to be some premium small town gossip fodder."

Archie bobbed his head in agreement. "And now his spirit is flitting all over Florida in a furious tempest. Ayla will have a devil of a time getting any useful information out of him."

"The intensity of his anger and confusion is hindering his ability to communicate, she said." I chewed my lip. "I need to figure out who could have wanted Marcus dead enough to kill him. He was disliked, sure, but murder?"

"Politics stir up the darkest passions in people," Archie replied sagely. He turned his piercing golden gaze on me. "But enough mooning over the murder. Not our problem unless Harmon does think you and Ami whacked the guy. We have more pressing issues to discuss."

I raised an eyebrow at him. "Oh? Like what?"

"Like why you haven't noticed what's bothering Althea."

I blinked in surprise. That wasn't the topic I'd expected. "What are you talking about? She's just been in a bad mood."

Archie ruffled his feathers. "Typical witch blindness. You're all hopeless without familiars. You have a divine familiar, and you still don't get it."

I crossed my arms, leaning against the window frame. "Okay, wise guy. Enlighten me."

The owl puffed out his feathered chest. "Isn't it obvious? Your sisters are all happy and infatuated. Ami has Wyatt, Ayla has her Melvin boy, and you have that wolf who makes cow eyes at you."

I felt my cheeks flush at the mention of Lothian. "All right, and your point?"

"My point," Archie continued in his lecturing owl tone, "is that Althea has no romantic interest of her own. She's lonely, you daft woman."

I stared at him, caught off guard by this observation.

As I turned this possibility over in my mind, I realized he had a valid perspective. Althea spent most of her time isolated in this big, empty house, with only her books and potion recipes to keep her company. She showed no interest in dating or socializing, seemingly content in her solitary bubble.

Archie waited, no doubt feeling quite smug at having to explain my own sister to me.

"That...actually makes sense," I said finally.

Archie puffed up even more. "Naturally. Like I said, you witches never notice anything."

I shot him a wry look. "Okay, enough gloating. But maybe you're right. I'll talk to Althea and see if that's the issue." A thought struck me, and I frowned slightly. "Although, now that I think about it, I don't know that Althea's ever shown interest in anyone before. Romantically, I mean."

Archie twisted his head upside down to peer at me. "You truly are oblivious, aren't you?"

"What are you talking about now?" I asked in exasperation.

"Think, Astra," he said patronizingly. "Perhaps Althea doesn't discuss her romantic interests with you all because she's worried how you would react."

I stared at him blankly.

What interests would Althea feel she needed to keep secret from us?

Archie heaved a dramatic sigh. "Because they don't involve men, you silly human! Honestly, it's a wonder your species manages to function at all."

My eyes widened in understanding. "Oh! You mean she's..." I trailed off, feeling rather dumbstruck. "How on earth do you know all this?"

Archie gave me a withering look. "Yes, as the crow told me, Althea is quite enamored with a certain broody customer that frequents the shop. But she's uncertain of her feelings and too afraid to confide in any of you about it."

I rolled my eyes, but had to admit he might have a point. There had to be a reason Althea never talked to any of us about this. Maybe the owl was right.

"I may owe you an apology on this one," I told Archie. "And I'll talk to Althea as soon as I can."

Archie inclined his head. "I'm just pleased I could provide you with some perspective. Gotta earn my keep around here, right?"

"Like if you didn't, I could send you back?" I asked with a raised eyebrow.

He ruffled his feathers indignantly at my joke and snapped his beak, falling into wounded silence. For a pretty sarcastic bird, he could dish it out far better than he could take it.

"Oh Archie, I'm only teasing and you know it," I said soothingly, reaching out to stroke his head. "I'd never dream of sending you away. You're part of the family now."

At my reassuring touch, he leaned into my hand, his feigned annoyance dissipating.

I stood then and started getting ready for the

day, my thoughts swirling. Archie had left me with plenty to mull over, and I hoped I could have an open and understanding conversation with Althea soon. Having unspoken personal struggles was difficult enough without feeling like you had to hide part of yourself.

I resolved to do better by my sister from here on out.

And to make sure she knew, whoever she loved, her sisters would always fully support her.

* * *

I SHUFFLED into the cheerful kitchen, stifling a yawn. The coffee pot gurgled promisingly on the counter.

As I poured myself a mug, I glanced at the calendar hanging by the window. Wednesday, October 26th. Two days until Forkbridge's Halloween festival, and just over a week until the actual holiday next Tuesday.

This year, the last October days seemed to fly by at an alarming pace.

Probably because I had a dead body and worrying about Harmon on my plate on top of the usual seasonal chaos.

Speak of the devil...I had agreed to meet with

Chief Harmon later this morning to discuss the case, and I was already dreading it, given his brusque attitude last night.

Vince's warning echoed in my mind: "The chief can jump to conclusions pretty quick." That impulsive tendency was troubling, especially since the Harmon I once knew always weighed evidence before making judgments.

Though our relationship had been strained since Jason's death, I thought we'd begun mending things a little at Emma's wedding. There seemed to be some lingering mutual respect and affection still buried underneath the loyalty Harmon felt for Lillian Thornton and her hatred of me.

But based on last night, that fragile bond now felt irrevocably broken.

Shaking off those concerns for now, I carried my coffee to the table where Aunt Gwennie and my sisters were already eating breakfast. Archie swooped in to perch on my shoulder, helping himself to a piece of bacon from my plate.

"Good morning, dear," Aunt Gwennie greeted me warmly. "You look a bit peaked. Didn't sleep well?"

I attempted a smile. "Not really. My brain wouldn't shut off after everything yesterday."

Aunt Gwennie nodded sympathetically. She passed me a dish of fluffy scrambled eggs.

As I scooped some onto my plate, Ami spoke up in a subdued voice. "Finding Marcus like that was so awful. I kept thinking about it all night." She shook her head, looking troubled.

"None of us slept great," Ayla agreed. Even she seemed affected by the grim discovery.

"Eh, I slept just fine," Althea interjected.

I took a sip of coffee, appetite fading. "I wonder who could have killed him."

"Someone who didn't want that festival to happen," Althea said. She aggressively sawed into a pancake as if it had personally offended her. "This town has a bias against paranormals. We've always known that. Some of them know we're here, and they hate us."

"While true, what does that have to do with Marcus?" Ayla asked Althea.

"What do you mean? Doesn't anyone read the paper anymore?" she asked in disbelief.

We glanced around at each other shiftily, mumbling a chaotic chorus of "Uh, not really" and "I just read the headlines" and "Does digital count?" Even Aunt Gwennie murmured that she only cut the coupons.

Althea rolled her eyes so hard I thought they

might get stuck pointing backward into her head. "I swear, you guys are hopeless," she snorted, waving her newspaper at us like a disappointed schoolmarm. "This Cassandra-crushing Halloween festival? It was all his idea."

Ami's eyes widened. "You think someone killed him because he pushed the festival?"

"He was found in one of the displays. It's as good as any other theory."

"True. One valid theory," Archie remarked. He craned his neck to steal a chunk of bacon off Ayla's plate. She made a halfhearted shooing motion with her hand as Cerberus barked at the owl.

I nibbled my eggs, thinking it over. "Well, I'm meeting with Harmon soon to go over things again. I need to ensure that he won't try to blame me or Ami to wrap up the case and impress his girlfriend."

Ami's eyes widened anxiously. Aunt Gwennie tutted, shaking her head.

"That's ridiculous. The chief knows perfectly well neither of you would do something so horrible."

"Maybe under normal circumstances he'd know that," I said. "But with Emma gone, he doesn't have her balancing him anymore. And we all know Lillian has been poisoning him against me, and she can't be happy with this festival as a whole, anyway." I stabbed a honeydew melon ball, frustration bubbling up. "My bet is his accusatory attitude stems from a desperation to appease her. Who knows what rash decisions he'll make?"

"You think his objectivity is compromised?" Ami asked.

"I think it's possible. Yes."

The table fell silent at my words. I knew they were all thinking the same thing—with his objectivity compromised, the chief really might wrongly arrest me or Ami just to smooth things over in Cassandra.

"Can't you ask Emma to talk to him?" Ayla suggested. "He'd listen to her, wouldn't he?"

I considered it. As Harmon's favorite detective, Emma did tend to have a moderating influence on him.

"Maybe," I said after a moment. "I'm not sure how much sway she still has now that she left the force. But it might be worth a try." I gave Ayla a grateful look. "I'll stop by the werewolf castle on the way back from the meeting with him. If I'm not in jail."

Ami reached over and put her hand over mine. "We won't let the chief railroad you, Astra.

If he blames you without cause, we'll figure something out."

I gave Ami's hand a quick squeeze.

"Here now, enough fretting," Aunt Gwennie said in her best soothing voice, rising to clear the empty plates. "Worrying yourself sick won't do any good until we know what the chief has in store. Just be forthright with him, Astra, and let things play out. The truth will come to light, dear."

Oh Aunt Gwennie. Always the hopeful optimist, seeing the world through rose-colored glasses.

So sweet.

So naive.

Archie ruffled his feathers. "And if the truth doesn't come out, I can always claw his eyes out as plan B," he offered.

"Hopefully it won't come to impromptu eyeball removal, but thanks for having my back, Archie," I said, giving him an appreciative scratch. "Well, no use putting it off. Time to go face the music."

And potentially tone-deaf interrogation tactics.

CHAPTER FOUR

The morning sun glared off the hood of my dusty Jeep as I pulled into the police station parking lot. Gravel crunched under the tires as I parked in my old familiar spot. But when I climbed out, locking the door behind me, it felt different this time.

I was here as a civilian now, not a consultant. No badge, no authority, no inside access. Just a witch with a complicated history who found a body.

With a resigned sigh, I pocketed my keys and made my way inside.

The blast of air conditioning washed over me as I stepped through the doors. Phones rang, keyboards clacked, and the ubiquitous scent of old coffee permeated the organized chaos. Head held high, I prepared for the uncertain reception that awaited me.

A few officers looked up as I entered.

"Astra!" Officer Blake waved me over, smiling warmly beneath his bushy mustache. "Good to see you. We've missed you around here."

"That's nice to hear." I smiled back. "I miss you guys, too."

He leaned in, lowering his voice. "The situation that occurred between you and the chief wasn't right. None of us thought you had anything to do with Jason and his mother using the boss to off your job? Not cool."

Before I could respond, Officer Ramirez approached, nodding in greeting. "Hey, Astra, I heard Emma went on permanent leave. Did she —" She glanced around furtively. "Was it because of how things went down with you and the chief?"

I shook my head. "I doubt it. I'm not sure if—"

"Arden! In my office. Now."

Chief Harmon's gruff voice barking my name made me jump. I turned to see him glowering from his office doorway, bushy brows drawn together and jaw clenched tight beneath his mustache.

The chief disappeared back into his office.

"Good luck," Ramirez murmured, giving me a sympathetic glance as I passed her and headed toward Harmon's office.

"Good morning, Chief," I said evenly, stopping in the doorway. The newly minted Detective Vince Briggs was already seated across from Harmon's desk. "Detective Briggs. Fancy meeting you here."

Harmon scowled. "Get in here, close the door, and sit down."

I did as he ordered, taking a seat across from him.

Old habits and all that.

Harmon settled his imposing bulk behind the desk but remained standing, palms planted on the scattered files like he was claiming his territory.

"Okay. What brings me here today?" I asked politely, even though my hackles were rising at Harmon's gruff manner. I turned to Briggs. "Congrats again on the recent promotion, Briggs. It does amaze me you managed to snag it a year before mandatory retirement age, but hey, better late than never, right?"

To my shock, pink tinged Briggs's weathered cheeks. "Ah, well, yeah." He rubbed his neck almost shyly. "Well, I arrived at the late-breaking personal insight that being the neighborhood eccentric elderly grouch in my waning days is far from my ideal. And that's where I was headed."

This uncharacteristically Zen attitude was quite a change from Briggs's usual cantankerous demeanor. When I left the force, he was still a grumpy patrolman with over twenty years under his belt and no hope of promotion because of his attitude.

"It's funny you should say something, actually," he continued. Briggs smiled a little self-consciously and cleared his throat. "I actually got one of those fortune telling readings from your sister. The blond one, Ami."

I sat up a little straighter. "Oh? And what did she see that inspired this change of heart?"

"Nothing too specific." Briggs waved a hand. "Just some thought-provoking things about my attitude and holding myself back all these years." His eyes took on a faraway look. "I put little stock in magic and all that, but I have to admit—her words stuck with me. Made me rethink things."

I studied him. However Ami's reading had affected Briggs, the shift in him was palpable. "Well, I'm glad it was a positive experience," I said.

Harmon snorted derisively. "Yes, I'm overjoyed to at least have rookie detectives now."

I turned my attention to Harmon. "Okay, let's try to wind this up before you get even testier. Why did you want to see me, Chief?"

His expression hardened. "I want to know what you saw when you touched Clinton's body last night. You and I both know you did."

I shifted under his flinty stare. "No clues about his death, if that's what you're after."

Harmon's eyes bored into me, as if trying to detect any deception. "So you didn't pick up anything useful?" Disappointment tinged his gravelly voice.

"If I had any relevant info, don't you think I would've mentioned it already?"

The chief gritted his jaw at what I said but held back a tart reply. Bowing over the desk, he let out an exhausted exhale that cast his features as far older. "What a mess."

"Yep," Briggs agreed. "It's a mess."

"I do not want to investigate everyone that was in city hall if I can help it. None of that will be good for my career." He scrubbed a hand over his face. "The whole damn business has the mayor breathing down my neck to make an arrest."

I felt a flicker of sympathy.

While he may have been quick to cast suspicion my way, at least he was willing to hear me out. There was a glimmer of the reasonable man I once knew behind that grump.

"I understand that pressure," I acknowledged in a softer tone. "Anything I can do to help, just say the word."

Harmon regarded me silently for a long moment. Briggs shifted uncomfortably in the tense quiet. Finally, the chief gave a single gruff nod.

The rest of the interview proceeded calmly enough. Harmon asked questions about my interactions with Marcus, which I answered candidly. Briggs took notes, brow furrowed in concentration.

When we finally finished, I stood to leave. As I reached the door, the chief's weary voice stopped me.

"Astra, despite...everything, I know you and your sisters are good people. You wouldn't be involved in a murder like this."

I turned back, surprised by this olive branch (and wondering what kind of murder he thought we would be involved in). Our gazes met in a rare moment of understanding.

"Thank you," I said simply. "I appreciate that, Chief."

With a parting nod, I left the office and made my way outside, feeling cautiously optimistic. My relationship with Harmon would probably never be fully repaired, but it at least hadn't deteriorated to the point of criminal suspicion. It seemed we could be cordial.

I could work with cordial.

* * *

AFTER LEAVING THE POLICE STATION, I headed for the secluded wooded road that led to the werewolf lair, my conversation with Harmon still fresh in my mind.

I pulled up the long, winding driveway that resembled a pine tree slalom course and parked between Emma's massive SUV and her beloved classic Malibu. As I climbed out of my comparatively plain Jeep, I wondered if getting a tank might help me compete with the werewolf vehicles dominating the parking area.

I let myself in and followed the sound of Emma's voice to the living room.

I paused in the arched doorway, taking in the cozy scene—Emma sitting cross-legged on the plush carpet across from baby Hunter, looking like they were about to host a tea party with their menagerie of stuffed animals. My best friend made a plush lion dance along the floor, bobbing and weaving dramatically, as she provided lively narration in a silly voice.

Hunter watched, utterly enthralled, as if seeing the best show on Broadway.

"Knock knock," I said, rapping gently on the door frame.

Emma and Hunter both glanced up in surprise, as if momentarily forgetting the world outside their stuffed animal soirée existed. "Astra! What a delightful surprise."

The baby squealed happily and pointed at me with a chubby little finger, his face lighting up. "Ta ta!" he exclaimed, bouncing excitedly in place.

I winced.

That nickname was going to stick.

But I also couldn't help but smile back. There was an easy joy to Emma and Hunter in these moments that warmed my heart. Motherhood suited her.

"Hey you two." I waved at Hunter as I sat on the floor. "Working on those animal sounds?"

Emma laughed. "More like teaching the art of imaginative play. He loves this lion." She made it prance again, eliciting a delighted baby chuckle from Hunter.

"Already learning improv skills. He'll make a great detective."

A cloud passed over Emma's face, her smile fading. She busied herself fussing with Hunter's sock.

"What was that?" My brow furrowed. "Everything okay?"

With a resigned sigh, she met my gaze. "Yeah, it's just...talking about Hunter being a detective one day reminds me I had to drop that dream for a while." She absently stroked the baby's downy hair. "I'm sorry again for not telling you, and maybe it was a rash decision, quitting the force. But the entire pack gave up their whole lives to move here just because I was stubborn, and..." Emma trailed off with a conflicted expression.

"You felt guilty after the fact," I finished for her.

Emma's eyes widened slightly in surprise. "Yeah, I guess I do. I feel a little silly admitting it. After all, it was my own behavior that forced Eddie into making a big gesture like coming here to Forkbridge. But now that they're all my family and I know what they gave up to come here, I feel like such a heel."

"You're not a heel." I told her off gently. "But it's also not a reason to give up something so meaningful to you. They did things for you in the past that your quitting won't make balanced, right?"

Emma's face flushed. She busied herself adjusting Hunter's shirt.

"It was my choice, Astra," she mumbled.

"Hey, I'm not saying it's not. I know. I just want you to be sure it was the right one for you," I said.

Emma's jaw tightened, eyes flashing. "Everything I do now, I do for this family. For Hunter. For the pack." Her voice hardened with an edge of warning. "I don't regret it."

Whoa.

I held up a hand. "Hey, I wasn't trying to criticize or judge. Just want to make sure you're doing what really makes you happy. That's all."

Emma let out a sharp breath, the tension in her posture easing. "I'm sorry. I know. And believe me, I gave it a lot of thought. I know it seems out of character for me but, honestly, Astra, having a kid changes you. It changes your perspective." She smiled softly down at Hunter playing with his lion. "Sure, I miss parts of the job. But I don't miss the chaos and crazy hours now that I have this little guy."

"I hear you."

She looked back up at me. "Being here for him is what I want. Truly."

I nodded, swallowing back any further arguments. If Emma was content with her choice, who was I to second-guess her?

"For what it's worth, the force isn't the same without you," I said. "But as long as you're happy, that's what matters."

Our conversation turned to more lighthearted topics after that, the tension dispelled. We chatted and played with Hunter, who seemed delighted by all the animated attention.

After a while, I heard voices approaching down the hall—Lothian and Eddie back from a run. As they entered the living room, shirtless and sweat-slicked, chatting casually about security measures, Eddie's face lit up at the sight of Emma on the floor with the baby.

"There's my little man!" He scooped up Hunter, kissing his forehead as Hunter babbled happily, grabbing at Eddie's stubbled cheeks. Eddie grinned at Emma. "And his beautiful momma."

Emma returned his adoring smile. "How was your run?"

"Good workout. The trails north of the property need some clearing, though."

Lothian nodded in agreement, then turned his attention to me with a cocky grin. "Well hey there, beautiful. To what do we owe the pleasure?"

"I just stopped by to chat with Emma," I said.

Lothian's grin faltered slightly when I said I was here to talk to Emma, not to him. His shoulders slumped a fraction, and the mischievous glint in his eyes dimmed. "The dead councilman?"

"Yeah. Though we hadn't gotten to him yet."

Sensing an opportunity, Eddie spoke up. "I'm gonna take this little guy out back. You all continue your conversation." He smiled supportively at Emma before heading out with the baby while Lothian moved further into the room.

"Any intriguing developments in town I should know about?" He raised an eyebrow.

"Other than a dead body in a fake display coffin in front of city hall, nope," I said. "I don't know much about the case, to be honest. I came from the station, and it doesn't seem like the chief has much of a handle on it."

Lothian nodded. "He's got one detective left, and I heard the guy is a hundred years old with almost no experience."

"It's Vince Briggs, and he's not a hundred years old."

Emma looked bemused. "I just can't believe Harmon promoted Vince Briggs."

I nodded. "I met with him today. He's a detective. I think he might be their only detective, actually, since you ran off all the others by being a woman in their department."

Emma shot me a chiding look. "Ease up, Astra."

"Anyway, they don't seem to have a clue."

"You know, I played golf with Marchand yesterday," Lothian said. "He mentioned that Marcus Clinton would not be a problem as far as approving the zoning development for the shopping center I'm involved in."

"You play golf with Paul Marchand?" I asked, unable to keep the surprise from my voice. Lothian hobnobbing with the mayor seemed an unlikely pairing.

"It's business," Lothian shrugged, as if that explained their unlikely camaraderie.

I regarded him curiously. The cocky, anti-authority werewolf I knew hobnobbing with politicians seemed an unlikely pairing. "Last I checked, you called him an ego-tripping windbag."

"He is." Lothian scratched his chin sheepishly. "But there are opportunities, for the pack and for me personally, if I play nice with the powers that be. We do what we have to."

Emma piped up sourly. "Can we get back to the murder please?"

I shot her an apologetic look. "You're right, sorry. The mayor stuff just threw me a little."

Lothian held up his hands. "Hey, I'm happy to talk murder any time. I just thought the golf thing was an interesting tidbit. How did the mayor know he wouldn't be a problem? The guy wasn't up for re-election this year."

"You raise an excellent point," Emma said, a barely perceptible furrowing of her brow the only external sign of the rapid analysis happening behind her cool gaze.

"I know that look, and I'd like to point out we're not on the force anymore," I pointed out. "I only looked into it—barely—because Harmon seemed to think we—my sisters and I—were suspects in the murder just because we found the body, but he said outright this morning that he doesn't think that."

"Did he, now?"

"He did. Why is any of this our problem?"

Emma gestured for me to follow her down the hall. As we walked, she nodded toward the security feeds lining the wall—various cameras positioned around the property. I scanned the monitors as we passed—the back porch, the tree line, the garage.

Jeesh.

This place was a fortress.

Then a familiar face jumped out at me from the feed trained on the street in front of the front gate. Sitting in an old Buick parked just outside the gate was none other than Detective Vince Briggs. I'd recognize that hawkish profile anywhere.

She fixed me with a knowing look and then followed my gaze. "People lie. Ignore the fluff and focus on the facts. Evidence reveals far more about motives than anything someone tells you."

* * *

THE SUN FILTERED through the towering pines lining the driveway, casting a scenic dappled glow on my unexpectedly leisurely stroll. I took in the idyllic surroundings, enjoying a rare peaceful moment with Lothian. I'd learned the hard way in my relationship with Jason that neglect can lead to resentment, and I didn't want to make that mistake again, so when the werewolf asked me for an impromptu walk, I agreed.

After a few moments of surprisingly not awkward silence, Lothian slid his gaze my way.

"So...you gonna tell me what that was really about back there?"

I kept my eyes fixed ahead with a noncommittal grunt. I wasn't sure which part he was talking about, but I was enjoying the silence and I didn't want to ruin it with talking.

Lothian nudged me with his elbow. "Come on, Astra. I know you well enough to see when something's eating at you. What's going on in that brilliant mind of yours?"

I shrugged, pulling my hand from his and shoving both in my pockets. As much as I cared for Lothian, I wasn't about to pour my heart out to a card-carrying member of Queen Emma's werewolf pack.

Don't get me wrong, I liked the guy.

A lot.

But confessing my concerns about his pack's alpha female?

Yeah, that could end up biting me in the behind.

"Just a minor disagreement between friends. Nothing for you to worry about."

Lothian stepped in front of me, blocking my path. I nearly crashed into his bare, sweat-sheened chest and took a hasty step back as he searched my face intently.

"It's clearly bothering you. And anything that bothers you, bothers me." His voice softened. "Let me in, Astra. I'm here to listen, no judgment."

"I'm just...concerned about Emma," I said, choosing my words carefully. "I feel like she gave up her career too easily."

Lothian cocked his head, considering. "You mean to focus on motherhood and Eddie?"

"And the pack, hence my hesitance at wanting to discuss this with you." I nodded, feeling like I was tiptoeing through a minefield here. "She made it sound like she quit mostly to accommodate Eddie and the pack. I want to be supportive, but..."

"You think she made a mistake," Lothian finished. His expression remained neutral.

"I don't know," I admitted. "Maybe? I just want

her to be true to herself. Does that make me a terrible friend?"

Lothian placed his hands on my shoulders, compelling me to meet his earnest gaze.

"Not at all. It makes you a caring friend who wants the best for someone she loves." His voice resonated with conviction. "But people change priorities. Emma's happiness is for her to define now."

I stared up at him, conflicted emotions churning. He had a valid perspective and somewhere in my stubborn head, I knew I should let it go and trust Emma's judgment.

Lothian's hands slid down to rest gently on my upper arms. "I get it. Change is hard to accept. But you have to let people make their own choices, even if you don't agree." His lips quirked in a crooked smile. "I'm actually surprised we're having this conversation at all. I would have thought you—of all people—wouldn't need to be told that."

Despite myself, I huffed out a laugh. "That's fair."

His smile widened at getting me to crack. He pulled me in for a hug, his bare skin hot against me. The woodsy scent of pine and musk enveloped me, familiar and comforting.

"Give it time," he murmured into my hair. "Everything will work out as it should."

I nestled against the hard planes of his chest, tension draining from my shoulders. Lothian always seemed to see right through to the core of things.

I was lucky to have him.

CHAPTER FIVE

I pushed open the carved wooden door of the Spellbound Emporium, breathing in the calming scents of herbs and incense. After the tension of my conversation with Lothian, I was looking forward to the peace of the shop.

That peace was short-lived.

The moment I stepped inside, angry voices assaulted my ears and I halted in surprise at the sight of my sister Althea locked in a heated argument with none other than Angela Hayes, Forkbridge's persnickety party planner and the absentee co-organizer of the Forkbridge Halloween Festival.

I stifled a groan.

Dealing with Angela was the last thing I wanted to do right now.

"For the last time, Angela, my sister is not available," Althea insisted through gritted teeth, fists clenched at her sides.

In response, Angela jabbed an accusing finger toward Althea. "Don't give me that, Thea! I know Astra lives right in the house attached to this place. She works here, and the only other thing going on in her life is the festival she's failed at setting up, so march yourself up there and get her down here. I need to speak with her!"

I saw red as Angela's words registered, my hands clenching into fists. For a brief, satisfying moment, I fantasized about zapping her smug behind with a lightning bolt. That would wipe the sneer off her face.

Taking a calming breath, I approached, my voice icy cool. "No need to shout. I'm right here," I said. "Though if I had been upstairs, I no doubt would've heard your dulcet tones just fine with no extra amplification."

Both women whirled to face me with matching startled expressions. Althea's surprise shifted to relief at the sight of me. Angela, on the other hand, affixed me with her signature glower that could have curdled fresh milk.

"Astra! Finally." She marched over, placing her hands firmly on her wide hips. "Would you care to explain why I arrived at city hall this morning to find the festival grounds abandoned and exposed after you left them in complete disarray last night? There's crime scene tape everywhere, police lights. The place looks terrible!"

I crossed my arms, arching an eyebrow. My temper still simmered below the surface, but I kept it contained. "You make it sound like we egged the place and toilet-papered the trees, Angela. We were done decorating when we found a dead body, if you recall. The police had things they needed to do."

She waved a hand. "Yes, yes, tragic about Marcus. But leaving debris everywhere, half-hung lights, police tape cordoning off the lawn— it's unacceptable! Do you have any idea the liability issues you've caused?"

By now, the entire shop was watching our confrontation. A hushed silence fell over the customers browsing the shelves. In my peripheral vision, I noticed Ayla and Althea staring daggers at Angela.

"The police sent us home so they could investigate," I said. "If they didn't clean up their tools, that's on them. It's not my responsibility to clean up after them. I'm sure you agree."

Angela let out an exasperated huff. "Police orders or not, I expected more professionalism from you and your hippie sisters, Astra. Honestly, just walking away from your job because of a dead body." She tsked in disappointment. "I want city hall cleaned up and redecorated by nightfall. The festival starts tomorrow, and people are already arriving today. I want it fixed or you're fired!"

That tore it.

This self-important windbag had some nerve.

I stepped closer, voice deathly quiet. "Fire us, then. We're volunteers, Angela, not your employees. And we found a body. That murder investigation is far more important than the impression Forkbridge city hall makes on visitors. Nobody cares about city hall."

Angela pushed her chin forward, although I perceived a slight unease in her eyes. "I don't care about the murder investigation, or Marcus. I want that festival running perfectly, and I hold you responsible for the state of city hall."

"Then you're a muddle-headed nitwit," I growled. "I'm done being your whipping post. Find someone else to bully."

Angela opened her mouth, but before she could respond, the shop door jingled as it swung open. We both turned to see a familiar willowy figure sweep inside, rainbow skirts rustling around her ankles.

Serena Bliss—thirty-one years old, with long, corn silk blond hair and piercing ice blue eyes. She was second-in-command to Lillian Thornton, the mayor of Cassandra and Guru Bernie, the spiritual leader of the spooky town. Former girlfriend of my dearly departed ex-boyfriend Jason Bishop, too, though no one spoke of that much anymore.

"Good morning, sisters," Serena said, gliding up to the counter, seemingly oblivious to the tension she'd interrupted. "I hope I'm not intruding." Her pale blue gaze zeroed in on Angela. "Well now, what do we have here?" she asked.

Angela stared back. "Miss Bliss. What are you doing in Forkbridge?"

Serena smiled. "Just picking up some herbal remedies. Althea's potions rival anything we make in Cassandra, I'm mortified to say." She drifted closer, dabbing at the crystals dangling from the ceiling. They chimed softly. "This lovely shop has so many treasures. Each crystal has its own vibration. Like a personality. Did you know that?"

Angela shifted under that mild gaze.

For some reason, I could sense Serena's unexpected presence rattled her.

"I couldn't help but overhear your lively discussion," Serena continued. "I believe you were talking about your attempt to sabotage my town's livelihood, and the importance of a particular festival aesthetic while doing so?"

Oh, snap.

Angela sputtered. "Now see here, I never said—"

"Stop," Serena told her.

To my stunned surprise, Angela snapped her mouth shut, swallowing back whatever retort she'd been about to unleash.

"There's no need to explain in front of all these people, dear." Serena turned her placid gaze to me. "Astra, would you mind if I borrowed your office for a chat with Angela? I believe we should discuss...respecting our neighbors."

I nodded. "Of course. It's right through that doorway."

As Serena steered a dumbstruck Angela toward the office, Althea appeared at my side looking deeply satisfied. "Was that magic?"

I chuckled. "I think it was confidence. I didn't sense anything."

"Serves Angela right. The nerve of that woman." Althea shook her head.

"No kidding." I watched them disappear into the office. "How long had she been here?"

"Long enough." Althea's scowl returned. "She barged in ranting about you not finishing decorating after finding Marcus. Said she's going to make sure you pay for the 'headache' you caused her."

I rolled my eyes. "At this point, I'd send her a thank you card if she fired us."

Althea smiled. "I bet Serena knocks that entitled attitude down a few pegs."

"Here's hoping." I glanced around the now-empty shop, the argument having scared off the customers. "Well, this should be an interesting rest of the day."

With the shop empty, we busied ourselves straightening displays. I fluffed the purple velvet pillows in the reading nook, imagining Angela's outrage at being dressed down by the mild-mannered Serena. A grin tugged at my lips. That image definitely brightened my mood.

* * *

THE OFFICE DOOR flew open and Angela came storming out, face flushed and pinched with anger. She stomped past without sparing me a glance, the bells above the shop door jangling violently as she flung the door open to leave.

I winced at the loud bang.

Whatever happened in that office, Angela was furious. Her anger seemed to linger in the air even after she'd gone, like the threatening rumble of a distant storm. I exchanged a surprised look with Althea.

She shrugged. "No idea."

Serena emerged from the back office, smoothing her flowing skirts. "We just had a thoughtful discussion about respecting our fellow communities." She smiled. "I'm sure Angela left with a new perspective."

"I'm sure," I said. Having been on the receiving end of Serena's gentle but pointed wisdom myself, I could well imagine how the conversation went.

Serena's face turned worried as she looked at me. "I must confess, I'm troubled to find you supporting Forkbridge in this tasteless spectacle, Astra. Especially after what happened to Marcus." She sighed. "That poor man had so many dark spirits feeding on him. As does Angela."

I stiffened, bristling at the implied criticism. "Serena, it's just a Halloween festival. Nothing sinister. Our festival is just a bit of fun, not some spiritual conclave of mediums taking appointments for the dead. Just pumpkin pies and hay rides and games. The two festivals are totally different."

Serena clasped her hands. "You think the crowds we gather are all there to commune with their beloved dead? Most are coming just to peek at the strange psychic town and the weird cult that lives in it. If you attract even half of the people we attract, you'll be stomping on Cassandra's livelihood like a booted thug squashing a bug. Is that who Forkbridge wants to be?"

Before I could respond, Ayla strolled in from the side door nearest the house. "Serena, last I checked, Cassandra was the only place that houses fifty people who could talk to the dead," she remarked. "You've got the spirits lining up right now, and you don't give those readings away for free. Forkbridge is not trying to compete with you. You don't own Halloween."

"She's right. I mean, technically, we do," Althea added with a smirk.

Serena bristled, her piercing eyes flashing.

"Now see here, the origins of Halloween are not something to be trivialized," she began. "It arose from the ancient Celtic festival of Samhain, when it was believed the veil between the spirit world and our own grew thin. Over time, it developed into the commercialized holiday it is today, but we must not forget its sacred roots and the communion with divine forces—"

"Yeah yeah, ancient forces, sacred veil thinning, we know," Ayla cut in, unfazed by Serena's imperious tone. "We're witches, Serena. We don't need a Halloween history lesson. What's your point?"

Serena blinked as if holding back tears. "You're right, of course. I'm sorry. It's just that Cassandra depends on our Halloween festival. Most residents don't work outside the town. Our businesses earn most of their income from that event. Without it..." she trailed off, distressed.

Guilt gnawed at me. Ayla had mentioned Bill Platt's concern, but I hadn't really considered how losing festival revenues could affect the people of Cassandra and the town as a whole.

Just then, Ami entered from the back room. Her smile faltered when she saw Serena's anguished expression.

"What's going on? Are you okay?" she asked, moving to Serena's side.

Serena grasped Ami's hands in desperation. "Please, I know your family means no harm, but you must call off this festival. Cassandra needs those Halloween revenues to survive. To support our work guiding spirits to healing and peace. I'm begging you."

I shifted uncomfortably.

While Serena made fair points, canceling the entire festival now would create chaos. The town had already invested significant resources into the event based on the council's directive. We couldn't just pull the plug.

And besides, I didn't have the power to do what she was asking.

I didn't have enough influence to try effectively.

"Serena, I understand your concerns," I said gently. "But realistically, Forkbridge's festival isn't likely to make much of a dent in Cassandra's Halloween attendance. People travel to your town for the experience you provide. Ours is just a small local thing."

Serena gazed at me while Ami squeezed her hands in reassurance. I could tell my sister ached to give Serena the answer she desired. But this decision was something we didn't have the magic to affect.

I met Serena's pleading eyes. "And the simple fact is my mother was the Forkbridge mover and shaker. None of us are. We don't have the ability to influence anyone's decision on this. I'm sorry, but there's nothing we can do this late in the game."

Serena's shoulders slumped in defeat. With a resigned sigh, she pulled her hands from Ami's and moved to the door. But as she left, she looked back at us, her expression sorrowful.

"I expected more compassion from you. I really did. I hope you'll reconsider."

With those parting words, she slipped out, the door falling shut behind her with an air of finality.

* * *

THE SHOP DOOR closed with a soft tinkle of bells, leaving a heavy silence in Serena's wake.

Ayla let out a breath, deflating a little as the tension seeped from the room. "Well, I kinda feel like I just kicked her puppy," she admitted, looking mildly guilty.

At her feet, Cerberus gave an affronted woof,

as if taking personal offense. He butted his gigantic head against Ayla's hand.

"Oh don't worry, not you, you adorable beast," Ayla assured him, scruffing his ears. Cerberus' tail thumped against the floorboards.

A gentle touch on my arm drew me from my thoughts. I glanced up to see Ami regarding me with her deep, kind eyes.

"You did your best, Astra," she said softly. "She has a point, and this situation isn't ideal, but the festival plans are already in motion. We'll find a way to make it work for both towns. There's always a middle path."

I sighed, wishing I shared her optimism. "I hope you're right."

Across the room, Ayla flopped into one of the cushioned chairs with a huff. "Well, that was dramatic," she muttered, stretching her legs out before her.

Althea shot her a quelling look. "A little sensitivity wouldn't hurt, Ayla. She's clearly upset about the festival."

Ayla held up her hands. "Hey, all I'm saying is, guilting us won't change anything. The town already made their choice. She's a day late and a dollar short with her concerns." She idly spun a crystal from the nearby display, watching it fractalize the light. "I don't know what she expected. Both festivals are tomorrow."

I moved to sit beside her with a tired exhale.

She had a point, blunt as it was.

Ami perched on the chair arm beside Ayla, brow furrowed in thought. "I do wish the timing hadn't ended up pitting the towns against each other, though. Especially now, with tensions already running so high after Marcus was murdered."

Althea crisscrossed her arms, settling into the sales counter. "Speaking of Marcus, you don't think his killer is connected to Cassandra, do you?" Her sharp gaze took in each of us in turn. "Maybe someone who wanted to stop the festival?"

I considered it, then shook my head. "As much as Serena wants it canceled, I can't see her or the other Cassandrans resorting to murder."

"Boy, you forget the past quick," Ayla snorted. "It's one heck of a coincidence," she mused, rolling the crystal between her palms. "Guy that pushed for the competing festival Cassandra thinks could torpedo their little spiritualist town winds up dead right before opening night? Little suspicious, if you ask me."

I had to admit, she made a good point.

Just then, the silvery wind chimes above the front door announced a customer's arrival. We all briefly raised our heads to spot Mrs. Henley, the elderly widow who lived down the street, shuffling in. Her keen dark eyes peered at us from behind thick bifocals as she leaned heavily on her carved oak cane.

"Good morning, girls," she greeted in her creaky voice. "I heard about the ruckus earlier with that dreadful Hayes woman. Everything all right?"

Ah, small town gossip. It spread faster than a viral cat video. Give it an hour, and everyone from the grocer to the little old library lady would know if you so much as sneezed funny.

"We're fine, Mrs. Henley," Ami assured her with a warm smile. "Just a minor disagreement, nothing to worry about."

The old woman harrumphed. "If you say so. Though I never did care for that one. Far too big for her britches." She winked conspiratorially. "Glad your visitor from Cassandra took her down a peg. These young folks today could use some old-fashioned discipline."

Okay, give it less than an hour.

"Was there something we could help you find

today?" Ayla asked, though I could tell her patience with the interruption was thin.

"Oh yes, I'm here for my usual nerve tonic." Mrs. Henley rapped her cane. "These creaky old bones need all the help they can get."

Once we had Mrs. Henley taken care of, I did a quick scan of the shop floor. A few browsers wandered the aisles, including young Megan Wright examining the crystal pendulums. But otherwise, business remained slow after the earlier disruptions.

I gathered my sisters with a glance. Pointing at Ami and Althea, I said, "Why don't you two go grab some lunch? Ayla and I can hold down the fort here."

Ami checked her delicate gold watch with a frown. "Are you sure? It's barely past eleven."

I waved off her concern. "I'm fine. You should take a break, get some air."

Truthfully, I needed some time alone to process everything swirling through my mind—Marcus's murder, Serena's plea about the festival, the brewing tensions in town. My sisters had witnessed enough turmoil already today without me offloading on them now.

Ami looked uncertain, but Althea took her by

the arm. "Come on, let's try that new café down the street you wanted to check out."

After they headed out, I occupied myself assisting the few customers present. I helped Megan select a rose quartz pendulum "to attract love," and Althea mixed up a batch of Mrs. Henley's nerve tonic for her aching joints so it would be ready the next time she needed it. The methodical work brought a sense of calm, allowing me to clear my restless thoughts.

The shop door chimed, and I looked up to see Detective Briggs striding in, his usual confident attitude replaced by evident concern and uncertainty.

"Hi Detective," I greeted warily.

"Astra." He approached the counter, hesitation in his body language. From his pocket, he produced a pendant on a silver chain, setting it down before me. "Maybe you can explain this."

CHAPTER SIX

I picked up the amulet by the silver chain, turning it over in my palm as if handling crucial evidence were once again part of my daily routine. It was a cheap metal disk engraved with pseudo-mystical symbols, the kind of mass-produced necklace someone might buy at a pop-up Halloween shop with a pentagram, runes, and other markings attempting to give it a distinctly witchy vibe.

"It's inexpensive metal, probably aluminum or a blend," I said, peering at it closely. "Stamped design, not hand-carved. A pentagram, some Norse bindrunes, a few alchemical symbols. Like someone cracked open an occult encyclopedia and slapped a few symbols on there. It definitely has an occult aesthetic, but no genuine power." Lifting my head, I met Vince's gaze. "What's the story here? Where did you find it?"

"There were about fifty of them scattered all over city hall. Under people's desks, behind books," Briggs explained, his brow furrowed with concern. "Hidden away like someone didn't want them to be found."

"Fifty in different places sounds like the opposite. Seems to me someone wanted to make sure they were found."

Vince's gaze flicked between me and the object in my hand, his forehead creasing. "You're sure there's nothing...magic about it?" He made air quotes when he said 'magic,' looking slightly embarrassed.

I raised an eyebrow.

"Look, I know I'm not part of the magic in-crowd you and Emma have going on, but I'm not stupid." He shifted his weight, mouth twisting as he searched for the right words. "It's obvious you can tell things from...from, uh, things. I just want to know if that thing has something in it. You know, like...something I can't see. That would kill someone." He waved a hand vaguely. "I don't know."

I couldn't help but chuckle. "Hate to break it to you, but this is just meaningless kitsch. The kind of thing you can buy at one of those Halloween specialty stores that appear out of nowhere and vanish just as quickly."

"Are you sure?" Briggs looked incredulous. "But it looks so...witchy."

"That's the idea—it's meant to look mystical, so they use real magical symbols," I explained. "But in reality, the message on that charm is nonsensical."

I held the amulet up closer so Briggs could inspect it.

"See the mold lines and rough edges? The symbols are just etched on, not finely engraved. And the metal is some cheap alloy, not silver. Finally, this message roughly translates to 'I put my phone in the fridge.' Trust me, this thing has no magical properties whatsoever."

Briggs furrowed his brow, clearly trying to reconcile his assumptions about the amulet's mystical nature with my expertise. "Well, that's disappointing."

"What is?"

"There were so many of them, and they were hidden away so secretively," he reasoned, gesturing with his hands as he spoke. "Are you absolutely sure they're not some kind of magic evidence?"

I offered him a sympathetic smile. Briggs was a good cop, and his instincts were right—the presence of the amulets likely did mean something significant. Just not, in my opinion, what he thought.

"You're right to think the amulets are important," I said, meeting his gaze. "But it's not because of any magical properties." I held up the amulet, letting it twist back and forth on its cord. "Here, let me show you why I'm so certain this thing came from a factory, not a spellbook."

I fished a magnifying glass out from under the counter and held the amulet under it, gesturing for Briggs to look.

"See the tiny writing here, stamped into the metal? It says 'Made in China.' And this serial number is from the manufacturing mold. I'd bet a box of pumpkin spice donuts these were bulk ordered from an online retailer or picked up from a Halloween pop-up store in Orlando."

Briggs looked closer, realization dawning on his face. "Ah, okay. I see what you mean," he said, straightening up. "So if these aren't magical items, why do you think someone stashed a bunch of them at city hall?"

"My guess? These were just props—decorative pieces to make some place look more 'magical' and mysterious as part of a larger plan. Like if you were staging an occult ritual scene or wanted to throw off investigators. The amulets themselves aren't dangerous, but their presence could point to someone's deceptive intent."

Briggs nodded, following my logic. "That makes sense. Misdirection to make something seem ritualistic and supernatural when it's not. Clever." He paused, thinking carefully before continuing. "Does this mean someone was trying to blame you and your sisters?"

"It's very possible," I agreed. "Everyone knows I was fired, everyone knows Emma's no longer with the force—or at least they knew she was on leave. Making a murder look witchy or supernatural when it's actually mundane is the oldest trick in the book. Now, the amulets alone don't prove that's what happened, but they definitely suggest you should re-examine all the 'witchy' elements with a skeptical eye."

Briggs sighed, clearly dissatisfied with the lack of straightforward answers. He was hoping the amulets would break open the case, not just muddy the waters further.

"I don't suppose you could...you know..." He

made a swirling gesture with his fingers that I guessed was meant to signify using magic. "Do a reading on one of the amulets to see if you can pick up any traces of who handled them last?"

"I can try, but you need to realize I can only get something juicy if that specific amulet was present for something significant, like a crime or other emotional event. These are just factory-made knickknacks. There might not be any genuine history to glean."

I flipped the circle over once more, feeling the smoothness of the metal warming under my touch.

I looked back up at the detective.

The gruff Vince Briggs was an experienced cop, not one to easily swallow his pride and come to me for help—but he wasn't an experienced detective like Emma. This case had him out of his depth, and he knew it.

It didn't seem likely that such an ordinary trinket would hold any profound secrets, but I was willing to try for Briggs' sake.

"I'll see what I can uncover," I promised, meeting his eyes. "No guarantees, but I'll do my best."

Briggs' shoulders relaxed slightly in relief.

"That's all I ask." He managed a small, grateful smile. "Thanks, Astra."

* * *

I CAUGHT Ami's eye and subtly lifted the amulet, letting her know the situation. Then I gestured for Briggs to follow me through the side door into the back rooms of the house.

"We can try scrying in my reading room. Maybe I can sense something about where that amulet's been," I explained as I led Briggs through the kitchen, our footsteps echoing on the tile.

I slid aside the curtain and waved him into the cozy, tapestry-draped space we used for readings and meditation in the house. Briggs hovered in the doorway, looking vaguely uneasy amid the crystals, tarot cards, goddess statues, and incense burners.

"Have a seat," I encouraged, motioning to the cushions around a low table.

Before he could sit, a dramatic fluttering sounded from above as Archie ruffled his feathers. "Astra! Is that Briggs?" The owl peered down at the detective, giving him a critical once-over with his large yellow eyes. "He shaved his beard. Briggs with no beard and no uniform! That means the donut crumbs already dropped."

I sent Archie a frustrated gaze, mouthing "shut up" at him.

"Did you just shush me?"

I shot Archie an exasperated look. "We're helping Detective Briggs with an investigation," I explained, turning back to Briggs with an apologetic shrug. "Sorry, he's a little loud. Do you want me to send him out? He doesn't bite."

Briggs stared up at the owl, eyebrows raised in surprise. "You can...understand what that owl is saying?" he asked slowly.

"Every sarcastic word, unfortunately," I sighed.

Archie let out an indignant hoot at the insult.

"Just try to tune him out if you can," I said to Briggs. "I know it's easier said than done, though."

I gave Archie a pointed look.

The owl rustled his wings in a feathered shrug, blinking innocently as if to say, "Who, me?"

I settled myself cross-legged on a large purple cushion, laying the amulet in front of me. Closing my eyes, I took a few deep, centering breaths, letting the bustle of the outside world fade away.

Then I opened them.

It dawned on me that Vince Briggs didn't actually have a clue about my gift.

"I don't know how much you know about what I do, but I'm going to try psychometrically connecting with the amulet, to see if I can get any impressions from its history," I explained to Briggs. "If I connect, I'll be able to see what it sees and hear what it heard. If it's been mostly sealed away in a bag, though, I may only get snippets of sound or emotion rather than full visuals."

"Did you say psy-cho... psychomet..."

"Psychometrically. My skill is called psychometry," I explained to Briggs. "I can pick up impressions and information from objects by touching them. It's kind of like the object has an energy imprint or memory that I can tune into."

"Psychometry. Got it."

I turned the amulet over in my hands. "Every person who has handled this amulet has left a little psychic residue behind. Their thoughts, emotions, intentions—all of that can linger on objects they've touched. I'm going to tell you what I see, hear, feel. Later, you can try to figure out what it means."

Briggs nodded, taking a seat on a cushion

facing me. "Any insight you can provide will be helpful."

"Okay. Here we go."

I took a slow breath, filtering out all distractions as I attempted to form a psychic link with the amulet. Fleeting glimpses of imagery skipped along the edges of my mind—hazy shapes and emotions imprinted on the metal surface beneath my seeking fingertips.

At first, I just felt a faint buzz of energy, like an echo left by the many folks who'd handled the cheap amulet. But then faint voices emerged, muted and indistinct. I focused harder, trying to resolve the blurry sounds into coherent words.

"...can't find...looked everywhere...you sure...brought enough?"

I relayed the fragmented phrases I could make out to Briggs. He scribbled down notes, brow furrowed.

"Only getting partial sentences," I told him regretfully. "The bag and the other amulets are muffling the psychic imprints."

I reached out cautiously even further with my mind, probing the cheap metal. Suddenly, a vivid barrage of emotions hit me, making me gasp—furtive excitement, tense anxiety, simmering resentment...

I told Briggs what I sensed. "And these are some potent emotions, but I still can't see who felt them," I reported with a frustrated sigh. "Only sensing their psychological state."

"Hmm...so whoever handled these amulets was up to no good," Briggs mused. "Nervous, secretive, on edge."

"Gee, aren't we lucky you provided that utterly useless factoid," Archie snarked, sarcasm coating each syllable.

"I don't think you needed me to tell you that, but yes, maybe." I looked up. "Why don't you try being helpful?"

"Moi, unhelpful?" Archie gasped dramatically, ruffling his feathers in feigned indignation. "I'm wounded by your cruel words."

"Uh huh."

I hovered my palm over the disk, delicate as a fortune teller, and sent a subtle probing tendril of star magic into the cheap, coin-sized amulet. I didn't normally use that agenda-laden magic, but I needed to amplify the visions and I hoped Astraea's justice magic would determine I was needed to see them.

"Astra, there's electricity coming from your fingers!" Vince's worried voice broke my concentration.

"Well, aren't you just the next Sherlock Holmes," Archie deadpanned.

I opened my eyes, the visions of the amulet fading. "Shhhh. Let me concentrate," I chided gently, not breaking my psychic connection with the disk.

"But—" Vince protested.

"It's fine, Vince," I reassured him, meeting his concerned gaze. "I promise. You asked for my help. Let me help."

Taking a deep breath, I focused my mind and magic on the amulet again. The electric tingle resumed beneath my fingertips as the connection reestablished. Vince remained blessedly silent this time, allowing me to direct my full focus back to the psychic impressions lying dormant within the metal.

At first, there was only silence.

Then suddenly, indistinct voices erupted in my mind, growing louder and clearer as the star magic connected with the psychic imprints slumbering within the metal disk. I focused intently, straining to make out the words and discern their meaning.

Voices overlapped in urgent, hushed tones. "...can't just stand by..." "...won't let them keep..."

"...teach them a lesson they won't forget..." A lowkey current of fury and defiance rippled through the fragmented exchanges. Male and female speakers, their words obscured but emotions raw.

Flashes of dim rooms fluttered through my mind's eye. Furtive meetings, makeshift plans. Hands placing the amulets deliberately, meaningfully. I concentrated harder, willing the disjointed images to coalesce into coherence. The magic thrummed, aligning past and present.

"...find the others...?...stashed in the closet...said not to touch...get the money..."

I opened my eyes and repeated what I heard.

"Wow, I'm so glad you contributed that totally useless information," Archie said in an overly sweet voice dripping with sarcasm.

I ignored him.

"That's something, I guess." He scribbled excitedly in his notebook. "How many voices were there?"

"Two, I think? I could swear it was a man and a woman." I shot Briggs an apologetic look. "Sorry, that's as much as I can get from something like this."

Briggs nodded thoughtfully as I finished

relaying the impressions I'd gleaned from the amulet. "That's more than I had when I came here. I appreciate it." He paused, looking concerned. "You know I'm not going to be able to talk to Chief Harmon about where I got this information. I mean, he'll probably know, but we've been told not to deal with any Arden people on cases anymore."

I frowned at the mention of Chief Harmon. The man's emotions regarding me seemed to bounce like a rubber ball. At Emma's wedding, I'd thought we were making progress. "I don't do this for credit, Briggs," I assured him.

"That's good, because no one would believe it anyway," Briggs replied bluntly.

"Since that's the case, maybe we just don't mention this to anyone, then."

Briggs stared down at my hands, brow furrowing. "What was that, by the way? That white light when you were holding the amulet?"

"I could tell you..." I raised my hand, letting sparks of star magic dance across my fingertips. Briggs's eyes went wide. "But then I'd have to kill you," I finished dramatically.

All the color drained from Briggs's face, which was expressionless.

"I think you killed him," Archie said.

"Forkbridge is going to run out of detectives if you keep going like this, Astra."

"Briggs, I'm kidding!" I quickly reassured him, dispelling the star magic sparks with a shake of my hand. "It's nothing. Just a parlor trick," I lied.

Briggs just shook his head, looking torn between amusement and utter confusion. "I'm never gonna get used to you people," he muttered. "But I appreciate the help."

"I wish you could get Harmon to appreciate the help."

Briggs shook his head, stowing his notebook.. "I wish I could, too, Astra. I don't know what's going on with Harmon, but he's really got trust issues where you're concerned. This, though, is definitely helpful." He stood and offered me a hand up. "Seriously Astra, thank you. I know I gave you a hard time before, but you've been invaluable today."

Well, at least someone on the force liked my detective work.

Even if it was just newly minted Detective Vince Briggs.

* * *

As Briggs and I walked back into the main shop, Ami looked up from arranging crystals in a display case.

"Oh good, you're done with the amulet stuff," she said. "We should really head over to city hall soon and clean up the decorations from the other night." Ami shot Briggs an uncertain glance. "The police are done with that entire area now, right?"

Briggs nodded. "Yeah, we cleared out this morning. The festival team should be able to go in and salvage any decorations that weren't taken for evidence." He hesitated, then added, "I did hear Angela Hayes came storming in here earlier, making a big stink. Everything okay?"

Ami rolled her eyes. "Ugh, don't get me started."

I leaned against the counter with a sigh. "Angela insisted we should have stuck around last night and fixed the Halloween decorations like her reputation depended on it. Got pretty heated."

"I was more worried about Serena, though," Ami said and turned toward Detective Briggs. "She came in and wanted us to shut down the whole Halloween festival."

Vince Briggs raised his eyebrows, flipping open his notebook. "Really? She wanted you to shut down everything, just a couple of days before the holiday?" He jotted down some notes. "Guess I shouldn't be surprised someone from that nutzo town would come over here and stir up trouble."

Briggs's pen flew across the pages as he took it all in.

"The town's not nutzo," I told him. "They're just scared we're going to affect their income, that's all."

"That might be enough to whack the guy that proposed it all. Maybe I should go have a chat with Ms. Bliss myself, get her side of things," Briggs mused once we'd finished the recap. He shot me a faint grin. "By the way, I know I'm no Emma Sullivan, but I hope you feel you can come to me if Angela causes any more issues."

Ayla waved a hand dismissively. "Please, we don't need police input to handle Angela. She's all bark and no bite, I'm sure. Besides, Astra's got several talents. Not just psychic."

Briggs looked mildly surprised by Ayla's confident tone. "Oh really? And what talents are we talking about here?" He regarded us curiously, one eyebrow raised.

Before I could respond, Althea appeared from the rear of the room holding an armful of potions. "Astra was in the military," she said matter-of-factly. "She can kill someone with her little finger in two seconds flat."

I sighed, shaking my head. "No, I can't," I said, giving Althea a look.

Briggs shifted uncomfortably, clearly unsure how seriously to take Althea's claim.

"She doesn't have to. Don't let my petite size fool you. This fierce appendage can skewer an eyeball like a grape," Archie noted matter-of-factly, feigning nonchalance about the grisly fact.

I sighed.

"What? It may look dainty, but this little talon can just pluck an eyeball right out. No problem," Archie said airily, waving his foot.

Grateful that Vince could not hear Archie's proclamations, I said, "Anyway, I think once Ami and I fix the display, Angela will be off our back." I started helping Althea sort through the box of potions so we could place them in the display case. "We're still going to have a spooky city hall and our haunted trail walk. She'll be fine once it's all ready."

"Well, I'll let you all get to the clean up," he said, tucking away his notebook. "And I'll keep an eye on Angela, in case she stirs up any more trouble. Call if you need back up."

"Will do, officer," Ayla said with a mock salute.

"Detective," Briggs corrected, standing a bit straighter.

"Well, he's certainly not letting that promotion go to his head or fuel his ego," Archie drawled sarcastically.

CHAPTER SEVEN

*A*mi and I pulled up to the front of the city hall.

Evidence of yesterday's chaotic events were strewn across the usually pristine lawn, drooping crepe paper streamers fluttering in the breeze. Yellow police tape cordoned off sections of the yard, crime scene markers still scattered about like morbid confetti. "Well, this is more of a mess than I expected," I remarked, hands on my hips. "It wouldn't look bad if the decorative theme was crime scene, but the theme was not crime scene."

With a confirming nod, Ami pursed her lips as she scanned the front yard and took stock. "I don't think it will take us too long. We just need to clean up all the crime scene stuff, then take a good look and see where there are holes in the scene. Plug 'em. Then go home and put on our costumes." She smiled. "Simple."

The Forkbridge town square was already bustling with activity as festival attendees gathered in full Halloween regalia. Under the watchful eye of early arrival costumed crowds, we busied ourselves tidying up our vandalized decorations, sorting through damaged items to see what could be salvaged.

I stood on a ladder re-hanging strands of orange lights along the exterior staircase railings when a woman's voice called out behind us.

"The decorations look wonderful. Very festive."

I glanced over and saw a statuesque woman with long, wavy blond hair smiling at us. She was dressed in an elaborate Greek warrior costume, complete with bronzed armor, helmet, and shield. I figured she must be heading to the costume party that was part of tonight's festival kickoff event.

"Thanks, we're still trying to get it all back in order after the police were here," I explained.

As she approached, the craftsmanship of her outfit became even more impressive. Intricate metalwork adorned the breastplate, which looked to be real bronze, hammered and etched by hand rather than a cheap plastic imitation. Her sword in its scabbard appeared authentic as well, the leather-wrapped hilt and gleaming metal blade seemingly fit for actual combat rather than a party.

I glanced at her wrists and fingers, expecting chunky bangles and rings to accessorize her costumed glamour. But her only adornment was a plain silver cuff bracelet on her right wrist.

"Well met, sisters," she greeted in a melodic voice. "I am glad to see you embracing the old ways and keeping the spirit of these holidays alive."

I shared a glance with Ayla, puzzled by the stranger's oddly formal speech. Before I could respond, she continued.

"You have my blessing to go forth and spread merriment throughout this town if you wish." The woman touched her helmet in salute. "May your efforts stir wonder in mortal hearts on this hallowed eve. When the sun sinks below the horizon and darkness blankets the land, we shall convene once more. Until then, may the gods watch over you."

With that cryptic pronouncement, she graced us with one last enigmatic smile before striding off toward the town square, her golden shield glinting under the afternoon sun.

"She really committed one hundred and ten percent to that cosplay costume," I remarked to Ami as the mysterious woman strode away. "Gotta respect the dedication to staying in character."

Ami turned to me, her eyebrows raised. "You don't think that was—"

"Don't even finish that sentence," I warned.

"But listen, you've never seen her—"

"Nope, not hearing it," I interrupted, plugging my ears theatrically. "That was just a Halloween reveler enjoying the spirit of the holiday. Let's leave it at that."

Ami opened her mouth to protest further, but I silenced her with a look.

"Now let's finish decorating so we can spread merriment throughout this town," I declared with exaggerated cheer, tossing her some fake cobwebs.

I glanced back once more to watch the formal woman's retreating form.

There was no way the actual Greek goddess Athena had just randomly shown up to bless our decorations...right?

I mean, it's not that it was impossible. My own father was Apollo, so I knew the Greek gods still popped in to meddle with mortals when the fancy struck them. But running into a goddess face to face, especially Athena? That seemed about as likely as finding a unicorn grazing in my backyard.

Had I received gifts from Athena over the years? Sure. I'd been given my owl by her, straight from her Menagerie of Animal Companions. A fact which, by the way, the bird never let me forget.

Had I been injected with star power (without my consent), a power previously belonging to her dead sister, Astraea? Yep. And had she followed up that "gift" with vague quests to save random people at her behest? That, too.

But met the goddess herself?

Never.

Dad would have given me a heads up if Athena planned on appearing in Forkbridge for Halloween...right?

As much as the rational part of me wanted to dismiss it as an eccentric Halloween reveler, I couldn't shake the thought that Ami might be right—I may have just met the actual goddess of wisdom in the flesh.

My skepticism, I realized, remained steadfastly selective.

* * *

WE WORKED STEADILY over the next hour as the cloudless sky kept temperatures warmer than usual for late October. I wiped sweat from my brow, grateful for the slight breeze, as rapid footsteps sounded on the stairs behind us.

I turned to see a grinning Lothian jogging up the steps toward us.

"Well hey there, beautiful," he said, giving me an admiring once-over as he reached the landing. "Don't you just look radiant doing manual labor out here in the heat."

I cocked an eyebrow, fighting back an amused smile. "Don't even start with me, mister. I'm sweaty and gross."

"Impossible," Lothian declared, moving closer to slide an arm around my waist. "You're gorgeous, as always."

Lothian's grin only widened. Before I could react, he swept me up in his arms, spinning me around and eliciting a surprised yelp.

"Lothian Pennington, don't you dare!" I gasped out. "Put me down, you lunatic!"

He didn't.

In a flash, I grabbed his arm and spun out of his hold, using his momentum to flip him onto his back on the lawn. He landed with a thud and an "oof!"

I stood over him, hands on my hips, fighting back a smile. "I warned you, didn't I?"

"You did." Lothian laughed. "Remind me not to sneak up on you again."

"Maybe that will teach you." I extended a hand to help him up.

"What, I can't even say hi to my girl without getting assaulted?"

I swatted his chest, unable to keep from smiling now. "Assaults involve spinning people around without their consent."

Lothian just laughed, unrepentant. His gaze turned serious then as he noticed the state of the decorations. "You guys are still fixing stuff up after everything yesterday?"

I nodded. "Angela made it abundantly clear it's our responsibility to have this photo-ready by tonight." I gestured toward the thin crowd. "People are already here."

Lothian's mouth twisted in distaste. "Don't let her push you around. She's got no authority over you. You're a volunteer."

Ami walked by carrying a damaged scarecrow that needed refastening. "I know, but it's easier to just do it than argue," she said as she passed. "We're almost done, anyway."

"Well, let me help you ladies finish up," Lothian offered. He strode over and untangled a strand of lights Ami was working on.

I watched him, a fond smile creeping over my face. For all his cocky bravado, Lothian never hesitated to lend a hand when needed. It was one of the things I lov—

Whoa.

I slammed the brakes on that runaway train of thought.

Lothian was a great guy, sure. Charming, loyal, intuitive.

But love?

Way too soon for anything like that.

I busied myself adjusting decorations to distract my racing thoughts. Love was a big, serious word I did not need to be tossing around, even internally. Lothian and I were still figuring things out.

No need to get ahead of myself.

We continued stringing up lights, the task moving swiftly with Lothian's help. As I secured the final silvery strand to the roof's edge, movement caught my eye. A petite blond woman was racing across the street toward us, her flowy skirt and long hair streaming behind her.

"Lothian!" she cried, her voice ringing out. Before I could even blink, she catapulted herself at Lothian, throwing her arms around his neck. He stumbled back a step from the force of her exuberant embrace, letting out a surprised laugh.

I couldn't help but arch an eyebrow as I watched the ecstatic blond shower Lothian with affection.

"I've missed you so much!" she crooned, nuzzling against his cheek like an overeager puppy. "You never call me anymore, you big meanie." She pouted dramatically, peering up at him through thick lashes. "I decided to come and find you since we never see each other anymore!"

Lothian detached himself from her vice-like grip, taking a subtle step back. He cleared his throat. "Uh, yeah. Hi, April. Long time no see." He shot me a sheepish, apologetic look over her shoulder.

I kept my arms crossed, staring at Lothian with as deadpan an expression on my face as I could manage while he shifted his weight from side to side under my silent but obvious scrutiny, a light flush creeping up his neck.

"We, uh, used to know each other," he explained, avoiding meeting my gaze.

"You don't say," I replied.

"Well, we still do. She manages one of my Palm Beach businesses."

"Uh huh."

April finally seemed to notice me standing there. She gave me a once-over. "Oh, Lothian, you didn't tell me you started doing charity work. That's so thoughtful of you to help...these people." She smiled at him.

I stared at her, irritation simmering, and reminded myself that exposing someone's face to blunt force trauma via my fist still qualified as battery.

Who exactly was this overly friendly woman, and what history did she and Lothian share?

Before I could ask for a better explanation from Lothian about his relationship with this mystery woman, April latched onto his arm, clinging to him.

"Lothi, you must come chat with me!" she exclaimed. "I have so much to tell you." She started tugging him toward the café down the block. Lothian dug in his heels, trying to resist.

"April, hang on," he protested, shooting me an apologetic look. "Let me just—"

But April was having none of it. She continued dragging him along, chattering as if I wasn't even there.

"It's been ages since we caught up. I want to hear all about what you've been up to." She batted her eyelashes up at him coquettishly.

Lothian craned his neck to look back at me, his expression a mix of frustration and apology.

"I'll just be a minute, okay?" he called over his shoulder as April pulled him onward. "Don't go anywhere!"

I stared after them, irritation simmering toward a full blown boil.

Lothian hadn't even properly introduced me before allowing himself to be carted off by Hurricane April.

Ami touched my arm. "I'm certain there's a logical explanation."

I grunted, watching April steer a helpless Lothian into the bustling café. "I'm sure he would have remembered to give me that explanation if April's bosoms hadn't been so close to bouncing out of her shirt," I added cattily.

"Come on. Let's finish, then we can go rescue him," Ami said.

"Right."

Lothian may have let himself be dragged

away, but I wasn't about to sit idly by while some random woman from his past monopolized his time.

I didn't need his help to do what I needed to do.

* * *

MY DETERMINED DECORATIVE whirlwind faltered as I caught sight of a familiar unwelcome figure storming toward the city hall display—Angela Hayes.

Just my luck.

The last thing I needed right now after pseudo-Athena's visit and perky April's absconding with Lothian was Forkbridge's persnickety party planner distracting me from everything I needed to get done today.

Angela spotted me and her pinched face lit up with barely contained fury.

"Astra Arden!" she screeched, jabbing a furious finger in my direction. "Just who I was coming to find."

I bit back a sigh, coming to a reluctant stop in front of a hay bale display. I noticed Ami shift uneasily beside me with a fleeting glance. Neither of us were eager for another confrontation with the abrasive Angela, but it looked unavoidable now.

"Hello, Angela," I said, keeping my voice calm despite her obvious ire. "What can I do for you?"

Angela stalked closer, practically vibrating with indignation. "You can explain why the festival grounds still look like a crime scene!" she exploded. "There is police tape everywhere!"

There was a pile of police tape in the corner, ready to be hauled off.

I clenched my jaw, tamping down the urge to unleash a scathing retort. I was sure yelling back would only provoke her further.

"We were just on our way to bag all that up," I explained, gesturing to the supplies Ami carried. "It'll be done well before the party tonight."

Angela thrust her pointy chin out. "It had better be. This sloppiness reflects terribly on me and the entire planning committee." She jabbed her finger into my shoulder for emphasis. "I will not have my reputation tarnished because you witches can't handle basic event cleanup."

I swallowed back the angry words on my tongue.

Losing my temper would only delight her.

Before I could fire back a response, the city hall door opened and out strode the mayor himself, Paul Marchand. He glanced between Angela and me, taking in the tense standoff.

"Ladies, is there a problem here?" he asked.

Angela whirled on him. "Yes, there is a problem, Mayor Marchand. These...these women," she spluttered, "have left the festival grounds in complete disarray even after I instructed them to have the decorations repaired."

I opened my mouth to defend myself, but the mayor held up a hand.

"Now I'm certain these lovely ladies are doing their utmost under less than ideal circumstances," Mayor Marchand said. "And after all, the Ardens are volunteers generously donating their time and energy to Forkbridge during their own busy Halloween season at the Spellbound Emporium." He smiled benevolently, like a kindly father. "They lost their beloved mother barely a year ago, too. So let's not be too quick to jump on them, shall we?"

His tone was light and cheerful, but there was a glint of steel underneath.

Translation: Back off, Angela.

Angela could not cover her surprise at his words, and had the lip-smacking look of a lemon connoisseur sampling an especially puckery specimen.

I had to admit, I was just as surprised by his reasonable attitude. Paul Marchand was an ambitious politician through and through. I figured he would have jumped at the chance to throw me under the bus and gain favor with someone like Angela.

Perhaps there was more to him than I thought.

Angela recovered her voice. "Mayor Marchand, the festival starts tonight! We can't have the grounds looking so sloppy and unprofessional. It's unacceptable."

Marchand's placating smile didn't waver. "I understand your concern, Angela. However, I'm sure these ladies completed all they could last night before the police needed full access to the area. We're fortunate they're willing to come back and restore things to order at all." He turned to me. "The grounds will be presentable by this evening, I presume?"

"Of course," I assured him, hiding my surprise at his willingness to give us the benefit of the doubt. "We just have some finishing touches left, and we'll haul off anything the police left behind. It won't be an issue."

"Excellent. See, problem solved." The mayor beamed at Angela—who looked ready to spontaneously combust from sheer frustration. "Is there anything else I can help you with, Angela?"

Angela sputtered, then whirled on her heel and stomped off. I didn't bother hiding my smirk as I watched her go.

Mayor Marchand shook his head. "My apologies for her behavior."

"It's okay," I said, feeling my opinion of him improve. "I know tensions are high after everything that happened."

The mayor nodded. "Yes, Marcus's passing has been difficult, especially with the festival underway. This was, after all, his idea. But we must carry on." He checked his watch. "Now, if you'll excuse me, I'm already late for a meeting. I appreciate you ladies tidying up the grounds." With a parting smile, he hurried back up the walkway and into city hall.

I turned to Ami, eyebrows raised. "I have to admit, I'm impressed by how Marchand handled Angela."

"Right?" Ami agreed. "He seems much more reasonable than I realized."

Just a half an hour later we surveyed the

center of the festival grounds with a satisfied smile, hands on hips. We had managed to transform the wrecked decorations into a festive Halloween scene, despite multiple disruptions.

"Well, I'd say our work here is done," I declared.

Ami nodded in agreement. "It looks great. Now let's get out of here and start enjoying the festival ourselves!"

"I like the way you think." I paused, looking around. "You know, it's been quite an eventful and bizarre day already. A possible Greek goddess walking the streets, one of Lothian's old girlfriends showing up, and a reasonable politician that doesn't hate us or blame us for something. What are the odds?"

Ami chuckled and linked her arm through mine. "With our history of weirdness and oddness and unexpectedness? I'd say pretty good, actually."

CHAPTER EIGHT

"And then, can you believe it, that little blond bombshell came bouncing over and just threw herself at Lothian right in front of me," I fumed, practically slamming the front door of the Spellbound Emporium closed and flipping the 'Open' sign to 'Closed' with more force than necessary.

"Maybe she didn't know who you were," Althea called.

"I dislike girls that bounce." Ayla raised an eyebrow as she wiped down the sales counter. "Was she an ex-girlfriend or something? Did he say who she was?"

"So, first, he said he used to know her. Then he said she worked for him. Which is it? Either he knows her, or used to know her. It didn't look like the relationship was all that 'ex' judging by the way she was draping herself over him," I said.

I started straightening the shelves of spell books and herb jars, channeling my irritation into tidying. "And if she 'manages one of his businesses' down in Palm Beach, what's she doing jumping on him?"

Althea made a sympathetic noise as she swept the floor. "I'm pretty cynical, but I'm sure it was all innocent. Lothian wouldn't disrespect you like that."

"Wouldn't he?" I muttered. After the enthusiastic reunion I'd witnessed, I wasn't so certain. "Just because he's a charmer now with his loyal boyfriend and werewolf baby protector act doesn't mean the old Lothian isn't still in there."

Lily gave an indignant caw, ruffling her inky black feathers. "Men are scoundrels, the lot of them. Present company excluded, of course." She inclined her head toward Archie, who was perched on his branch near the cash register.

He bobbed his head in return. "Naturally."

Ami entered from the back room. "I don't think Astra's being paranoid here. I still can't believe how that woman hung all over Lothian like that," she remarked, shaking her head. "It was so inappropriate."

"Right?" I threw my hands up in exasperation, nearly whacking Archie in the process. He ruffled his feathers. "Thank you!"

"Maybe we should invite her to the festival kickoff tonight. You know, to be polite," Ayla suggested with a devious grin. "See how touchy-feely she gets with Lothian while you're standing right there."

"I was standing right there. She was pretty touchy-feely."

Ami shot us both a reproachful look. "Getting violent won't help anything."

"Who said anything about violence?" Ayla and I shared a knowing smirk as I replied.

Ami rolled her eyes. "I'm a seer, remember?"

"If you see my fist meeting her nose, just look away."

"Stop it. It's not funny. Why can't you just trust him?"

Althea laughed. "Seriously, Ami? Have you met Lothian?"

"Look, it's not that I don't trust him, but he does have a past. Again—just because he's all 'supportive boyfriend' now doesn't mean the old Lothian doesn't exist anymore," I said, stuffing colorful silk scarves back into a drawer. "I don't think April Long Legs was jumping on the supportive boyfriend version of Lothian."

With a smirk, Althea crossed her arms, leaning back against the now-gleaming glass sales counter. "Well, I guess you're over your commitment issues, at least. That's something."

I tossed a scarf at her in response.

She caught it, lips twitching in a smile.

"Shake her hand if you're so concerned. Read the woman. That will settle everything once and for all." Ami smoothed her skirt, redirecting the conversation. "That woman in the Greek warrior costume earlier has been nagging at me since we left city hall. Do you think there's any truth to what I said about her maybe being the actual goddess Athena?" She looked at us. "Have any of you heard from your fathers about Athena attending the festival?"

"I have heard nothing from Dad about it, but he doesn't keep me informed of stuff like that," Ayla said with a shrug. She plopped down in one of the plush chairs we kept for tarot readings, propping her feet up. Cerberus padded over and plopped his gigantic head on her lap. "Why not ask Archie?"

"I'm not here to gossip about the gods to

witches—I chronicle your foibles to the gods. Not the other way around," he explained in between preening.

"Thanks, Archie."

"No problem."

Althea shook her head. "Poseidon hasn't been in touch either. But communication isn't his strong suit, being underwater and all."

They turned expectantly to me.

"No word from Apollo on the goddess front. But you guys know he's been pretty hands off with me since Mom and Jason passed away, even though he moved here."

My throat tightened.

"I understand. Well, that's all our otherworldly contacts, since my dad, Hermes, doesn't acknowledge my existence." Ami nodded. "Maybe we should call Mom and see what she knows. Ayla, hand me the magic mirror polish. I'll ring up the underworld and see if we can get anyone on the line."

Before any of us could make a move, the side door leading from the shop to the house swung open and Aunt Gwennie bustled in, her cheeks flushed and eyes sparkling with excitement.

"Oh good, you're all here," she exclaimed, barely containing her enthusiasm. "Your father is waiting for you in the living room, Astra. And he brought someone very special along. Someone divine! So sophisticated, so well-mannered and gracious. And quite the looker too, I must say." Aunt Gwennie looked at Ami. "Though I can't say I'm surprised."

Ayla and I exchanged surprised looks.

Dad—the god Apollo—rarely made house calls anymore unless something major was up. And him bringing another god unannounced—which is what I thought Aunt Gwennie was implying—qualified as major.

"Who is it?" I asked.

"Just come see. All of you."

Anxious thoughts swirled through my mind as we filed into the house. I didn't want to see my father. Our relationship remained strained in the aftermath of my mother's death and Jason's loss. A few of the Olympus gods had created olympic-sized problems in my life. I didn't need any more of them.

Most of all, I hoped this unexpected visitor wasn't who my sinking gut feared. I wasn't ready to deal with Athena face to face.

* * *

AND I WOULDN'T HAVE to.

It wasn't Athena.

I halted in surprise when I spotted not only my father, Apollo, standing by the fireplace, but a lanky blond man beside him I'd met briefly before.

Hermes looked just as I remembered—tan and athletic, with artfully tousled golden hair framing his classically beautiful yet masculine face. His sky blue linen shirt matched his piercing eyes, which glimmered with immortal radiance and vigor.

Those piercing eyes landed on me, crinkling at the corners. "Astra," he greeted warmly. "It's good to see you again."

Before I could respond, Ami gasped beside me. She was staring, transfixed, at the blond stranger that bore an uncanny resemblance to Ami herself.

Ami's absentee father, Hermes, stared back at his daughter.

"You," she whispered.

"Amethyst, as beautiful as the stone for which you were named," he began, taking a step toward her, hand extended. "Lovely daughter. How are you?"

His overblown prose was a bucket of ice,

snapping me alert. I moved to block his path, fixing the newcomer with a frosty look.

"Don't you dare," I warned, shielding Ami behind me. "Every other god in this dysfunctional divine daycare made at least some effort to connect with their kid early on. But not you. You stayed silent, you stayed absent, and you didn't even bother to introduce yourself. You have a lot of nerve."

Hermes withdrew his hand uncertainly under my blistering stare.

"What makes you think you can just show up unannounced years later and everything will be all hunky-dory?"

The messenger god had the grace to look embarrassed by my blunt reproach. "You're right," he acknowledged. "I have no excuse for being absent for so long. All I can say is time is not the same for us, and I didn't realize I had put this off so long. But I'm here now to make amends, if you'll allow it."

"That's up to her, not me," I replied. "But know this—you hurt her. Intentional or not, what you did was not right."

"I agree." Althea crossed her arms, eyes flashing.

Even Ayla looked disturbed, shaking her head

at Hermes' audacity. "I know you're our uncle and all, but what you did to Ami sucked."

Hermes held up his hands in a placating gesture. "You're right, and I know I can't make up for the absence. But doing nothing would be worse, would it not?" His voice took on a pleading note as he looked between me, Ayla, and Althea as if we were the three Cerberus heads guarding the gate. "Please, have mercy. Grant me a chance."

Before I could unleash a scathing retort, Ami's soft voice spoke up behind me.

"It's okay." She moved out from behind me and approached Hermes, searching his face as if for any resemblance to her own. "I'm open to giving you a chance," she said, choosing her words with care. "But my sisters are right about what you did. We have a lot to discuss first."

I gaped at her calm reaction.

After being ignored by Hermes since the whole divine daddy debacle, I'd expected Ami to react with more anger.

Or at least hesitance.

But nope.

My cool as a cucumber sister met his betrayal with calm and forgiveness.

I hoped he had the capacity to appreciate her.

Hermes nodded. "Of course. I understand this will take time to mend. But I'm thankful you're willing to try."

Apollo smiled at Ami and Hermes. Neither returned it, absorbed in studying each other with cautious curiosity.

"I appreciate you coming here to meet me," Ami began. "But showing up after ignoring me the whole time my sisters were building relationships with their fathers...it's a lot to process."

Hermes nodded, contrition etched across his fine features. "You're right, and I'm sorry for the shock of my sudden arrival." He hesitated. "I've been a terrible father. There's no denying it. But if you're willing to give me a chance, even just to talk, I swear on the River Styx I want to know you and be a part of your life from now on. However you'll have me."

The earnest-sounding promise echoed through the room.

Ami searched his face a moment longer, then gave a single nod.

"Okay. We can talk."

I met my father's gaze. "I still don't like this. But it's Ami's call."

Apollo exhaled, relief smoothing some of the

creases from his brow. "I understand your protective instincts are strong, Astra," he said. "You've always looked out for those you care for. It is, no doubt, why Athena chose you to bear Astraea's starlight." He gave my shoulder an approving squeeze. "But trust that all will unfold as it should with the fates' guidance. Have faith, my daughter."

Have faith, he tells me.

He might have just asked me to turn blue spontaneously..

I managed a jerky nod, even as uncertainty still gnawed at me. For Ami's sake, I could attempt to temper my skepticism.

Even now, faith did not come easily to me, not when those I loved were involved—and that was before I found out my high priestess mother had been lying to all of us our entire lives and the gods we were supposed to worship were not exactly infallible.

Maybe in time, faith would come more readily, but for the moment, I had full faith in just one thing.

Me.

* * *

AFTER AN AWKWARD SILENCE, Apollo suggested Ami and Hermes sit on the back porch to become acquainted while he spoke with me and my sisters. I sent a quick prayer to the universe that Ami and Hermes' conversation went smoothly.

She deserved that much, at least.

Once they'd slipped outside, my father turned to us. "I know Hermes' sudden arrival is a shock," he acknowledged. "But try to understand, he has good intentions."

"Does he?" Althea challenged. "Seems like he's about a year too late for 'good intentions.'"

"This is not my disagreement to interject myself into or to defend," my father told Althea—although he had already inserted himself into the situation. "My brother may owe all of you explanations, but they are not mine to give."

Apollo gave my shoulder another gentle, reassuring squeeze, his usual serene confidence returning now that the tension had calmed somewhat.

"Dad, do you know if Athena's in Forkbridge?" I asked. "For the Halloween festival?"

"Athena attending a mortal festival?" Apollo asked, settling back in the plush armchair. "I doubt that my esteemed sister would ever mingle so casually. It's just not possible."

Ayla straightened in her seat, eyes flashing. "Who are you to say what's possible or not for Athena? Or for any of you, really?" she challenged.

Apollo blinked, looking taken aback at her confrontational tone.

"Ayla, what—"

Ayla cut me off and barreled on, ticking points off on her fingers. "Let's review, shall we? The Greek gods did 'impossible' things. Zeus turned into animals to seduce mortals. Poseidon caused destructive storms and earthquakes on a whim." She narrowed her fierce gaze on Apollo. "And you? Didn't you impersonate a woman to get close to a boy you were obsessed with?"

"Now see here—" Apollo tried to interject, but Ayla would not be deterred.

"Face it, divine or not, your pantheon loves meddling in mortal affairs and you never do what anyone predicts you're going to do. If you were even the slightest bit predictable, a lot fewer people would be turned into stone and spiders and who knows what else." Ayla sat back, looking pleased with herself. "Am I wrong?"

"Aren't you the youngest one?" Apollo asked politely.

"And yet she makes excellent points," Archie noted.

My father shot him an irritated look.

"Yep, I'm the youngest one. And the daughter of Hades. By the way, you know what else should be impossible?" Ayla asked. Without waiting for a response, she pointed at Cerberus, snoozing by her feet. "A three-headed hell hound the size of a tank being housebroken and shrunk down to bull dog size."

At his name, Cerberus's singular bull dog head perked up. He woofed in agreement.

"Yes, thank you for your contribution to the debate," I told him.

The dog sneezed.

Apollo held up his hands in mock surrender. "Very well. You've made your point. Perhaps I spoke too hastily." He grimaced, looking mildly embarrassed at being schooled by Ayla. "I found it hard to fathom my sister taking an interest in a quaint mortal celebration in the small town of Forkbridge, Florida."

"The small town where four demigod sisters, one god, lots of pixies, lots of vampires, and one werewolf pack live?" I pointed out. "Yeah, no, can't imagine why she would take an interest in this neck of the woods." I held up my hand and sparked starlight from my fingers. "Remember this?"

"Fine, fine." Apollo waved a dismissive hand. "Yes, Athena has always had peculiar hobbies and pet projects. So perhaps she is here to see what her interest in this little town has produced."

Did my father just call me a peculiar hobby or pet project?

Ayla certainly thought so, since she chuckled. "Astra's getting a job review."

I frowned, not finding the joke all that funny.

That the goddess of wisdom herself could be evaluating my efforts in Forkbridge made me uneasy—because I didn't think she would come here just for that. It seemed my sisters forgot that my mother had been Athena's high priestess and since her death, no one had stepped into the role. We had been the first and last coven of the goddess Athena. Our house was her temple.

Was.

I wasn't sure it was only me she was here to see if, in fact, the woman was Athena at all.

Before I could reply, the porch door opened and in walked a smiling Ami arm-in-arm with Hermes. I searched Ami's face for any signs her father had upset her, but she seemed relaxed and content. Hermes, too, looked far less tense than before their talk.

"So?" I asked, not wanting to push.

Ami's answering smile soothed my concerns —for the immediate moment, anyway. "It was nice. We're going to keep talking and get to know each other." She gave Hermes' arm an affectionate squeeze.

As long as Ami was happy, I would keep my misgivings about Hermes to myself. She deserved the chance to build a relationship with him, if that's what she wanted.

"So, Dad," I began, steering us back on topic, "you have no idea why Athena would be interested in our little Halloween festival?"

"Athena?" Hermes asked.

"The girls think they may have seen her." Apollo shrugged, looking exasperated about being back on this topic. "I couldn't fathom my sister's motives. But I doubt she is attending your mortal celebrations, especially unannounced. Visiting temples and sacred rites, perhaps, but costumed revelry?" He shook his head. "It seems rather beneath the dignity of a goddess."

"With all due respect, you popping in out of nowhere after all this time, with brother in tow, comes off just as arbitrary," I pointed out. I didn't point out he seemed to feel confident speaking for Hermes over there—or that he was sitting in Athena's former temple.

"Perhaps. Perhaps it is." Apollo's eyes shone bright. "In any case, let's make the most of our time together, shall we?" He rose, clapping his hands together. "Come now, your festival awaits! We can't miss a moment of the merriment."

With simultaneous casual snaps of their fingers, Apollo and Hermes transformed all our outfits into elaborate ancient Greek costumes, as if we were about to partake in an ancient ritual rather than a modern festival kickoff.

I glanced down to find myself dressed in a flowing ivory chiton pinned at the shoulders with intricate gold brooches. A braided gold belt cinched my waist, with leather sandals lacing up my calves. My hair was arranged in an elegant braided updo adorned with gold leaves and coils.

The others wore similarly resplendent attire— gowns of linen and chiffon, leather sandals, and gilded accessories. The intricately draped fabrics, hand-wrought jewelry, and historically accurate details made even store-bought costumes look cheap and garish by comparison.

Even Aunt Gwennie was decked out.

"Whoa," Ami breathed.

"Right?" Althea agreed.

"You could pass for goddesses straight off Mount Olympus," Archie declared, bug-eyed with wonder.

And as out of the blue as this paternal visit was, I couldn't deny it was kind of nice having the family together to share in the holiday fun.

Even messed up, partially immortal families like ours.

CHAPTER NINE

The town square was alive with excitement and revelry as we made our way through the bustling crowds. People thronged along the cobblestone streets and open green spaces around the city hall, all decked out in colorful costumes and laughing faces. The strands of twinkling orange lights crisscrossed overhead like glimmering spiderwebs just above gentle wafts of hot cider, pumpkin spice, and sugary fried treats.

As we wove through the costumed revelers, I caught sight of Eddie and Emma waving at us.

"There you are! And holy wow!" the un-costumed Emma bellowed in her trademark loud voice designed to carry over police sirens. She surveyed our flowing gowns and intricate gold accessories. "Killer costumes, ladies. Let me guess —Greek goddesses?"

I glanced down at my ivory gown. "Courtesy of an unexpected visit from two of the divine dads."

Emma's jaw dropped.

"I'll tell you all about it later."

"You'd better." Emma smiled, jostling a lightly bundled baby Hunter in her arms. "Now I kind of regret not dressing up this year—I'm jealous of how fantastic you all look. I can barely get this little guy to keep a hat on, let alone an ancient Greek getup."

Hunter babbled happily at the sight of me, waving a chubby little fist in my direction.

"Hi there! There's my cheerful boy!" I cooed as I booped his little baby nose.

His enormous eyes crinkled with delight and he gave me a toothless grin, kicking his legs.

Hunter's innocent joy and love never failed to lift my spirits. No matter what else was going on, time with this sweet little baby always melted my heart.

As I pulled back, I noticed Briggs making his way through the crowd toward us out of the corner of my eye.

"Evening all," he said as he approached us. Despite the casual tone, the new detective's posture was ramrod straight, shoulders squared as he surveyed the lively festival scene. His sharp gaze scanned the crowded square, watchful for any signs of trouble.

"At ease, detective," I teased. "It's a party, not a crime scene."

"It was a crime scene," he pointed out.

"Good point. But it isn't anymore and it won't be the rest of the weekend."

"From your lips to the public safety gods' ears." Briggs gave me a wry half-smile and his expression softened a bit. "Can't be too careful. I got Chief's orders to monitor things." His smile faded. "Especially after...well, you know. So that's what I'm doing."

An uncomfortable silence settled over our group at the mention of Marcus's murder. The discovery still cast a pall over what should have been a lighthearted event.

"Are you making any progress in the investigation?" Emma asked.

Briggs gave a noncommittal shrug. "Well, I'm not you, Detective. As Harmon is very fond of reminding me daily."

"And I'm not a detective anymore." Emma squeezed Hunter.

"I hear you. Just big shoes to fill," Briggs said with a self-deprecating huff. "I could make some progress if I wasn't constantly getting tangled up in all that bureaucratic red tape."

"And I hear you." Emma gave him an understanding look. "Sounds like you're a real detective to me, Briggs. It's not an easy role, but you're up to the task. Trust your instincts. And you can always come to us for help if you need it. I hope you know that."

"You and Astra?"

"Me and Astra, me and Eddie—Eddie was a detective in Palm Beach, Astra was a skip tracer in the military. All of us have experience, and we're always happy to give you some help or advice. Especially since you work in a town as unique as Forkbridge. Off the record."

Briggs nodded, seeming grateful for the supportive words. But then he paused, brow furrowing as though he'd just processed Emma's full statement. "What do you mean 'unique'?" he asked, eyeing Emma with sudden wariness. "Unique how?"

"I think what Emma meant is that with her investigative experience and my...unique skill set and knowledge, we may be able to glean insights that conventional methods could miss," I said.

Emma laughed. "Yeah, sure, that's what I meant."

Briggs swiveled his gaze between us, eyes narrowing with suspicion. "Why do I feel you two aren't telling me something?"

"We just want to help however we can, Briggs," I said. "Emma has her investigative instincts. I have my areas of obscure expertise. Together we hope we can aid in your efforts. That's all there is to it."

After a tense beat, Briggs nodded.

Ami touched my arm. "Hey, can we go try to find Wyatt and the rest of the pack?" she suggested. "I want to introduce him to my father."

"I think I saw them over by the food stands near city hall earlier." Emma's eyes glinted. "You should go find them. You need to witness Wyatt's costume choice for yourself, Ami. Your eyes are going to bug right out of your head when you see it."

I glanced between them. "Why, what did he dress up like?"

Ami looked bemused as well. "Should I be concerned?"

"Oh no, it's nothing bad," Emma said, her grin

widening. "But let's just say he committed to an...interesting look, and it's one my brother will not be very pleased about."

I let Ami steer me away toward the food stands.

In short order, we found Wyatt and the other werewolves (aside from Lothian) gathered around a picnic table laden with caramel apples, pumpkin pie, and other tasty treats.

Wyatt was dressed up as a stereotypical vampire, complete with fake fangs and a billowing satin-lined cape.

"Has Rex seen you in that getup yet?" I asked.

"No, I wanted it to be a surprise." Wyatt tilted his head. "Do you think he'll like it?"

No.

No, I didn't.

"You know what? I'm sure he'll appreciate the effort you put into it," I said.

As we stood beside their table, I caught a glimpse of Gordon Schmidt a few feet from us. He was one of Marcus's political rivals, and he moved through the crowd shaking hands and chatting people up with his politician's smile. His sharp eyes met mine before he pivoted on his heel to head in the opposite direction, vanishing into the ocean of costumes like a fish darting away into murky waters.

I frowned.

That was weird.

It almost looked like he went the opposite direction to avoid shaking my hand.

Ami gave me a quizzical look, but I just shook my head. "Nothing, just thought I saw someone. Forget it." Tonight wasn't the time to worry about Schmidt.

"Welcome, everyone!" Mayor Paul Marchand's voice boomed out suddenly over the loudspeakers. He stood on a makeshift stage near the pumpkin patch, beaming out at the audience.

"What a glorious night to launch Forkbridge's first annual Halloween festival!" More cheering erupted, and Marchand waited for it to die down before continuing. "We have many people to thank for making this wonderful event happen..."

As the mayor spoke, I spotted Angela Hayes elbowing her way to the front of the stage in her Elvira costume, ready to take over the mic. Sure enough, after a few more generic "thanks to the community" comments, Marchand introduced her.

Angela strode up the steps, blowing kisses to the crowd. "Wasn't Mayor Marchand's speech just delightful?" she trilled into the mic. A few halfhearted claps sounded from the audience.

I rolled my eyes.

"I know if Councilman Marcus Clinton were here, he would be so pleased to see all of you enjoying the festival he championed into being." Angela placed a hand over her heart, casting her gaze heavenward. "Let's have fun tonight in Marcus's memory!"

With that brief speech, she flounced off stage to scattered, obligatory applause.

* * *

ONCE EMMA ARRIVED at the picnic table with Eddie, I grabbed her and steered her away from the lively festival crowds, needing a moment of quiet with my best friend. The merry din faded to background noise as we ducked into a secluded grove of trees strung with twinkling lights.

"It looks like it's a success for the most part," I said. "Except for the dead body in the coffin."

Emma nodded, shifting the sleepy baby in her arms. "It's definitely been eventful. But everyone seems to be having fun, regardless." She raised her eyebrow. "Which doesn't say a lot about Marcus, actually."

"He was a politician. Do politicians have genuine relationships with people?" I leaned back against a tree, watching the costumed crowds wander past our hideaway. "I'm glad the murder isn't overshadowing things. Maybe it's just because I'm a witch, but I love Halloween."

"For sure." Emma followed my gaze, her expression thoughtful. After a moment, she glanced back at me. "How are you guys doing with everything else going on?" She pointed toward the extra Greek god hovering over Ami. "Hermes, yeah? That must've really thrown Ami for a loop."

I took a long exhale. "That's the understatement of the year. I still can't believe he just breezed in unannounced with Dad and expected instant forgiveness."

Emma uttered a soothing murmur of commiseration. "I'll never understand the way your gods handle things. So entitled and oblivious sometimes."

"First, they're not mine, and second, right?" I threw my hands up like I just won an invisible championship of frustration. "Here we were, living peacefully with no sign of him, and suddenly Hermes decides Halloween is the perfect time to introduce himself to the daughter he's been ignoring for months. With no notice."

"I don't blame you for being annoyed," Emma said. "Especially with how much Ami has struggled with his lack of reaction."

"She needed him back then. Needed him to at least acknowledge her. She doesn't need him now and his showing up better not do more harm than good." I crossed my arms. "I hope Ami doesn't just let him waltz all entitled into her life after one conversation."

Emma shifted Hunter to her other arm, patting his back gently. "Well, it's her decision who she allows in her life and on what terms." Her tone turned wry. "As you know too well, Ms. 'I ran away to join the military.'"

I sighed. "You're right, I know. I'm trying not to meddle too much, but I just worry about her getting hurt again. She was inconsolable after Mom died, and that divine jerk didn't help matters."

"You'll watch out for her. That's what family is for—having each other's backs." Emma smiled. "Ami's lucky to have you."

I managed a small smile in return. "I hope so."

We fell into a comfortable silence then, watching masquerading revelers wander past. My thoughts turned to Lothian, and I realized I hadn't seen him at all.

"By the way, where is he?" I said.

"Who?"

"Lothian."

"Oh, I'd rather not get in the middle of...whatever this is," Emma hedged, raising an eyebrow. "But I'm mated to the alpha werewolf and I'm holding the next generation alpha in waiting, so I suppose I can spare some opinionated comments on the subject without worrying too much. Let me guess—you've already met a certain bouncy visitor?"

"I think classifying what happened as an introduction or a meeting might be stretching it." I shook my head, irritation flaring. "April dragged him off once she found him in town and he never came back to talk to me. He hasn't called me. He didn't show up here with everyone else, even though he was supposed to meet me here an hour ago. Explain to me why I shouldn't think they're off canoodling somewhere?"

"Well, listening to the situation listed out like that? I sympathize," Emma said. "I can empathize with your annoyance."

"Right?" I threw up my hands. "Who acts like that when they're in a relationship? Who the heck is this woman, anyway? Do you know anything about her?"

"Not much. I wish I did." Emma made a sympathetic noise. "Look, there's a few things I've learned about these guys since Eddie and I got together. One? There's still some aspect of them that will always be mysterious, calculating, and predatory. It's a part of them. With Eddie, it creeps in when he's chasing a bad guy. With Wyatt, it's when he's protecting someone. With Lothian, it comes out in business. Dude is ruthless when it comes to business."

"Thanks for the pack personality lesson," I quipped, arching an eyebrow at Emma's attempt to school me.

"You're welcome." Her lips curved into a sly grin. "And don't get saucy with me, Bearnaise. I've heard from my brother how little you witches mingled with the other species and races when your old bosses were in charge. I probably know more about werewolves than you do, at least as far as how to have an interpersonal relationship with one of them."

"I'll have you know there was an entire class on werewolves and I got an A."

"How to catch them, you mean?"

With a huff, I crossed my arms. "Your point?"

She leaned in, her tone a mix of confidence and amusement. "I could teach you a thing or two about werewolves. And you know it."

"You think? Let's give that a whirl, then." My face probably looked as sour as if I'd downed a straight shot of lemon juice. "Is there some kind of species-specific excuse for Mr. Mysterious disappearing on me and not even bothering to dial a phone to apologize or explain?" I waved a hand in an exaggerated flourish, mimicking a magician's act. "Poof! Off he goes, chasing after Miss April Bouncy Bosoms in the middle of Forkbridge town square. Go. Explain it."

"Well..." Emma hesitated, then exhaled a defeated sigh. "I can't. He should have at least called. I said I could tell you about things Lothian might do. I didn't say I could explain or justify why he does everything he does."

"Uh huh."

"Honestly, I don't know who she is."

"I don't care who she is. It's about Lothian's behavior. Not hers."

"Preach," Emma agreed.

Just then, Gordon Schmidt peeked through the gaps in the bushes, his head popping in like a curious jack-in-the-box. "Evening ladies," he greeted cordially. "Quite the celebration, isn't it?"

I extended my hand for a friendly shake, but his gaze dropped to it as if my hand were a hot potato he wanted nothing to do with. "Oh, goodness, no. I can't do that. I've had a cold for the last week and I'm sure my sanitizer has worn off. Wouldn't want to give you a cold, Ms. Arden."

I managed a polite smile. "Not a problem, Mr. Schmidt. But yes, it's something. People seem to be having fun."

Twice, Gordon Schmidt pulled this odd move —like he was totally averse to a simple handshake from me. The first time, I shrugged it off, but this time, a prickle of curiosity ran up my spine.

"They sure do." Schmidt nodded. "Say, I overheard you mention Lothian Pennington. I just wanted to tell you how grateful I am for his generous donation to my city council election campaign."

"How nice," I said flatly.

News of Lothian cozying up to politicians soured my mood even further.

Like a true politician, Schmidt was oblivious to my tone and charged on. "With Lothian's support, I'm confident the voters will make the right choice to give me back my city council seat. Good man, Lothian. He understands the importance of picking reasonable leaders to move this town forward."

"Does he?" I asked, unable to keep the skepticism from my voice.

If Schmidt picked up on it, he didn't let on. "Absolutely. Lothian is a man of vision and integrity. We're of a similar mindset on key issues. Given the unfortunate passing of Marcus and our town's modest size, I'm confident we can expedite an election. Lothian's gracious backing assures I'll be back in my seat, possibly within weeks. Your late mother, may she rest in peace, would be proud of the outcome."

Oh, that's right, now I remembered—Marcus had defeated Gordon just a couple of years ago, ousting him from a ten-year reign of power. It happened just a month or two after I first moved back. I'd heard my mother talk about the fact that Gordon was irate over the defeat—and despite old Gordon's claim, my mother couldn't stand him.

He didn't seem so irate now.

As if sensing my skepticism about dear old Mom's afterlife position on Forkbridge politics, Schmidt frowned. "I understand you and Lothian are...close. I hope I haven't overstepped by complimenting him to you."

"Not at all," I replied. "I agree Lothian is very civic-minded these days. All that matters is Forkbridge thrives, right?"

"Right," Schmidt said. He shifted from foot to foot, perhaps realizing I wasn't as enamored with Lothian at the moment as he'd assumed. "Well, I should mingle. Enjoy the festival!"

With an awkward parting smile, he slipped back into the crowds.

Leaning against a nearby tree, I watched him go. "Did you notice Georgie avoided my handshake? He did that earlier, too. Saw me and did an about face like his butt was on fire and he needed to sit in a rain barrel," I told Emma.

"Astra, you do have a reputation thanks to your time with the police. Maybe he's taking those newspaper articles at face value and thinks you're capable of all they claimed. There could be something he's caught wind of, or something he knows that he's determined to keep under wraps."

Like killing Marcus?

The idea was a giant leap, I had to admit. But the timing of it all and his apparent gains from the councilman's death added an unsettling layer to the puzzle. If it was him, though, why would—

"Stop," Emma interrupted, a knowing smile

playing on her lips. "I can practically hear your brain gears grinding. Remember, we're here to enjoy ourselves."

Linking my arm through Emma's, I smiled. "You're right. Let's get back to everyone and have some fun. Time enough to think tomorrow."

Leaving thoughts of fickle boyfriends and clueless politicians behind, Emma and I made our way back toward the festival lights and music.

The night was young, and I was determined to enjoy it.

With or without my boyfriend.

CHAPTER TEN

Stepping out after Emma, I took in a deep whiff of the pumpkin spice perfumed breeze. My exasperation with Lothian and Schmidt had receded for now, and I was intent on enjoying the festivities alongside my sisters.

I was, that is, until an unwelcome voice grated behind me like the screeching brakes on a speeding city bus. "Astra Arden! Just who I wanted to see."

I immediately recognized the dulcet tones of Angela Hayes.

So much for a peaceful night out.

Hastily plastering a pleasant smile on my face, I turned to find her glaring at me, hands planted judgmentally on her wide hips. Her beady eyes bored into me like twin drills behind her ostentatious cat-eye glasses.

"Hello, Angela. Everything okay?"

"No, everything is not okay," she snapped. "I've been getting complaints all night from party goers about the poor state of the decorations near city hall. And, of course, that's where everyone is going because Marcus was found there."

She was dressed in a tight, low-cut black gown, her overly peroxided hair sprayed black and teased within an inch of its life. Crimson lipstick and fake lashes completed her attempt at channeling Elvira, Mistress of the Dark—though the costume looked more gaudy than sultry on her.

"I'm so sorry to hear that," I responded.

I prayed she was commiserating and that my tone was off-putting enough she would find some other shoulder to whine on, but knowing Angela, she was more likely getting warmed up to launch into a litany of petty grievances. Fake smile frozen in place, I steeled myself for the onslaught.

Angela let out an exasperated huff. "Well, I certainly doubt that since you and your sister did such a slapdash job on setup. Why did only two of you bother to help? Weren't we supposed to have four of you?"

"Now hold on," I said, irritation rising. "Ami and I worked hard on those decorations under pretty challenging circumstances, and it was just us because Althea and Ayla needed to keep our shop open at the busiest time of the year. It's not our fault if some decorations got damaged or moved by the crowds tonight."

"No? Well, whose fault is it then?" Angela challenged, peering over her nose at me imperiously.

"Angela, we're unpaid volunteers doing you a favor, remember? We finished the job to the best of our ability. If there are issues, take it up with the actual event staff the city is paying during the festival to handle stuff like this."

Angela thrust her pointy chin out indignantly. "Marcus involving you people was such a mistake. I knew we shouldn't have relied on a bunch of pretend witches for a job requiring competence and professionalism."

Her mocking "pretend witches" barb made me burn to show precisely how fictional my powers were, but before I could fire off an angry retort, Ami touched my arm, giving me a subtle shake of her head.

I knew she was right. Losing my temper would only delight Angela.

"You clearly have concerns about how things were handled," I said evenly. "Why don't we discuss this in the morning when tensions aren't running so high?"

"High tensions are no excuse for shoddy work and stubborn refusal to fix mistakes," she lectured, fueled by too many pumpkin spice lattes and too much self-righteous indignation. "Honestly, I don't know why Marcus ever thought involving charlatans like you in this event was a good idea. This town should work to put Cassandra out of business, not work to replace it as the hotbed of devilry."

I raised an eyebrow. "What do you mean?"

Angela blinked, looking briefly wrong-footed by my sudden focus, but she recovered quickly. "What do I mean? Well, obviously, it was Marcus's plan to use you four to generate buzz and draw people away from that other Halloween festival. He was obsessed with beating Cassandra's festival turnout. Poor man."

"Was he?" I watched her closely.

Angela averted her gaze, flapping a hand dismissively. "Yes, yes, everyone knows the overarching obsession with eclipsing Cassandra's festival was his."

Everything I'd heard about the festival's

development pointed to it being chiefly Angela's baby—yet now she seemed intent on distancing herself from the planning and laying the credit—or blame—on Marcus.

There had to be a reason.

Angela put her hands on her hips. "Why are you interrogating me about this? I don't have time for a bunch of pointless questions when there's work to be done."

I shrugged, keeping my tone casual. "Just making conversation. But back to the decorations—we followed all the instructions we were given to the letter. If changes needed to be made, that's on you as lead coordinator. We were on the setup crew." I stretched out my arm and pointed. "It's set up."

Angela swelled indignantly, gearing up for a fresh tirade about our supposed incompetence, no doubt. Before she could launch into it, Ami jumped in.

"We're happy to talk to the event staff and work with them to fix any issues," she interjected smoothly, giving me a quelling look, and then turned her most placating smile on Angela. "I'm sure we can get everything picture perfect again."

Angela pressed her thin lips together, reluctantly mollified by Ami's diplomatic offer.

"See that you do," she sniffed. With one last glare at me, she whirled and flounced off into the crowd.

I watched her disappear, eyes narrowed.

Something about her attitude tonight struck me as a smidge forced and evasive. Almost guilty.

Almost.

"What was that about?" Ami asked me.

"I don't know, honestly," I murmured. "But the more Angela tries to lay responsibility for this whole thing on Marcus, the more convinced I am she might have something to do with what happened to Marcus."

Ami's eyes widened. "You don't think she—"

"I'm not sure yet," I admitted. "It's just a feeling. But her insistence that it was all Marcus's vision when she'd driven the whole thing and is now the one running around obsessing over every little detail? What she said just makes little sense."

Ami bit her lip, looking troubled. "Do you really think she would have killed him over a festival?"

"She certainly had opportunity if they were working together." I gave my head a quick shake from side to side. "No. I don't know. Maybe I'm grasping at straws. But something felt off about her demeanor tonight."

"Should we tell Briggs?" Ami asked.

I considered it. While Angela's behavior struck me as odd, I had nothing solid to implicate her yet.

"Let's hold off for now," I decided. "I'd rather not send Briggs on a wild goose chase without more proof." I met Ami's concerned gaze. "But we'll monitor Mrs. Hayes. Something just isn't adding up with her."

* * *

I STILL HADN'T GLIMPSED Lothian at the festival and a few hours in, my earlier devotion to distraction had faded, replaced by simmering hurt and irritation.

I told myself I should probably just text him to find out where he was, but despite that brilliant and obvious idea, my phone remained in my pocket.

He knew my number.

If Lothian wanted to talk, he could call me.

"Looking for someone?"

I spun around and caught sight of Wyatt sneaking up to my side, his Dracula cape swishing behind him. I had to smile once more at his costume choice—a vampire getup seemed highly ironic for a werewolf, but Wyatt pulled it off with his typical understated flair.

I shrugged. "Just people watching. Where's Ami?"

"She's off talking to Hermes. Your father is doing his family therapy psychology thing with them, too—which is weird, I don't mind saying." Wyatt followed my gaze, which kept involuntarily drifting toward the festival entrance as if I could will Lothian to materialize through sheer mental effort. "She asked me to check on you while she was talking to them."

"I'm fine."

"Uh huh," Wyatt said, clearly unconvinced. He elbowed me gently. "You know, you could just call him yourself instead of waiting around here all mopey."

I bristled slightly at the implication. "I am not being all mopey."

"Brooding, then. Or maybe sulking is the right word." Wyatt grinned, dodging the halfhearted swat I aimed at his shoulder. His expression turned serious. "Want me to track him down for you?"

I wavered, pride warring with longing.

After a moment, I sighed, shoulders slumping. "No. I shouldn't have to hunt him down. I'm just..." I trailed off, struggling to verbalize the hurt I felt. "I don't trust easily, Wyatt. I trusted him, and now I'm standing here wondering if that was a huge mistake."

Wyatt nodded, eyes gentle with understanding. "You're wondering where he ran off to without an explanation. And who this chick even is who seems awfully handsy with your man. Am I right?"

"No." I exhaled, mortified someone could see what I was feeling.

"No?" he asked, and chuckled.

"When you say it like that, I'm embarrassed for being so bothered by it. But yes, it bothered me. How she jumped on him bothered me. How he walked away bothered me. Is that so unreasonable?"

"Not at all," Wyatt said firmly.

He gestured toward a picnic table off to the side, away from the crowds. I followed and gratefully sunk onto the bench, the cheery festival atmosphere feeling at odds with my melancholy mood.

Wyatt settled across from me, expression thoughtful. "Look, Lothian's my brother now, but that doesn't mean I always agree with how he handles things." He leaned forward, elbows resting on the table. "Especially with relationships. Subtlety isn't his strong suit, and consideration is something he's still learning."

Despite myself, I huffed out a short laugh. "You could say that again."

Wyatt grinned before growing serious once more. "I can't excuse what happened earlier, and you're justified in feeling angry. But don't write him off just yet. Talk to him first."

As if summoned by our conversation, I spotted a familiar blond head weaving through the crowd toward us. My pulse quickened, equal parts anticipation and nerves.

Sensing my stare shift, Wyatt looked to see what caught my attention.

"Speak of the wolf and he will appear," he remarked wryly. Wyatt stood and clapped his hands like a conductor signaling the last note of a symphony. "I'll give you two some privacy. But remember what I said." With an encouraging smile, he walked off into the festival commotion.

I watched Wyatt go, then turned to face Lothian as he reached the picnic table, an uncertain smile teasing his lips. His sapphire blue eyes were clouded with guilt.

"Hey," he greeted softly.

"Hey yourself," I returned, voice cool. I crossed my arms, pulse thrumming as I waited to see how he would explain himself.

Lothian exhaled, running a hand through his tousled blond hair. "Look, Astra, I'm really sorry about earlier. Ditching you like that was a jerk move, no question." His beautiful eyes stayed locked with mine, contrition evident in his expression. "I messed up. And I'm hoping you'll give me a chance to explain everything."

I considered him for a prolonged beat, searching those sparkling blue eyes that usually made me feel cared for and protected. He seemed genuinely contrite. With a curt nod, I agreed. "Fine. Explain, then."

Looking relieved, Lothian sank onto the bench across from me. "You have every right to be upset," he began earnestly, echoing Wyatt's words. "When April showed up out of the blue, I guess I just got overwhelmed and didn't handle it well."

He took a breath before continuing.

"April manages one of my clubs down in Palm Beach. We had a..." He shifted, avoiding my gaze. "A brief fling awhile back. But it never amounted to anything serious, and we both moved on, or so I thought. I guess she didn't get the memo. That's all ancient history now. She caught me off guard seeing her here—but that's no excuse for brushing you off."

Lothian reached across the table, taking my hand in his.

I let him.

"You are the only one I want to be with. What we have is real." His eyes stormy with emotion stayed locked on mine. "I know I made a mistake today, but I promise you have nothing to worry about with April. She's just a colleague. That's all."

She was a colleague that whisked him away from me with no effort.

A colleague that distracted him so much he never called to explain.

A colleague that made him late without so much as a text.

I studied our joined hands, turning his words over in my mind.

The hurt and questions swirling inside me had quieted somewhat. I was soothed by the candor I sensed through our joined hands, and I believed Lothian regretted his thoughtless actions.

But I didn't like what had happened today.

And I didn't like how it made me feel.

"Thank you for explaining all that. I appreciate you being honest." I met his earnest gaze. "I just need a little time to process everything."

Relief broke across Lothian's face as if I'd fully forgiven him. He gave my hand a grateful squeeze. "Of course, take all the time you need. I meant what I said, though." He smiled hopefully. "You're my priority. My partner. As long as you're by my side, nothing else matters."

"You can stop pouring it on like a broken faucet with the handles stripped off."

"Nope. I can't." He smiled.

Lothian could be infuriating, but it felt like his reckless heart was in the right place. The depth of his feelings for me shone through the nagging sting and doubt, lighting a flame of hope inside me.

* * *

THE FESTIVAL WAS WINDING down for the night, costumed revelers drifting away in small groups. I lingered near the perimeter listening to my family and extended family chat and laugh, no one quite ready to leave.

Ami appeared at my side, stifling a yawn behind her hand. "You ready to head home?"

I started to reply when a gruff voice spoke from the shadows.

"Astra. Got a minute?"

I turned to see Chief Harmon step from the darkness surrounding the road, his face unreadable in the dim glow of the street lamps. Surprise rippled through me, and I wondered what on earth was with tonight. Is Forkbridge Halloween when all the issues of the past year show up to be dealt with like zombies lumbering out of the shadows?

If so, it would not be very successful.

No one would sign up for this.

"Of course, Chief. What can I do for you?"

He jerked his head toward a secluded grove of trees nearby. "Let's talk over there. Away from prying ears."

I nodded and followed him into the relative privacy of the grove, curiosity mingling with wariness. I felt like I was approaching a coiled rattlesnake barefoot. Over my shoulder, I said, "I'll be back in a minute, Ami. Then we can go."

Ami raised her eyebrow, eyes questioning. I gave her a subtle nod of assurance, and she reluctantly left us alone among the trees.

Harmon turned to face me, rubbing his jaw. He seemed to wrestle with how to begin, and I waited, silently, for him to gather his thoughts.

"Look, Astra, I know things have been...strained between us since Jason passed." He held my gaze, regret shadowing his flinty eyes. "We patched things up a bit, and then when Emma quit—" He paused abruptly. "Look, she was a damn excellent investigator, and losing her was a blow to the department."

I stood silent.

"But you were, too. And while she was there, I knew we had access to your abilities, even if I wasn't paying you. I knew you'd help if we really needed it. Now, with you both gone?" He looked out over the crowds. "I'm struggling a little."

I blinked, shocked by this uncharacteristic admission. "I'm sorry if Emma's choice made things more difficult for you, but I didn't quit the department, Chief," I said carefully. "You fired me. I enjoyed helping people. I liked my job."

Harmon nodded. "And you did help many people. There's no question. Including me." He cleared his throat gruffly. "Which is why I need to explain myself and try to make things right."

He paused, jaw tightening. I sensed this

vulnerability didn't come easily to the taciturn chief.

"When Emma first partnered with you, I'll admit I had my doubts," he confessed. "Letting a civilian with no law enforcement training advise on cases seemed like a fool's errand. But it quickly became clear your contributions were invaluable. Your niche expertise cracked multiple tough cases. You proved yourself to me again and again."

Despite myself, I smiled slightly at the rare compliment. From Harmon, that amounted to a glowing endorsement.

"So what changed?" I asked bluntly, but not unkindly.

Harmon's shoulders slumped a fraction. "After Jason died, things with Mayor Thornton grew...complicated. As you know."

I nodded.

No need to rehash that turbulent history.

We both remembered his girlfriend almost shot me.

"She made it very clear if I wanted to maintain a relationship with her, you could no longer be involved with the department in any capacity. I know you know this already, but I needed to say it to you directly. I chose her over you. For personal reasons." His jaw clenched, a crack appearing in his stoic facade. "It was an impossible position she put me in. But you have to understand, Astra, I love her...I lost my wife years ago, to Cancer. I don't know if you knew that."

I shook my head. "No, sir. I didn't."

"Few people do. It's not something I talk about. But I just couldn't lose Lil, too, and I was willing to do anything I could to help her pain. Anything. Even if it was wrong. I thought she'd come around as she worked through what happened, but..."

But she never came around.

Harmon's raw admission stunned me. A wave of empathy washed over me, cooling the lingering hurt and resentment his actions had fostered. We'd both suffered painful losses in our lives, and I could relate to that soul-deep fear of further grief.

"I'm sorry for your loss, Chief. I can't imagine how difficult that was."

Gratitude flashed across Harmon's weathered face. "Thank you. It's no excuse for how I handled things, but hopefully it provides some explanation." He met my gaze. "I let Lil pressure me into making a decision I regretted. I should have stood by you, and Emma told me how I treated you was part of the reason it was so easy for her to walk away. I got angry at you for her quitting, even though it was partly my fault."

Emma had never told me I'd played any role in her decision to leave the force, and I felt a swell of guilt. "I didn't know."

"No reason you should. Jason pulled me aside through one of the other mediums in Cassandra and gave me a what for earlier today, though, for even thinking about throwing you in jail. Which I did think about." The gruff cop looked sheepish, and I met his remorseful gaze with an amused but understanding smile. "I'm ashamed it took me this long to understand what I did. And I'm sorry."

I blinked back tears.

Jason was still looking out for me.

Even now.

I considered Harmon for a long moment as he awaited my response. The anger and mistrust I'd carried faded away as I realized the chief was as flawed as any of us. But he had sought me out tonight and shown humility I wouldn't have thought him capable of—that courage spoke louder than any words.

Finally, I extended my hand. "Apology accepted, Chief."

Relief broke across Harmon's face.

"Does this mean you'll consider lending your skills to the department again?" Hope tinged the chief's voice. "Discreetly, of course. We're drowning without Emma, and I could use your instincts on the Clinton case." His mouth twisted wryly. "Clearly Briggs is not making much headway."

"I've already been helping Briggs a bit."

A rare smile crinkled the corners of his eyes. "Thank you, Astra."

"What about Jason's mother?" I asked, unable to let go of my lingering doubts.

"That's not your problem," Harmon said gently but firmly. "And I promise to stop making it your problem."

I chewed my lip, conflicted emotions swirling within me. Part of me understood I couldn't continue shouldering the blame and anger Jason's mother directed my way. What happened to her son was tragic, but ultimately not my fault, regardless of the role my mother played.

At the same time, I couldn't help but feel for her even now. If it brought her some measure of comfort to vilify me as the cause of her loss, wasn't it kinder to allow it? Keeping the peace had always been my priority.

But the chief was right—Jason's mother would likely never forgive me, and we all needed to stop accommodating her misplaced fury. All we could do was live our lives with compassion and hope she found some sliver of peace one day.

Until then, her hatred would have to remain her own burden to carry.

CHAPTER ELEVEN

I tossed and turned in bed, unable to quiet my restless mind. The day's events kept replaying—the unexpected arrival of Hermes, Lothian's thoughtless behavior, Angela's odd insistence that the festival was all Marcus's idea, the chief's—

"What's it going to take for you to pipe down and get some rest, a magical sleep potion?" Archie quipped from his perch near the open window. "I already had to stay home with the bird and the dog. Now you want to rob me of my beauty sleep, too? Just close your eyes and snooze already."

"If you don't like it, go hunt or something." With a frustrated huff, I punched my pillow and flipped over again, kicking off the sheets twisted around my legs. Sleep remained elusive. The old house creaked and settled around me in the darkness. "Aren't owls nocturnal, anyway?"

"You're thinking of owls that don't have witches to give them bacon. Besides, a heavy meal before bed? What am I, a masochist looking for a night of searing heartburn and restless tossing and turning like you?" he said. "I think I'll pass on inflicting pain on myself, but thanks for the awful suggestion."

I sighed and threw an arm over my eyes. "You're annoying."

"I'm annoying? Says the worrywart who's stressing over everything and nothing. Your anxiety is so loud the dolphins off the coast are wondering what's wrong."

I sank into the mattress, the sheets cool against my skin as Archie's words echoed in my mind. I opened my mouth, a barbed reply on my lips, but clenched my jaw before it could slip free.

He was right.

Of course, he was right. If I continued churning over every detail of the day, sleep would remain as distant as the moon.

I squeezed my eyes shut and focused on the rise and fall of my chest the way they'd taught me in the military. Soldiers could sleep anywhere.

Inhale.

Exhale.

Like waves smoothing the sand, the frenzied activity in my mind ebbed as an abnormally cool breeze drifted through the open window. I shivered as it raised goosebumps on my bare arms.

"Archie, are you too cold?" I mumbled.

Silence. That was weird.

"Archie?" I called out more insistently.

More silence.

Propping myself up on my elbows, I peered through the inky blackness toward the window bathed in moonlight. To my surprise, a figure stood silhouetted against the lunar-lit frame. I bolted upright, heart pounding.

"Who's there?" I demanded.

The shadowy figure stepped forward into a shaft of moonglow. I recognized the woman's flowing garments and winged helmet—it was the blond woman from the festival, the one dressed as Athena.

I slid back against the headboard, staring. "Well, I guess that answers the question of whether you're human." I narrowed my eyes. "But just because you're supernatural doesn't mean you're a goddess." I looked around. "Where's my owl?"

"My owl." The woman's ice blue eyes glinted. "Did you really believe it mere happenstance that brought someone to your celebration clad in the vestments of divine Athena herself? Though you comprehend little of the gods' grand designs, Olympus ever turns around you, child."

"Um, yeah, I was pretty sure it was a coincidence. It's Halloween. People dress up for Halloween," I said. "A goddess doesn't just pop in for a Halloween festival unannounced. That would be ridiculous."

"Would it? The ways of the gods are obscured to mortal minds. The tapestry of fate is woven with threads mortal eyes cannot discern. Even witches can only see but a hint of the magic."

"What do you want?" I asked. "I'm tired. So either tell me what you want or see yourself out."

The woman tilted her head. "My knowledge encompasses all, yet questioning is beneath you. My wisdom is thy torch in the night, and yet you choose to sit in darkness. Disappointing."

"I'm in darkness because I'm trying to sleep. Something you're making impossible." I was tired, and cranky, and just plain irritated at the dramatics. "Why are you here?"

The woman pressed her hand over her heart. "I am she who gifted you purpose. She who entrusted you with celestial might to mete out justice." Her eyes flashed like lightning. "I am Athena. My gifts will guide thee if thou trust in me."

I stared at Athena and though I knew somewhere within me this was a dream, I also knew that just because it was a dream for me didn't mean this visitation wasn't real. I sensed the truth of her words, the reality of her presence.

"You must be kidding me," I told her. "My mother screwed up our family trying to earn favor and power using the whims and vagueness of immortal beings who saw mortals as mere playthings. You are fickle and self-serving at best, cruel at worst. I don't worship gods. Don't follow them, don't worship them. Apollo will be damn lucky if I bother to buy him a tie for Father's Day."

I met Athena's gaze, feeling more boldly confident than I ever thought I would feel in her presence. Let her judge me unworthy—her validation meant nothing, and I had no plans to validate her by pretending a piety I didn't feel.

"I seek not rituals nor tributes. For eons beyond count, I have steered heroes, counseled kings, roused artists. For you, I offer only gifts freely given. I wish for you to be discerning, to be prudent, to walk in light—this is reverence enough. Should you tread the path of truth and virtue, you shall have my favor, even though you bend no knee before me. Vain glorification holds no appeal for me. I desire only the enlightenment of humankind." Her voice echoed with ancient authority, yet infinite compassion swirled in her stormy gaze.

"Look, Athena, I—"

Before I get the sentence out of my mouth, the woman glowed from within with a blinding golden radiance that lit up the entire room. I shielded my eyes against the searing brightness. Then, just as quickly, the light receded. The woman stood serenely watching me, not a hair out of place.

I lowered my hand, blinking away residual flashes.

"Well, that was dramatic and pointless," I managed. I took a steadying breath. "Why appear to me like this now? I've had the star power for a few years now, and I never heard from you except when you wanted me to run around saving someone you decided shouldn't die."

The goddess smiled. "I appear in my own

time, according to my own wisdom. I am Athena, peerless among immortals, born not of a woman but of thought itself. The affairs of men are like dust motes in my eternal gaze."

I blinked.

That wasn't an answer.

"Seek me in wise judgment, in skill hard-won, in battles justly fought. Thus shall you find me, in glimpses and glimmers, long before your eyes behold me." Athena clasped her hands. "Darkness stirs in this mortal town, niece. Sinister forces seeking to threaten all you hold dear."

Oh, jeez.

That's right.

Athena's technically my aunt on my father's side.

I sat up straighter. "What are you talking about? What sinister forces?"

Auntie Cryptic looked troubled. "Since the passing of your mother, my vessel in this realm, the protections she wove to protect this temple now fray and fail."

Her words sent a chill down my spine. "Fray how?"

Athena pressed on as if she hadn't heard me. "Powerful interests seek to exploit the fragility left in her absence. On the surface, matters appear calm. This conflict of festivals seems none but petty civic posturing." The goddess raised her chin. "But probing deeper reveals corruption rooted at the heart of this town's power structures. Rotten—and spreading."

"Are you saying Marcus's murder is connected to some kind of larger corruption?"

Athena's ageless gaze remained cryptic, her expression unreadable. "All will become clear in due course," she said.

"With all due respect, could you please just give me straightforward answers?" I asked through gritted teeth. "No more riddles or vagueness."

But Athena was already retreating toward the open window through which pale moonlight spilled onto the floor.

"You have courage, and a passion for truth," she said. "You will find what you need. My time here is ended, but we shall meet again." The goddess held my gaze, her ageless eyes reflecting the eternal wisdom of generations. "Trust in the stars. Stay true to your heart. The light of justice still burns within you. Let it guide your way to what machinations simmer beneath the surface."

As she began dematerializing, her edges grew

hazy, blurring into a silvery mist swirling toward the wide open window.

"Wait!" I cried, lunging forward.

My grasping hands met only empty air as I jolted awake, my own gasp piercing the still darkness of my bedroom. As Archie's soft snores from his perch reassured me I was awake once more, I sank back with a shaky exhale, the goddess's cryptic words echoing through my mind.

* * *

I AWOKE to sunlight streaming in through my open bedroom window. Had that surreal midnight encounter happened, or was it an especially vivid dream?

It happened.

Somehow, I knew.

It happened.

I dressed and headed downstairs, eager to compare notes with my sisters about everything that had transpired yesterday. As I entered the cozy kitchen, the comforting aroma of coffee and sizzling bacon enveloped me.

"There you are, sleepyhead," Aunt Gwennie

greeted me over her shoulder while manning the stove. "I was about to send out a search party."

I smiled as I slid into a chair at the table. "Sorry, rough night. My brain wouldn't turn off."

Ami passed me a steaming mug. "I don't think any of us got much rest after the way yesterday went down."

"No kidding," Ayla agreed through a mouthful of pancake.

"I bet I had a weirder night than you did," I said.

"Oh?"

Once Aunt Gwennie bustled over with a plate of food, I summarized the unexpected late-night encounter with the goddess Athena.

Ayla's eyes went wide. "Whoa. Athena herself just casually popped by your bedroom to chat? That's insane."

"Not my bedroom. In my dreams."

"What did she want?" Althea asked, leaning forward.

I speared a chunk of honeydew melon. "Oh, the usual goddess nonsense. Vague ominous warnings about nameless 'dark forces' lurking in Forkbridge." I rolled my eyes before continuing. "She did say something that was pretty important, I think. She lost her 'conduit' here when Mom died, and now evil is creeping in or our divine shields are messed up or something."

My flippant tone drew reproachful looks from Ami and Aunt Gwennie.

"Astra, dear, far be it from me to tell you how to process a divine visitation, but if it was Athena, perhaps you should take her words a bit more seriously," Aunt Gwennie said.

"I did. And I..." I sighed. "Look, you're probably right. It's just frustrating getting mystical mumbo-jumbo instead of anything concrete I can do something about. On the one hand, sure, that was interesting—on the other hand, she barely said anything. And I don't even know if it was her. It could have just been a dream. I mean, that's possible, right?" As the words left my mouth, I felt a swell of conviction I was telling a big lie.

Aunt Gwennie glared at me.

"Okay, I know it wasn't a dream. Happy now?"

"Well, Athena must have had a reason for the sudden visit and dramatic warnings," Ami pointed out.

"We'll figure it out," Althea said. "Archie can probably clarify what the visit was about."

I nodded. "Where is he?"

"Looking for a capsaicin-free rabbit."

Ami had initially taken offense at Archie's innate owl instinct to snack on the bunnies inhabiting our backyard. To address this, she teamed up with Althea, concocting a plan and a potion to give those nearby rabbits a fiery twist by infusing their natural rabbit flavor with the essence of Carolina Reapers.

Ami snorted. "Good luck with that."

Across the table, Ayla leaned back in her chair with a huff. "Okay, enough about the Greek gods. I want to talk about Lothian pulling a disappearing act yesterday." She fixed me with an expectant look. "What was his deal?"

I quickly recapped my talk with Lothian at the festival and his attempts to smooth things over. "He apologized. Said this April woman was just an old fling and a current colleague. Said he was overwhelmed."

"All day? He was overwhelmed all day?"

I shrugged. "I guess."

"And you bought that line?" Althea asked skeptically.

I bristled at her bluntness. "I'm reserving judgment for the moment."

Ayla laughed. "Wow, he fed you some garbage apology and you're already letting him off the hook?" She shook her head. "Melvin isn't even out of his teens yet and he wouldn't pull that crap with me. Never took you for such a pushover, Astra."

Stung, my mouth parted, ready to slap a stunning retort on my little sister, but Ami interjected.

"It sounds like they're working through a difficult situation. Let's not judge." She gave me an encouraging smile. "Communication is key. I'm sure Astra has plans to talk through the situation further when we aren't so busy."

"Yep, absolutely." I smiled and agreed.

Although I hadn't really made any plans of the sort.

"All I'm saying is, he didn't explain anything," Ayla argued. "Who is April? How well does he know her? Why did she show up out of nowhere during the Halloween festival weekend? Why did he go off with her and not even pick up a phone and call you? He gave you zero relevant details."

Ayla raised a valid point.

Well, points.

Lothian's apology, while seeming heartfelt, was noticeably light on specifics about his history and relationship with April.

"You're right," I acknowledged. "There are still unanswered questions."

"And yet you seem ready to just trust his non-explanation and move on." Ayla shook her head, exasperated by my willingness to potentially excuse Lothian's thoughtless behavior. "No wonder you're almost forty and you haven't made a relationship work yet."

My gaze locked on Ayla, a mixture of surprise and annoyance washing over me.

"Oh, leave her be," Ami chided. "Astra's a big girl. She can handle Lothian."

Ayla held up her hands in mock surrender. "Fine." She stood and dropped her plate in the sink with a clatter. "I'm going to walk Cerberus before we open the shop. Another male in my life, I'll remind you, that exhibits complete loyalty."

Ami's hand shot out in an instant, intercepting my fury before I could unleash my reaction on Ayla. "Just let her go," she whispered.

As my youngest sister left the room, I bit my lip, doubt creeping in as I mulled over her (rather hurtful) words.

Had I been too quick to dismiss Lothian's conduct yesterday? Hearing my sisters' perspectives cast his apology in a less flattering light. While sweet, he explained little—and I walked away without getting many answers.

I didn't want to be critical of Lothian over one

mistake—but perhaps now that we were getting serious, I needed to be more mindful of unhealthy patterns going forward. At the time, I'd accepted it, glad to have the awkwardness behind us.

But Althea and Ayla had a point—Lothian hadn't explained.

Sensing my self-doubt, Ami touched my arm. "Don't let Ayla make you second-guess yourself," she whispered. "Trust your instincts with Lothian. And remember—at least he's trying to make amends."

"You're right," I told her. "Thanks, Ami."

She nodded, looking relieved I wasn't going to write off Lothian at the first bump in the road. I knew she wanted to see me happy with someone, even if that someone was the infuriating and perplexing Lothian Pennington.

After breakfast, we all pitched in tidying up the kitchen. My thoughts kept returning to Athena's dire warnings, though I tried focusing on the day ahead. With the festival underway, the shop would be busy.

CHAPTER TWELVE

The morning hours passed in a blur of activity at the shop as crowds of eager festival-goers streamed in seeking "real" magic wares and occult trinkets between Friday and Saturday night's parties.

Between assisting customers, restocking shelves, and mixing up potions, the afternoon flew by, and before I knew it, dusk was falling outside, with the setting sun casting a golden glow through the shop windows.

I flipped the 'Open' sign to 'Closed' and let out a tired, but satisfied, sigh.

Despite the chaotic lead-up and a murder, the first official day of the festival seemed to go smoothly—at least from what I could gather. No new grim discoveries or unexplained dramas had arisen.

"What a day," Ami remarked, voicing my thoughts while cleaning the sales counter. "I don't think I've ever seen the shop so consistently busy, even at peak times."

"No kidding." I grabbed the broom to sweep the day's dust and clutter. "At this rate, we'll sell out half our inventory by the end of the festival. Frankly, if Cassandra sells this much? I can see why Serena's worried."

"They sell access to ghosts, not stuff." Althea emerged from the back room, already bundling herbs for replenishing the most popular potions. "We sell stuff, and we better start restocking. I don't want to run out of anything with the crowds we're getting. It'll be just as bad tomorrow."

As we worked, I found my thoughts straying to Athena's surprise visit.

Had she come to warn me about a threat to the festival specifically? If so, everything seemed peaceful enough at the moment. I couldn't shake the nagging feeling I should be more vigilant, though—scanning for potential dangers lurking beneath the cheery exterior.

I swept the last of the loose herbs into a pile,

thoughts swirling like scattered leaves when the door bell jingled.

"Knock knock," a voice spoke up behind me. "Mind if I come in?"

I turned in surprise as the shop door swung open, revealing Detective Vince Briggs's tall frame silhouetted in the doorway. Leaning the broom against the counter, I waved him inside with a smile. "Detective Briggs! What brings you by?"

"Well, I wanted to give you ladies a quick update," he said. "We've identified a new suspect in Marcus Clinton's murder."

I quirked an eyebrow. "That was fast. Who is it?"

"Angela Hayes."

"Angela?" Ami's disbelief was as clear as the crystal ball on our counter.

"I knew something seemed off with her," I muttered, more to myself than Briggs.

"I'm sure it has nothing to do with your distinct lack of fondness for her," Althea said.

"Well, there's that, too."

Briggs nodded. "Hold on to your hat for this one: the mayor stumbled upon her and Marcus having a no-holds-barred tiff in the city hall corridors on the day he met his maker. And right before he kicked the bucket, they're locked in a heated, knock-your-socks-off argument in his office."

"Mayor Marchand told you this?" I crossed my arms. "What did he say they were arguing about?"

"The Halloween festival," Briggs said. "Marchand said Angela was furious Marcus was taking all the credit for planning it when she did most of the work. She threatened to make him regret trying to steal the spotlight from her. Pretty incriminating stuff."

"Do you think she really would have killed him over something like that, though?" Ami asked uncertainly. "That seems really petty."

Briggs shrugged. "Folks have murdered for less, and when politics gets mixed in, it's like pouring hot sauce on a fire." He gestured broadly, as if indicating the whole crazy situation. "Add in the tensions with Cassandra over this competing festival nonsense, and it's a volatile mix."

There I was, deep in thought, gnawing on my lower lip when I realized that pouring hot sauce on a fire would put it out. It might smell bad, but the fire would just go out. "I suppose she could have done it. She's mean enough. Is she strong enough to drag a body into a coffin, though?"

After seeing Angela's vindictive attitude toward us firsthand, I could easily imagine her lashing out violently if she felt slighted. Her haughty demeanor masked what I suspected was actually a very insecure person desperate for recognition and control.

"Well, don't go spreading this around just yet," Briggs cautioned. "She's still just a person of interest that may be a suspect at some point. But I'm hot on her tail, pursuing it aggressively."

"Of course," I assured him. "We appreciate you giving us a heads up."

After a few more quick updates, Briggs departed to continue investigating. I stood pondering this fresh development as Ami finished closing the register.

"Hot sauce would just put a fire out, wouldn't it?" Ami asked, brows knitted together in puzzlement. "If you pour hot sauce on a fire, wouldn't it just douse the flames?"

"Yeah, I don't know what he was trying to say with that. But yes." Althea grabbed a box and continued as she walked into the back. "Hot sauce would put out a fire. It's wet. It's not flammable. Flames, meet moisture, end of story."

Was I too quick to view Angela as the likely killer based solely on her difficult personality?

Her argument with Marcus gave her means and opportunity, but was her desire for credit motive enough for murder?

Before I could mull it over further, the shop door chimed cheerfully. My gaze shifted, drawn to the source of the sound, revealing none other than Mayor Paul Marchand himself stepping into the shop dressed sharply in a jacket and tie.

"Good evening, ladies," he greeted us genially. "I hope you're enjoying the festival's success so far."

"We are, thanks," Ami replied. "It's been wonderfully busy."

The mayor's nod was a measured gesture, his attention split between us and the myriad of magical products on our shelves. "Excellent. That's music to my ears." He turned his congenial smile on me. "I wanted to personally commend you all again for agreeing to help with setup and getting the grounds looking so festive, even after that nasty business with Marcus. I realize that was traumatic, finding the poor man like that."

I put on a polite smile and said, "Thanks. That means a lot. We were basically doing what anyone else would, you know, pitching in to help the town."

"Not everyone," he muttered. Marchand

cleared his throat delicately. "Yes, well, not just anyone would soldier on so selflessly after such a horrific ordeal. Please know your efforts have not gone unnoticed." He trailed his fingers along the shelves, casually picking up items, giving them a quick once-over, and then setting them back down. "Such interesting things."

"Thanks." I nodded, unsure how to respond to the effusive praise. Marchand seemed inordinately invested in commending our decorating abilities, considering everything else going on. This was the second time in a day.

"In any case, I won't keep you," he said with a sudden change in tone. "I'm sure you're eager to get home and change for the second night of the festival."

The mayor said goodbye, gave us a wave, and strolled out, tossing a last reminder to holler if we needed anything.

I watched him go, frowning slightly.

His super-attentive behavior toward us suddenly seemed over-the-top, almost weird. Why'd he stopped by at all? Yesterday I thought it was a nice politician's touch, but now it got me wondering: what's his game?

"Well, that was nice of him to stop by just to

thank us again," Ami remarked as she finished tallying the cash drawer.

"Was it, though?" I murmured.

She glanced up. "What do you mean?"

I shook my head, unsure myself what it was about Marchand's impromptu visit that needled my instincts. "Nothing. Just weird to me, I guess. We're going to the festival tonight. So is he. Why come out to the shop to say what he said? And when we're closed, too. No opportunity to shake hands or kiss babies. It doesn't strike you as odd?"

"I didn't really think about it like that." Ami looked mildly troubled by my response. "I guess that's why you worked for the police and I didn't, though."

I laughed. "I suppose so."

Despite Briggs's update on Angela's potential involvement, I couldn't shake the feeling that she wasn't our killer. Who stood to gain the most from Marcus's death? And just what lengths had they gone to in pursuit of their goals?

* * *

WE ARRIVED BACK at the bustling festival, the crisp night air filled with laughter and music. The crowd—slightly larger tonight—moved with a joyful fluidity, a tapestry of costumes weaving together beneath the soft glow of hanging lights.

I turned to Ami. "Where's your father?"

Ami shook her head, her gaze sweeping through the lively throng of festival-goers. "He mentioned the possibility of dropping by, but apparently, your dad and mine had some kind of meeting to go to. He didn't share the specifics."

The four of us strolled beneath the string of lights that crisscrossed the bustling square, soaking in the vibrant pulse of the ongoing festivities. A sudden flicker of motion drew my attention toward the queue for the haunted hayride and found myself face to face with an unexpected sight—a woman, donned in an owl costume, patiently standing in line.

Archie would have loved that.

Up ahead, I noticed Detective Briggs speaking with Mayor Marchand near the pumpkin patch. Marchand gestured emphatically while Briggs nodded, scribbling notes. As we drew closer, I overheard Marchand saying, "...yes, Angela and Marcus often butted heads over so many things I hardly have time to list them, but I can't believe she would resort to murder over one of their petty disagreements."

Gotta hand it to Mayor Marchand, I mused, he's got a point there.

He shook his head, looking grave. "This entire matter has been dreadful for our town's image. I want it resolved quickly."

Briggs reassured him they were pursuing all leads aggressively. After a few more exchanges, the mayor departed, shooting me a tight smile as he passed.

"Making progress?" I asked Briggs as Althea and Ayla wandered off.

"We're trying," he sighed, pocketing his notebook. "But this case feels like trying to nail jelly to a tree. Just when I think we've got something solid, it slips away."

I nodded sympathetically. Briggs seemed exhausted and overwhelmed trying to navigate this high-profile investigation solo.

"Let me know if there's anything I can do to help," I told him. "Really. An outside perspective might provide some new insight."

Briggs seemed grateful. "I'm thankful for that —and I caught wind you and the chief made amends last night. I'll likely call in that favor if I continue finding zilch." He peeked at his watch. "I ought to keep interrogating would be informants. You ladies enjoy your evening."

After Briggs left, I spotted a familiar blond head up ahead.

Lothian.

He stood with the rest of the werewolf pack, laughing at something Wyatt said. I watched him for a moment, conflicted emotions swirling. I knew my sisters were right and the two of us needed to delve deeper into his motivations for leaving me standing alone on the street, but I wasn't ready to continue our complicated conversation.

I also didn't want to avoid him completely.

Ami's soft voice broke through my spiraling thoughts. She placed a gentle hand on my arm, her eyes searching mine. "Why don't you just come with me to say hi?" she said. "You don't have to talk to him right now, Astra—like, talk to him, talk to him. You know what I mean? It's a festival. Just have some fun."

Not bothering to wait for my response, she spun on her heel and marched straight for Wyatt. I heaved a reluctant sigh, but sucked it up and approached Lothian.

He turned as I approached, face lighting up. "Astra! I was hoping I'd run into you."

"Hey," I said.

The silence descended as we regarded each other awkwardly.

Lothian cleared his throat. "Look, I know things are weird right now. But I meant what I said about fixing this. About us." He reached for my hand tentatively. "Emma said I did a terrible job apologizing yesterday and I owe you a better explanation. And she's right. You're what matters to me. I hope you know that."

I chuckled.

Considering my sibling sorority and ride-or-die gal pal were so vigilant about policing my love life, Lothian was thoroughly outmatched trying any nonsense.

"What's funny?" he asked.

"Nothing. I just feel a little sorry for you, that's all." Despite my lingering hurt, I softened at the sincerity in his voice and eyes. I gave his hand a gentle squeeze. "I know I matter to you. And you and I both have some sketchy history with healthy relationships. We'll figure it out and work through it."

Lothian's shoulders relaxed in relief. He stepped closer, lowering his voice. "Any chance we could go somewhere quiet to talk more? There's still so much I want to explain."

"Not now. I don't want to do this in the

middle of the festival," I said. "I think you're right —we do need to talk, and I want to know more about what the deal is with April and why it made you feel overwhelmed enough to leave me by the side of the road, but not right now." I adjusted my stance. "I'm dealing with some other stuff this weekend, too, and I just want a bit of a break from it."

Disappointment flashed across Lothian's face, but he quickly smoothed his features. "Of course. Whenever you're ready." He lifted my hand and pressed a kiss to my knuckles. "I'm here for you. However you need me to be. What's going on?"

"Greek god stuff." I offered him a small, grateful smile. No matter how infuriating he could be, Lothian cared for me. I needed to remember that. "Nothing big, honestly. Could you get me some of that purple punch over there?"

"Sure."

* * *

"HEY YOU TWO!" Emma called out, lifting baby Hunter's arm to wave it at us. The werewolf-costumed baby babbled at the sight of us approaching.

"You don't think that's redundant?" I asked, pointing at the baby.

"Weren't you dressed up like you were gunning for a spot on Mt. Olympus last night?" she asked. Emma was dressed as the resplendent queen of hearts. Her gown was a rich crimson, voluminous skirts swishing as she walked. Intricate gold embroidery glittered across the bodice and sleeves, catching the light with each movement. She even wore a delicate gold crown atop her perfectly coiffed curls, tiny rubies embedded throughout the metalwork and matching the shade of her lips. "Why aren't you dressed up today?"

"I am." I pointed to my old military outfit. "I'm dressed as a retired military witch."

"You know, I don't miss that outfit."

"Well, hello there, Mr. Hunter," I cooed, tickling his belly. He gave me a toothless grin that never failed to melt my heart. "Your Mom's skirts are so big I bet you could use them as a playhouse."

"Has Rex seen Wyatt's costume yet?" Ami asked, biting back a smile.

Ami's werewolf boyfriend was dressed once more as a kitschy vampire.

Emma rolled her eyes. "Oh, he saw it and he

was not a fan of the costume, to put it mildly," Emma said, gesturing toward Rex and his friend Tara chatting with Althea, Ayla, and Melvin beneath a large oak. "I think he was more embarrassed than upset, but the whole thing struck a nerve."

"That vampire costume had 'trigger' written all over it for Rex," I said.

"Which is likely what Wyatt intended," Eddie pointed out.

"Hopefully Rex can see it came from a place of fun."

"Oh right, because my brother is just a nonstop laugh riot," Emma said. "Vampires take themselves way too seriously, if you ask me."

We all chuckled.

"Hey, have you talked to Briggs tonight? I saw him earlier, and he implied he was more than a little suspicious of Hayes in the matter of Marcus's unexpected death," Emma continued. "The coroner said it was blunt force trauma to the head, but they don't know what whacked the guy yet."

"Yeah, I saw him earlier, but he didn't mention that," I told Emma. "He did mention that Marchand said something about Angela fighting with Marcus on the day he died."

"That wouldn't make any sense, though. Marcus is so much bigger than Angela," Emma said. Then her expression shifted, growing serious. "By the way, I talked to Lothian about what he did yesterday. I know I should have talked to you first, but I'm just cashing in my best friend and werewolf mom prerogatives here. I'll just abuse my prerogatives as I see fit." She looked at me. "I've got a lot of prerogatives, you know. More than you, apparently."

"Yeah, demigod with a side of lightning here. Don't hurt yourself patting your own back," I said.

"Wow, thanks for the reminder, Your Demigreatness," she quipped. "I'll be sure not to step out of line around your supreme lightening abilities." Emma nodded, but then sympathy filled her eyes. "I just want to remind you—despite the diapers and sleeplessness—I'm still here to talk about it anytime. I know you're still figuring things out." She nudged my shoulder playfully.

"And if you decide you need someone to knock some sense into him," Emma continued, "Eddie and I have absolutely got your back."

"We do," Eddie agreed, nodding.

"In fact, it would be a pleasure to slap Lothian around a little."

"Please, continue talking about me like I'm not here."

"Oh, you know I will," Emma said dryly.

Despite myself, I smiled. "Thanks, you guys." Her fierce protectiveness never failed to reassure me.

Glancing at her watch, Emma bounced a fussy Hunter gently. "Speaking of the baby extraordinaire, we should get this little guy to bed."

Eddie waved her off, reaching over to scoop up his fussing son. "I've got this—you stay and hang out with Astra for a bit," he insisted. "Norden and I will take this sleepy boy home."

Hunter let out a disgruntled whine as Eddie hoisted him up, his tiny face scrunching in displeasure. Emma leaned in to place a soft kiss on the baby's downy head, then Eddie headed with him toward the parking lot. The big man whispering soothing words to the overtired infant.

Lothian walked up and handed me an iced purple punch. "Thanks."

"He really is such a wonderful dad," Emma said watching Eddie and Hunter.

"And to think you made him crawl over

broken glass before agreeing to marry him," I teased.

"Ugh, that was definitely not my finest moment," Emma said. "Let's go blow a fortune on carnival games to spoil the baby rotten so I can pretend I didn't almost run off his father with my emotionally stunted rebellion."

I let her steer us toward the row of carnival game booths, lined up like a brightly lit, noisy avenue of chaos. The air rang with victorious shouts and giggles of delight from lucky winners as kids and adults cheered and groaned. Footballs sailed, milk bottles toppled, and rings circled prizes at the game booths.

I cracked my knuckles, sizing up the games. The balloon pop challenge looked simple enough —just aim darts at rows of colorful balloons pinned to a wall. I forked over a couple of dollars for five shots, hefting a red dart experimentally.

"Step right up, folks! Pop just one balloon and win a small prize," the attendant announced in a showman's booming voice. "Pop two, and you'll take home a medium. Pop all five and win our grand prize!"

I studied the balloons carefully. They looked barely inflated, as if most of the air had already leaked out. Of course, with less air inside, they'd be harder to pop.

The game was rigged.

I took aim at the front balloon with a dart and threw it with extra force—and a smidge of buzzy star magic. It pierced the thin latex and popped.

Well, technically, it was justice.

I threw the next magically-infused dart harder as well, compensating for the underinflation in a multitude of ways, and the balloon burst.

"We have a winner!" the attendant cried as the balloons burst.

Grinning, I let my final three darts fly in quick succession, each hitting their mark flawlessly. Ami cheered, giving me an impressed look. With careful aim, strong throws—and a little bit of magical justice—I had popped the rigged balloons and won the grand prize.

"Congratulations!" the attendant said, handing over an enormous plush unicorn with a sparkly silver horn and rainbow yarn mane.

"For your kid." I presented it to Emma with a flourish.

"My hero." She laughed and accepted the unicorn.

As we walked, I noticed a woman watching us from the shadows near the haunted barn. She stayed just out of sight, far enough away that I couldn't see her clearly.

Yet she seemed familiar.

Before I could study her further, she slipped away into the darkness.

A sudden uneasy feeling prickled the back of my neck, that instinctive sense that something ominous had occurred even though I couldn't pinpoint what. I tensed, my gaze scanning the festive crowd for any signs of trouble.

Lothian stopped abruptly and scanned my face, his playful grin fading. "What's wrong?" he asked, picking up on my tension.

"Everything okay?" Ami asked, noticing my distraction and Lothian's concern.

Wyatt stopped and moved closer to us. "What is it?"

"Jeesh, you guys, it's fine. I just thought I saw someone. It's probably nothing," I said, shaking off the uneasy feeling. I didn't want to ruin our evening over unexplained apprehensions. "Don't worry about it."

Up ahead, eerie music drifted through the air as we approached the festival's haunted barn attraction. Strobe lights flashed inside the open doors, revealing disorienting glimpses of lurking figures and disturbing tableaux. Dramatic screams and screeches pierced the night at random intervals, making me jump.

Ami eyed the spooky barn. "Should we go in?"

"If you want to," I said. If we could face down killers, gods, and magic, we could brave a silly haunted barn.

Probably.

"You guys go," Emma said, waving toward the barn. "Not my thing. I'll go find Rex and see what they're up to."

Ami still looked uncertain as we joined the queue to enter. Wyatt gave her hand an encouraging squeeze. "Don't worry, I'll protect you from the scary monsters."

"My hero," she laughed.

As we drew closer, the disturbing sounds and frantic screams from within set my nerves on edge. But there was no turning back now.

Hand in hand with our werewolf boyfriends, Ami and I plunged into the darkness.

CHAPTER THIRTEEN

The moment we stepped through the creaky wooden doors into the haunted barn, we were enveloped in inky darkness straight out of a B-horror movie. Strobe lights flashed, briefly illuminating leering clowns and disturbing figures designed to shorten lifespans by a good decade thanks to sheer terror.

I resisted the urge to judo-flip the clown into a hay bale when a fluorescent smile suddenly flashed in my face. Note to self: Avoid haunted houses when already on edge from actual murder.

"Don't punch anyone," Lothian said.

"Yep. Got it."

A fake corpse hanging from the rafters swung down suddenly right in front of me. Beside me, Ami shrieked and grasped Wyatt's arm.

"It's just special effects, don't worry," Wyatt soothed, although he looked unnerved himself.

We inched deeper into the barn, fog machines filling the air with sinister mist. In the intermittent strobe light, I caught sight of another deranged clown lunging toward us in a Tweety Bird patterned outfit wielding a huge butcher knife and letting loose a maniacal laugh.

"Oh, come on, a Tweety Bird?" I chuckled.

The clown faltered, looking offended. "Hey, I worked hard on this costume," he complained, breaking character.

"Yeah, Astra, he worked hard on that costume," Ami told me.

"Don't mind her, she's impossible to scare," Lothian told him.

We moved on to the next room, which appeared empty at first glance. But then a menacing growl sounded from the shadows. Two red eyes shone in the darkness, approaching slowly. As the creature stepped into the light, we saw it was a person in an elaborate werewolf costume, complete with a furry mask and claws.

Lothian threw his head back and laughed.

"Nice try," he chuckled. The faux werewolf swiped a clawed hand at him halfheartedly. "You're going to have to put a bit more into it than that, brother."

"Don't mind him. He's impossible to scare," I told the polyester-clad lupine apologetically.

"Why'd you guys even bother coming in?" the werewolf muttered.

In the next area, a mad scientist scene was set up with Jacob's ladders throwing off electric arcs and bubbling beakers and vials everywhere. The white-coated scientist cackled maniacally over a lab table where a body lay, hidden by a sheet. As we passed by, the scientist grabbed Ami's arm, causing her to shriek.

"Take your hand off my girlfriend, dude," Wyatt growled.

The scientist quickly released Ami, throwing his hands up in surrender. "Sorry, man, just having some Halloween fun," he mumbled.

As I suppressed a chuckle at Wyatt's show of protectiveness, we moved into a darkened maze-like passage. Fog swirled around our feet and creepy whispers echoed all around. The path forked, and Ami and I exchanged a nervous glance.

"Which way?" she asked uncertainly. A shrill

scream sounded from the left passage. Ami pointed in its direction and asked, "That way?"

I raised an eyebrow. "You want to go in the scream's direction?"

"Reverse psychology. I think the passage that looks and sounds less scary is probably more scary than the way trying to scare us off."

"Screams it is," Wyatt declared cheerfully, taking Ami's hand and leading us toward the blood-curdling sounds through a maze of baffling twists and turns.

After the third disorienting pivot, I was convinced we were going in endless circles designed to trap us in B-Movie horror purgatory forever. But then, rounding a corner, I was startled to find Detective Briggs lurking in the shadows.

He quickly pressed one finger to his lips. "Shhh, stay quiet," he whispered. "I'm following a lead."

I glanced around in confusion.

A lead?

Here?

He gestured for us to peek around the corner.

Peering through the haze, I glimpsed two silhouettes engaged in a heated exchange against the wall of the barn. As I leaned forward, the fog thinned just enough to reveal Angela Hayes and Gordon Schmidt.

Angela's face was taut, her eyes flashing as she jabbed a finger toward Gordon. "I'm telling you, the police are up my butt farther and harder than a proctologist looking for hemorrhoids, Schmidt!" Angela hissed at Gordon. "If they find out the two of us are having an affair, I'm going to wind up in prison—and I don't look good in stripes!"

He had his arms crossed, his shoulders hunched defensively. "You're being ridiculous, Angie. No one knows," he shot back. "We can still salvage this."

"Salvage what?" I murmured.

I focused hard, hoping to pick up on more of what was being said in the hushed conversation, but couldn't focus enough among the chaotic haunted barn sound effects. Turning to Lothian, I raised my eyebrows, but he gave a subtle shake of his head. Even with his superhuman hearing, the cacophony of shrieks, howls and clanking chains drowned out the pair's whispered words.

After a moment, Angela shook her head sharply and turned on her heel. Gordon watched her go, his jaw clenched and brows drawn, then slipped away in the opposite direction.

Briggs nodded, looking satisfied. He jotted a note in his little notebook. "Well, that's definitely suspicious," he remarked. "Good thing I followed them in here tonight."

"Are you going to arrest them?" Ami asked.

"Based on what we just heard? Of course not." Briggs sighed. "Not yet, anyway. I still lack any solid evidence linking them directly to the crime. But they know something." He checked his watch. "I need to run."

With that, he exited, fading into the mist as if he'd never been there.

Before we could say anything, a shrill cackle rebounded off the plywood walls. In a burst of color, a grotesque jester sprang out from a dark alcove, leering beneath his belled cap. "A jester is not a joke! I perform for kings!" He raised his arms up and cackled. "You are no kings and you have lain eyes upon me, so you must die!"

We looked at him.

"Nice outfit," Ami told him.

"It really is," Lothian agreed.

The costumed worker wilted under our collective stare, bells jingling as he shifted his weight. "Just gotta ask: what's the motivation behind you lot even stepping foot here?" he grumbled as the clown had before him, dropping the act. "Like, what's the point?" With an exaggerated huff, the jester slouched off in search of more reactive victims. "Happy Halloween, spoilsports," he called over his shoulder as he walked away.

"Well, now I feel bad," I said.

"Come on, let's get out of here," Lothian said, catching his breath.

Nodding, I followed as he led the way through the remaining haunted displays.

Ghastly faces leered from the darkness, eliciting no reaction from our stoic group. In the last room, Ami deftly sidestepped a lurching zombie while Wyatt batted aside strands of cobwebs. A chorus of unearthly howls and screams accompanied our exit, topped by a roared, "And don't come back!"

* * *

AFTER SURVIVING the haunted barn and destroying the experience for around ten haunt volunteers, we followed the scent of frying dough and sugar toward the food stands.

"Funnel cake, anyone?" Wyatt asked.

"Yes, please!" Ami said. "Let's grab a snack and then grab a table. There's one under that tree over there that seems pretty isolated." She looked at me. "I want to talk about what we saw."

As we neared the front of the line, I noticed Mayor Paul Marchand embroiled in an intense exchange just beyond the colorful festival lights. He stood rigid, gesturing sharply as he conversed with a figure obscured in shadow. Craning my neck, I struggled to identify the mystery speaker, but their back remained stubbornly turned, and their head was blocked by a tree branch.

"Ugh. I can't hear anything," I said to myself.

"What?" Lothian asked.

I pointed. "I can't hear them. Festivals are horrible for eavesdropping."

Snatches of Halloween music and laughter masked Marchand's words.

Still, his taut posture spoke volumes. He jabbed a finger toward his hidden companion, brows drawn severely. The shadowy outline handed something to Marchand—a small, indistinct object that disappeared into his suit jacket.

"Can you tell who that is?" I asked Lothian.

"With the mayor?"

"Yeah."

"No, not from here. Do you want me to get closer?"

Marchand seemed intent on the conversation, gesturing emphatically in a way that bordered on aggressive, and his body language radiated tension. After another minute, the shadowy figure slipped away into the darkness.

"I can follow them," Lothian prodded me again. "Should I?"

As Marchand glanced around, his eyes suddenly widened when they met mine. I glanced away, not wanting him to think I'd been spying.

"Next!" called the server at the funnel cake stand.

"He's watching us now. It'll be too suspicious," I told the werewolf. "Let's just get our funnel cake, sit down, and act normal." I frowned. "I need to look into getting one of those wildlife permits. Archie would have come in handy here."

We placed our order and made our way toward the empty picnic table. As we ate the warm, crispy confections topped with powdered sugar, I thought about the mayor's demeanor this weekend and wondered why it kept niggling at me.

Would the mayor have a reason to kill Marcus Clinton?

As mayor, Marchand frequently clashed with the city council over policy decisions. He was a traditionalist who resisted change, while Marcus had been more progressive and outspoken, often leading the charge on reforms Marchand opposed.

Last month, Marcus had forced through approval of new land protections over the mayor's objections. And he'd been gearing up for a big affordable housing proposal that Marchand bitterly fought against.

Marcus's death wouldn't undo any of that, though.

Would it?

I was so lost in thought I didn't even realize Wyatt had asked me a question until Ami nudged me gently. "Hmm?" I asked, refocusing. "Sorry, what was that?"

"You okay?" Wyatt asked, looking concerned. "You kinda spaced out there for a minute."

"Oh yeah, I'm fine," I assured them. "Just got distracted."

Lothian leaned forward, eyebrows knitting together. "You want to tell them what you saw that's bothering you?"

I waved it off. "No, it's nothing."

Lothian and Wyatt exchanged a look, clearly not fully convinced.

Ami's green eyes searched mine. "What did you see?" she asked.

"When we were waiting for funnel cake, I saw Mayor Marchand talking to someone in the shadows. I couldn't see who it was, but the mayor seemed really tense and upset about something. And then the other person gave him a small item that Marchand quickly stashed in his pocket."

"What kind of item?" Wyatt asked, intrigued.

I shook my head. "No clue. It was too small for me to make out from a distance. I couldn't even tell who the other person was. But something about the entire exchange seemed...off. Hinky. I don't know."

"Do you think it has something to do with Marcus's murder?" Ami wondered aloud.

I chewed my lip thoughtfully. "Possibly. But it also could have been totally innocuous. I don't want to jump to conclusions based on one semi-odd observation." I took a bite of the funnel cake. "Well, two. Not one. Him stopping by earlier today was odd."

Wyatt finished the last bites of his funnel cake and dusted the powdered sugar from his hands. "Here's what we should do," he said. "Let's monitor Marchand tonight. Watch his interactions, see if we notice anything else unusual. If he seems really suspicious, we tell Briggs." He looked at me. "We should probably find Emma and let her know what's going on."

I nodded slowly. "Okay, that's not a bad idea. And yeah, given the circumstances, a little discreet observation seems warranted."

We left the food area, keeping Marchand in our sights. He mingled with townspeople, all smiles and congeniality. Nothing about his current behavior seemed concerning.

After about fifteen minutes of subtle surveillance, Marchand made his way over to a gathering of local business owners. His public persona was on full display as he laughed and shook hands. But underneath the affable exterior, his smile seemed forced. His posture was tense and on edge.

As we watched, Emma entered the area. She made a beeline for the mayor, tapping his shoulder.

Marchand jumped, then quickly smoothed his features when he saw the former Detective Sullivan. They spoke for a few minutes,

Marchand shaking his head and gesturing in denial.

Whatever Emma was asking him about, Marchand wanted no part of it. After a terse back and forth, she nodded and walked toward us, expression almost jovial.

*　*　*

EMMA RETURNED TO OUR GROUP, mischief twinkling in her eyes. "I have an update," she announced. "Apparently Rex—with his handy dandy vampire hearing—was able to make out most of your conversation. A conversation you should have called me about so I could be part of it, by the way, but whatever."

"Sorry."

"I would have loved a funnel cake, too. But it turned out okay." She leaned in, lowering her voice. "Since he didn't see me with you, I took it upon myself to move things forward a bit." With a flourish, she produced a small object from her pocket. "I picked the mayor's pocket."

"Emma!" Ami admonished. "You can't just pickpocket the mayor!"

"Well, I can. Because I did."

"But that's illegal!"

"Former detective's prerogative," Emma said. She opened her palm to reveal one of the cheap aluminum occult coins, engraved with pseudo-magical symbols. "I figured Astra could tap into her psychic mojo and see if this thing gives us any clues about the mayor's shady dealings."

I took the coin from Emma, frowning down at the meaningless mishmash of etched symbols. "What is with these stupid trinkets?" I asked.

"No idea, but it was on Marchand, so read away." Emma made an exaggerated hand-waving gesture. "Use your powers, witchy woman."

I rolled my eyes but closed my fist around the coin, focusing on my psychic senses. Like with the previous coin, at first, all I perceived was a vague hum of energy, the residual imprint of the many hands that had touched the mass-produced amulet.

But then indistinct voices emerged.

"...too risky, you fool..." a man's voice, low and angry.

"...won't let her keep him..." a woman retorted heatedly.

I strained to hear more, but the impressions remained fragmented. "I'm only getting bits and pieces," I told the others with a frustrated sigh. "Their words keep getting drowned out by background noise, or it's too muffled to make out."

"Oh, come on," Emma said. She nudged my shoulder. "You have to be able to pick up more than that."

Before I could stop myself, a biting, "Are you an expert on all things supernatural now?" slipped out.

Emma snorted, unfazed by my sharp tone. "Maybe not an expert," Emma murmured. "But sister to a vampire, best friend to a witch, and mother and wife to a werewolf all have to count for something, right? I mean, just one of those things would count. A lot."

"You're letting all that go to your head, you know that?"

"The head that wears the werewolf lady crown? That head?"

I narrowed my eyes.

Emma grinned, giving me an encouraging thumbs up.

I took a deep breath and reached out with my mind once more, probing the cheap metal disk. Flickers of images danced at the edge of my mind as the scent of gardenias ticked my nose—hazy shapes and glimpses of furtive meetings and hushed plans. An undercurrent of anger and defiance rang through the exchanges.

"...find the others..."

"...not about the money or the..."

I opened my eyes as the visions faded. "Picking up some sketchy stuff, but not enough to pinpoint anything solid."

Emma's face fell in disappointment. "No smoking gun implicating Marchand?"

"I'm sorry. Did reality just pop your optimism balloon?" I shook my head. "No, there's nothing implicating anyone specifically. It's too fractured."

"It's still useful," Ami pointed out. "Now we know Mayor Marchand has been engaged in some sort of covert, ethically questionable discussions."

"He's a politician. Isn't that a given?" Wyatt asked.

"Fair point." Emma clapped her hands together. "Still—combine that with Astra seeing him be all furtive and tense during a cryptic exchange earlier, and I'd say that merits keeping a close eye on the esteemed mayor. And we still have no idea what those cheap pretend-magic coins mean."

"I mentioned this earlier, but I have to ask." Wyatt shifted in his seat, looking uncertain.

"Should we be doing surveillance on the mayor without actual proof he's done something illegal?" he asked. "Seems outside our purview as civilians, and I'm not sure why we're getting involved."

The werewolf pack queen waved a hand. "Technicalities. We're just concerned citizens watching out for our town."

"AKA, you miss being a detective," I remarked.

Emma grinned. "Is it that obvious?" She nudged Wyatt. Oh, don't be so tense, relax. Just so you know, we're not planning to turn into professional stalkers or start pulling any wild stunts."

Wyatt still appeared unconvinced.

Emma squeezed his shoulder. "Tell you what. We'll keep it low key, and if anything more concrete comes up, we'll loop in Detective Briggs to handle it. Deal?"

Wyatt considered this compromise, then nodded. "Deal."

"Great." Emma turned back, green eyes glinting. "So recap everything hinky you've noticed about Marchand so far. Loop me in."

I summarized the mayor's oddly effusive praise of our work on the festival decorations, and the tense exchange I'd witnessed earlier.

"He's definitely on edge about something," I concluded. "You know the guy better than I do. Do you think it could relate to Marcus's murder?"

Emma pursed her lips. "Possibly. As mayor, Marchand did butt heads with Marcus over policy issues frequently. And Marcus's death leaves a vacant council seat up for grabs."

"That points more toward Gordon Schmidt, though. He wants that seat and would likely get it. Schmidt is no fan of the mayor," Lothian said. He then gave Emma a rundown of what we saw in the haunted barn.

"Yeah, no, you're right—Schmidt and Marchand can't stand each other."

"How did you know that?" I asked Lothian, but he didn't answer.

"Maybe Marchand wanted Marcus gone to get a more allied replacement on council and wasn't doing it to benefit Schmidt?" Ami asked, looking troubled.

"It's a working theory," Emma replied.

I shook my head, doubtful. "I don't know. That seems like overkill. No pun intended. Oh! One more thing about what I saw from the pilfered coin. I smelled gardenias. Like a heavy, dense gardenia scent."

Just then, Lothian rose to his feet.

"What's wrong?" I asked.

"Nothing. Hey, sorry, you guys, I need to go...check on something. I just remembered," he mumbled. "I'll catch up with you guys later." Without further explanation, my boyfriend rushed off into the milling crowd.

I stared after him, confused by his sudden departure. Emma looked puzzled, eyebrows knitting together.

"What was that about?" Ami wondered aloud.

"Do you think he knows something about Marchand he's not telling us? Lothian is Mr. Plugged-In with the politics," Emma said.

"I don't know," I said. "But it was weird he rushed off like that."

Wyatt stayed quiet.

"Okay, Lothian being weird aside, let's stay on top of this mayor situation," Emma said, redirecting the conversation. "We'll keep eyes on him tonight. Look for anything else questionable."

"Ooh, stakeouts and secret missions?" Ami shook her head, amusement glinting in her eyes. "I've never gotten to do this before. This is so exciting! And I think Astra's right. You do miss being a detective, Emma."

Emma laughed. "Maybe I do a little. I like

puzzles." She nudged Wyatt. "Oh, come on, don't look so worried. We're not going to stalk the guy or do anything crazy."

Wyatt looked worried, and appeared unconvinced.

CHAPTER FOURTEEN

*E*mma pulled me aside, glancing around to ensure we were out of earshot of the others. "Okay, what was up with Lothian just disappearing like that?" she asked, eyebrows furrowing. "Did you two have some kind of fight?"

I shook my head. "He seemed his normal self right up until he took off in a rush. Nothing happened you didn't see. He was acting totally normal and then just took off without explanation." I met Emma's gaze, her eyes clouded with confusion. "I was actually going to ask you if he said anything to you or the rest of the pack about why he needed to go."

Emma looked as puzzled as I felt. "Not a

word. He mentioned nothing to me." She crossed her arms. "But that was weird, even for him. I wonder what spooked him."

"I have no idea." I frowned. "He seemed suddenly distracted when I mentioned the gardenia scent from the amulet, though."

"Hmm." Emma tapped her chin thoughtfully. "Maybe that triggered something?"

"Could be." I surveyed the lively crowd, but there was still no sign of Lothian's blond head. "Should we ask Wyatt if he knows anything? Lothian tells him stuff sometimes."

Emma nodded. "Good call. Let's go pry him off your sister."

It didn't take long to locate Wyatt back by the food stands, loading up a paper plate with fried confections. Golden corn dogs dripping with grease, elephant ears glistening with cinnamon sugar, and piping hot churros piled high on his plate.

Emma barreled up to Wyatt, propped her hands on her hips, and cocked an eyebrow at his loaded plate. "Where's Ami?"

"She ran to the restroom. She asked me to—"

"Fine, fine. Where did Lothian run off to just now?" she demanded without preamble.

"You're asking me?" Wyatt looked up as if he'd

been caught with his hand in the cookie jar. "How should I know?"

Emma fixed him with her classic "no nonsense" stare, honed from years as a detective grilling uncooperative suspects. "Don't you even try to pretend you all don't know everything about everyone else with a tail within three miles of this place. He's your pack brother. If something was up, he would have told you or you would have sensed it."

Wyatt shifted his weight, avoiding her gaze. "I mean, maybe he had to use the bathroom or something. I don't keep tabs on the guy."

"Yes, you do."

Wyatt's gaze darted away. "Not all the time! Come on, Emma—I don't know."

"Would you tell me if you did know?"

His eyebrows pinched together and his shoulders tensed, like a kid caught sneaking cookies before dinner.

But he didn't say yes.

I studied Wyatt. I watched his throat bob as he swallowed hard, a telltale sign of nerves. He shifted his weight from one foot to the other, subtly angling his body away from us. All the signs were there—the averted eyes, the tense posture, the fidgeting.

Wyatt was definitely hiding something.

Emma threw her hands up in exasperation. "Ugh, you werewolves and your code of secrecy. Just tell us where he went, Wyatt!"

"I don't know," Wyatt insisted—but the way his gaze slid away told me he wasn't being entirely truthful.

Emma's eyes narrowed. She jabbed a finger into Wyatt's chest. "Listen here, mister. I may be a wolfy pack queen now, but I was a detective first. I can spot a liar from a mile away. You may not know the exact answer to my question, but you know something you're not telling us. Spill it."

I raised my eyebrow. "Wolfy pack queen?"

"They don't have a title for me that's not completely misogynist, so I made up my own. Whatever they call me, they have to answer me because I'm married to the big kahuna. Wyatt's denials and dancing around the answer tells me he doesn't want to, and what's more? He doesn't feel like he has to. That can mean only one thing." Emma faced Wyatt. "He's protecting a pack brother."

Wyatt held up his hands, looking trapped. "Look, I don't know what this means, but Lothian thought about April when Astra said something about gardenias. That's it." Wyatt's gaze shifted slowly between Emma and I, the silent exchange stretching on for loaded beats without a word passing between us. "I know only that. I swear."

April, huh?

I studied Wyatt closely.

No flared nostrils, no clenching of fists, no sheen of nervous sweat. As far as I could discern, there were no tangible indications that Wyatt was anything less than truthful about what he did and didn't know. His body language betrayed no evidence of duplicity. He seemed to be telling the truth about his limited knowledge.

Emma seemed to read this as well because she deflated slightly. "Fine."

"Look, Astra, he's not having any kind of affair with her," Wyatt told me. "And I didn't get any sense he was happy about what you said. In fact, he seemed pretty concerned. He took off like it was urgent, whatever it was."

I crossed my arms over my chest, defiance flashing in my eyes. "I'm not worried he's having an affair with her," I retorted, my tone sharp.

Though his reassurance should have put me at ease, I still felt unsettled, my instincts nagging at me. Wyatt's reassurance meant little when my gut still churned with unease and mistrust.

Lothian was up to something with that woman.

I just knew it.

"Do you think I should try calling him?" I asked. "I mean, we could just ask."

Emma compulsively checked her phone again, even though the screen was still dark. With a frustrated huff, she shoved it back into her pocket.

"Let's kick back for a few ticks and let him deal with whatever made him rush outta here," the former detective (and current werewolf queen) finally said. "See if he comes back or shoots one of us a text. If he's a no-show for too long, then we go nuclear. Rapid fire texts, back-to-back calls, the whole nine yards." Emma cracked her knuckles, as if preparing for a fight. "We'll blow up his phone until he has no choice but to respond."

I nodded.

Emma clapped her hands together. "Okay, Wyatt? You and Ami are on Lothian duty. Let us know the second you hear from him or he gets back."

Wyatt nodded, a look of relief washing over his rugged features as he realized he now had an assigned task that didn't involve enduring further interrogation from Emma. His broad shoulders, which had been tense and rigid throughout our conversation, relaxed slightly as some of the pressure was taken off.

"Astra and I will keep tabs on Mr. Mayor." Emma looped her arm through mine. "Let Operation Shady Politician begin!"

I allowed Emma to steer me back toward the festival crowds, thoughts still swirling with questions about Lothian's abrupt departure.

* * *

Emma and I wove through the bustling crowd, searching for Mayor Marchand as carnival music and laughter rang out around us as people milled about, enjoying the festivities.

Scanning over the sea of faces, I caught sight of Rex's distinctive tall, lean frame over by the ring toss. His sleek dark hair fell across his forehead as he chuckled at something Althea said. She had her arm loosely slung around someone unseen standing behind Rex, leaning against them with casual affection.

"Emma, heads up. Our siblings are over there," I said, clasping her arm. I nodded toward the ring toss game, where Althea and Rex stood chatting.

Emma followed my gesture, her eyes landing on her lanky brother. Her face instantly brightened, lips curving into a wide smile that lit up her entire expression. "Rex! I'm so glad he came out to the festival," she said, gripping my arm. "His nocturnal nature keeps him from so many things in this town."

"Come on, let's stop by there real quick," I said, linking my arm through hers companionably. "We can give them a heads up about the mayor situation, at least."

As we made our way over, Rex broke into a grin. "Well, if it isn't my darling baby sister once more," he said, pulling Emma in for a hug. He kissed both her cheeks in an exaggerated European-style greeting. "As I mentioned before, you look radiant tonight. Queen of the wolf hearts—red is definitely your color."

Emma laughed. "Why thank you, kind sir." She gave a little curtsy, playing along. Then she turned to the unfamiliar woman. "And who is this lovely creature with you?"

The woman had jet black hair styled in an elegant side-swept bob, her alabaster skin stark against a form-fitting black dress. Dark eyeliner rimmed her pale blue eyes.

The raven-haired woman angled her body

toward us, extending a graceful hand in greeting. Blood-red nails glinted under the carnival lights looking dangerously sharp. "Tara Orlok," she introduced herself in a sultry voice. "Your brother and I go back a few years." She gave Rex a fond smile before turning. "Hello Astra. Lovely to see you again."

Emma's brows shot up, her gaze ping-ponging between Tara and me. "How exactly do you two know each other?"

"Oh, Tara's a regular at the emporium," Althea chimed in casually, though her eyes were watchful. "Once Mom passed, we stopped the vampire prohibition."

I nodded in agreement. "One of our best customers, in fact."

Tara exuded a hypnotic sensuality that made it hard to look away from her fox-like eyes and wine-stained lips, but I pulled my gaze from the sexy vampire to Althea shifting her weight beside the female vampire, arms crossed tightly over her chest. My sister seemed distinctly uncomfortable with the conversation unfolding.

"So what's on the agenda for you ladies tonight?" Rex asked in a friendly tone, though his eyes were cautiously assessing.

"Oh, just a top secret covert op," Emma said,

lowering her voice to a dramatic whisper. She leaned in close, eyes glinting with mischief.

Rex cocked an eyebrow, intrigued. "Do tell."

Emma mimicked, zipping her lips. "Can't dish the details, I'm afraid. Hush-hush."

I laughed, giving her shoulder a playful nudge. "Simmer down there, secret agent Emma. We're just keeping an eye on things, considering everything that's happened lately."

I gave him the SparkNotes version of spotting Mayor Marchand in a shady-looking exchange earlier that night. Rex's easygoing expression shifted to one of concern as he listened, arms crossed over his chest.

"I don't like the sound of that," he said, shaking his head. "What do you think he's up to?"

"That's what we're trying to figure out," I said.

Emma nodded, the humor in her eyes replaced by a somber glint.

Whatever mischief the mayor was stirring up, she was taking it seriously.

And so was I.

"If you need any help, I'd be happy to pitch in." Tara smiled. "I can be quite stealthy when I want to be." She winked.

"They're fine, don't worry," Althea said in a rush, waving her hand as if to brush away Tara's offer. Her usual stoic demeanor cracked slightly, eyebrows pinching together. "My sister's ex-military, you know, and Emma was a detective," she continued. "I'm sure they can handle themselves."

Althea folded her arms across her chest, hands gripping her elbows tightly. Her shoulders hunched inward, radiating tension. She shifted her weight from foot to foot, avoiding eye contact.

Seeing my normally unflappable sister so on edge seemed to worsen my unease. My eyes flicked back and forth between Althea and Tara. Finally, I caught my sister's eye. "You okay?" I mouthed.

Althea nodded, quick and jerky, shifting even closer to Tara until their arms pressed together. "I'm fine," she said under her breath, almost like a mantra. But the crease between her brows remained, giving away her true feelings.

Interesting.

Rex and Emma fell into easy conversation with Tara, discussing the recent murder and all the suspicious activity around the festival. He gestured animatedly as he shared his theories, while his human sister nodded along, interjecting quips that made Tara laugh throatily.

But Althea...

My normally confident sister stood slightly apart, arms wrapped around herself. She responded only in murmurs when Rex tried engaging her, her gaze downcast and eyebrows knitted. Noticing Althea's uncharacteristic quietness, Rex shot me a questioning look.

I gave a small, worried shrug.

After a few more minutes of stilted interaction from Althea, Emma decided to give us space so I could find out what was going on with my sister. "I want a mug of whatever's bubbling in that cauldron over there," she announced, linking her arm through Rex's. "Come on, you two. Let's see if you can guess the ingredients with those super noses of yours."

With a flutter of fingers in farewell, Emma steered Rex and Tara away, the trio soon disappearing into the swirling crowds around the food stalls.

Althea's shoulders seemed to slump in relief once they moved on—but she continued studying her boots, mouth tight, as if bracing herself for an uncomfortable conversation.

Watching Althea's body language, I suddenly understood why she had been acting so shifty around Tara. Memories flashed through my mind like slides in a viewfinder: Althea leaning in close to chat with Tara at the shop, finding little excuses to touch her arm or hand, an occasional blush coloring her cheeks.

How had I not recognized the signs before now?

As soon as we had privacy, I turned to Althea with a knowing look. "So, you and Tara seem pretty friendly," I said, keeping my tone casual.

Althea's shoulders tensed, her eyes widening briefly before she looked away. "So?" she responded.

I could tell she was nervous about opening up, so I pressed further. "Hey, you know you can talk to me about anything, right? What matters most to me is that you're happy." I reached out and squeezed her hand. "She seems nice. And she's beautiful." I nudged my sister. "I think she's great."

Confusion creased Althea's brow as she searched my face. "Wait, so you're...okay with it?"

"Of course I'm okay with it," I told her. "All that matters is that you're happy."

"You think Ami and Ayla will be okay with it? I mean, Tara's a girl. And a vampire." Her hesitant tone and questioning look made my heart ache. She was really worried about how we would react. "Mom cast wards against vampires, so...I mean, I just wasn't sure. And she's a female, so...yeah. I guess I'm pretty weird."

I gave her my warmest, most reassuring smile.

"Althea Arden, your sisters love you." I tugged her close and gave her a real spine-popping squeeze, hoping she could feel how much I loved her through my embrace. "You're not weird. You're uniquely you, and I'm so proud of you for being brave enough to be true to yourself," I told her. "Ami and Ayla will support you. Of course they will. Your happiness means everything to us."

I could see the relief washing over her as the anxiety left her body. Her shoulders lowered and a small, grateful smile turned up the corners of her mouth. This was clearly something she had been stressing over. I felt a pang of regret, wishing she had shared her feelings sooner, so she didn't have to feel this fear.

I met her gaze evenly. "All I want is for you to be happy, Thea. Guy, girl, vampire—it doesn't matter."

Althea's posture relaxed, relief smoothing the creases from her brow. "Thanks, Astra. I appreciate you saying that." A hint of vulnerability entered her eyes. "I had my doubts about how you all would react if you knew I, uh, don't only like guys. Or humans. When I priestessed to Hecate, I figured that was going to stress everyone out. This was just...I've been racking my brain on the right way to let you in on this, but kept coming up blank."

I pulled her into another fierce hug. "I will always love and support you, no matter what or who makes you happy. Never forget that."

Althea returned the embrace.

When we pulled back, her expression was lighter than I'd seen in ages.

CHAPTER FIFTEEN

The night air held a little bite as Emma and I marched through the lively festival grounds. Shadows danced around the glowing Ferris wheel, empty save a few brave riders, while we scanned the costumed crowd for any sign of Mayor Marchand's distinctive presence.

"You see him?" I asked, scanning the sea of revelers.

Emma shook her head, blond curls bouncing beneath her crown. "No, I haven't spotted him yet. This is like trying to find a needle in a haystack with all these people."

"You can say that again. The festival seems to be an enormous success, even with everything that's happened." I looked to the right. "I guess Marcus wasn't wrong."

"It really does," Emma agreed, green eyes thoughtful. "Hopefully, this will ease some of Serena and Cassandra's worries about losing business."

"How'd you know about that?"

"Ayla and Melvin told me."

I still felt a pang of guilt over how we'd left things with her. "I hope so, but I'm still feeling bad about how desperate and upset Serena was, begging us to call off the festival. It was an impossible situation, though."

Emma nodded, her expression somber. "I hear you. But maybe we can still build a bridge."

I chewed my lip, an idea taking shape. "You're right. I was thinking we could donate a portion of the shop's earnings this weekend to Cassandra businesses. To present it as a goodwill gesture between the towns." I met Emma's gaze. "It would show Serena we do care about their wellbeing, even if we couldn't outright cancel the festival."

Emma's face lit up. "I'm sure Serena would really appreciate a gesture like that. The mayor? Probably not. But Serena and the guru will like it. The last thing we need is to have a town war with the ghost whisperers over there." She nudged my shoulder affectionately. "See, this is why I keep you around."

"Oh, good. I was wondering if you just used me for my owl," I joked.

Emma's gaze suddenly sharpened, focusing over my shoulder. "Speaking of big-eyed insincere males, is that Mayor Marchand over by the apple cider stand?" She pointed discreetly. "See him over there in that corner?"

I followed her gaze to see the mayor accepting a steaming cup from a vendor. "Let's move a little closer," I suggested. "But subtly. We don't want him to notice us watching him."

Emma's green eyes glinted with anticipation. "On this night, I think we'll stealthily blend into the crowd without a problem."

We slowly made our way toward the apple cider stand, keeping the mayor within earshot, as we pretended to look over the offerings of a nearby jewelry booth. I strained to make out Marchand's words over the din of music and laughter surrounding us.

He'd moved away from the booth and was leaning against a tree on the edge of the festival grounds, looking furtive as he spoke with someone obscured (again) in shadow. Though he'd looked cheerful and friendly at the cider stand, now his posture radiated tension, one hand slicing the air in sharp gestures.

My steps quickened as I tugged Emma's arm and angled toward the tree. She followed my lead, eyes narrowing when she, too, noticed the mayor's agitated demeanor. His voice floated to us in urgent snatches.

"...getting too risky...need to be careful..."

Emma and I exchanged an intrigued look as we crept closer.

We slipped behind a bubbling brew booth, using its flashing lights and eerie soundtrack to mask our approach. Crouching low, we snuck up to the tree right behind the other tree and hid ourselves in shadow.

Between flickering strobe lights, I caught a flash of familiar blond curls—Angela. My eyes widened in surprise. What was she doing here with Marchand? Their voices dropped too low to discern words, so I risked leaning closer.

"...got Briggs breathing down my neck about that stupid argument at the festival," Angela was saying. "If he discovers we're having an affair, I'll wind up in prison. We have to be more careful!"

"Wait, what?" Emma whispered.

"I'm having déjà vu," I whispered back.

"Didn't you tell me she said that same thing to

Gordon back at the haunted house?" Emma looked at me. "Are you sure you weren't having some kind of vision of the future or something?"

"No. It wasn't a vision." She fed Gordon the same line.

Was she having a romantic affair with both?

And if she was, what did that mean?

Marchand ran a shaky hand over his head. "I know, I know! This whole mess is spiraling out of control." His voice dropped to an urgent whisper. "You need to get rid of that evidence. If the police find it, my career is finished."

My pulse quickened. Get rid of what evidence?

Angela crossed her arms, eyes flashing. "Don't tell me how to keep this a secret. I'm the one who got us this far, remember?" She leaned closer, tone dangerous. "Or should I remind you that you have a lot more to lose than I do?"

Were they talking about Marcus's murder?

"Keep your voice down!" Marchand hissed, glancing around nervously. Satisfied they were unobserved, he continued in a bare whisper. "Tell me you were careful disposing of everything. No traces left behind?"

Angela gave him a scathing look. "Of course I was careful. That's why you hired me." She jabbed a finger into his chest. "I've cleaned up your mess every time so far. But if you get sloppy and lead the cops back to us, no amount of cleaning will fix that." She stepped back, hands on her hips. "We had a deal, Paul. I expect you to honor it."

Marchand raked a hand over his face. When he finally replied, his voice was brittle and defeated. "You're right. I'm just on edge after everything lately. But I'll get you what I promised. Then this nightmare can finally end."

Angela nodded curtly. "See that you do."

With a swish of her long skirts, she strode off into the swirling crowd. Marchand slumped back against the tree, staring at nothing. The weight of the world seemed to press down on his rounded shoulders.

"So let me get this straight," I said, turning to Emma as we hurried away from the secluded grove of trees. "Did Marchand and Hayes basically just confess to not only having a sordid affair, but also being involved in the murder, bribery, and overall shadiness around Marcus's death?"

Emma waved off the idea with a firm head shake no. "No, that's not what we heard."

I stopped walking. "Wait, what? Of course we did."

"No." Emma held up a hand. "We heard suggestive remarks that could imply they were involved in something illicit, but nothing specific." She ticked the points off on her fingers. "Neither of them outright admitted to killing anyone or committing any crime."

We'd been so close to a confession, I could taste it.

But as I thought back over what we heard, I realized Emma was right; we had nothing solid. Yet. With a huff, I turned and continued down the path, visions of cornering Marchand and Hayes for the truth dancing in my head.

* * *

"Where could Briggs be?" Emma wondered aloud, standing on her tiptoes to peer over the sea of heads.

"No clue, but we need to—oof!" I stumbled as someone barreled right into me.

"Pardon me, darling!" a man's voice exclaimed. Strong hands grasped my shoulders, steadying me.

I looked up to see none other than Hermes smiling down at me, his bright blue gaze twinkling with amusement. The hands that had caught me slipped casually into the pockets of his linen trousers. Behind him stood a small gaggle of scantily clad men and women representing nearly every crude, sexy costume ever created.

Irritation boiled in my veins at the sight of Ami's absentee father living it up with a bevy of half-clothed firemen, nurses, and witches. He was knocking back neon cocktails without a care, oblivious to the fact that his daughter was somewhere at the chaotic festival.

"In a hurry, are we?" Hermes asked lazily, not bothering to peel his eyes off the barely clad nurse stroking his arm.

I clenched my jaw, biting back a scathing retort.

"We need to find Briggs," Emma said sharply, her lips drawn together. "No time to stop and chat, your highness."

Hermes finally glanced up at that, brow furrowing for only a moment before his attention was stolen by a busty witch shimmying up to refill his glass. "Oh, I'm sure it can wait. Come join us!" He smiled over his shoulder at the women. "We're having a delightful time over at the divination tent."

The women tittered, gazing at Hermes with adoring eyes.

A buff, sexy fireman sidled up to him, slipping a proprietary arm around his waist. "Yes, you simply must have him tell you the amazing prediction Hermes got from Madam Zelda."

That did it.

"Does Ami know you're here partying with your harem while she's off by herself?" I demanded, fists clenching.

Hermes looked taken aback. "Well, no, but—"

"Exactly!" I chimed in with a finger poke to his chest, making it clear I held him accountable. "You should spend time with your daughter at this family festival, not fawn over all these half-naked groupies." I swept my arm out, indicating the dozens of provocatively dressed men and women draped around him.

Hermes leaned back, nearly sloshing his neon cocktail down his front. "Hey now, I didn't mean any harm."

"You people never do, do you? Didn't mean any harm?" I repeated incredulously. "Do you have any idea how much Ami has needed you these past months? How much she's ached for a relationship with her father? Heck, she would have been ecstatic if you just bothered to stop by. But you couldn't be bothered to so much as send a birthday card!"

Hermes raised an eyebrow. "Now hold on, I—"

But I was too fired up to stop. "No, you hold on! She was devastated after Mom died. Devastated! And you ignoring her made it so much worse. Ami has been so patient—and forgiving—of your neglect, but I won't stand by anymore and watch you break her heart. You claim you want to make amends, yet here you are at the first chance living it up without a thought for her feelings. Some father you are!"

"Astra, take it easy," Emma tried to interject, but I barreled on.

"My mother used us to get to your power—we have trust issues. Obviously, right? But Ami has them most of all. That girl trusts even when she shouldn't, and she loves deeply. If you have no intention of being an actual father to Ami, then do her a favor and leave her the hell alone," I spat. "She doesn't need your halfhearted attention when the mood strikes you. Either step up or get lost."

The crowd of beautiful people's eyes ping-ponged between us as we stared each other down —the incensed witch and the impassive god. I doubted my tirade would change Hermes' ways, but at least this jerk would know I had Ami's back

—and now he can't claim no one ever told him what he was doing to her.

Emma's hand gripped my arm, a silent warning to rein it in. "Okay, I think you've said your piece," she murmured under her breath.

I gave a terse nod, even as I continued boring holes into Hermes with my glare. He held my gaze unflinchingly, standing tall and unruffled by my outburst. My diatribe didn't faze him—he was Hermes, the unflappable god of messengers and thieves. My words were a mere mortal blustering to his divine ears.

But I didn't care about his status.

Immortal or not, he needed to know how callously he was treating his own daughter. Ami deserved better than an absentee father who prioritized parties and groupies over spending time with her.

Hermes nodded. "You're absolutely right," he said after a long moment. "I haven't been acting like a proper father to Amethyst." He turned to the gaggle of worshippers still hovering behind him. "Ladies and gentlemen, thank you for a lovely time, but I'm afraid I must be off."

The arm candy groupies orbiting Hermes shot me looks of disappointment as my tirade ended their fun. With exaggerated pouts and trailing fingertips across Hermes' chest, they fluttered away one by one in search of entertainment elsewhere.

Gross.

Once alone, Hermes faced me. "When Persephone first told me about Amethyst, I'll admit I wasn't interested in her," he confessed. "I didn't know how to be a father, especially to a grown daughter. So instead of trying, I...didn't."

"No kidding," I shot back.

"Astra," Emma chided under her breath, "he's trying to explain."

I bit my tongue and gestured for Hermes to continue, tamping down the scathing remarks on the tip of my tongue. As much as I wanted to rail into him for neglecting Ami all these years, Emma had a point. If he was finally ready to take responsibility, the least I could do was hear him out.

But that didn't mean I had to make it easy for him.

"It was wrong of me. Amethyst deserves more. You're correct—she needs me to either step up or remove myself from her life. And though I know you won't believe this, I don't want to lose a chance to know my daughter."

My anger finally cooled as I saw genuine regret in his eyes.

Emma gave me an encouraging nod. She was right—screaming at him would fix nothing. If Hermes wanted to have a relationship with Ami, he deserved the opportunity to try. I had to at least give him that, for her sake.

"Okay," I relented. "But you need to actually try. No more flakiness or putting your needs first —especially not where she can see you. Ami needs a father, not another disappointment."

"I understand." His expression turned solemn. "I cannot change the past, but I can dedicate myself to her future happiness."

He extended a hand, and after a brief hesitation, I shook it.

* * *

WITH HERMES HAVING SET off to find Ami, Emma and I wove between food stalls and game booths, scanning for Briggs. Earlier tonight, I was tripping over him in haunted houses, and now I couldn't find him anywhere or get him to pick up his cell.

Where was he?

With a huff, I pulled out my phone again,

shooting Briggs yet another text demanding his location. "This is ridiculous," I told Emma.

"Yeah, a bit," she agreed, but her brow knitted with worry.

Just as I was about to combust from frustration, I spotted Lothian beneath the sprawling oak on the festival's edge, looking lost in thought while revelers streamed past him unnoticed. His hands were shoved in his pockets, shoulders slumped.

"What's he doing all by himself?" Emma murmured.

We picked up our pace, making a beeline for the isolated werewolf. Sensing our approach, his gaze lifted, eyes widening at whatever annoyed expression I hadn't managed to hide on my face.

"Hey there," Lothian said. "Everything okay?"

"No, everything is not okay." I stopped in front of him, crossing my arms. "You're going to explain why you rushed off without a word earlier. What aren't you telling me?"

Lothian shifted his weight, shoulders tensing under my scrutiny. "It's not a big deal. I just remembered something I had to take care of."

"Something so urgent you couldn't even tell your girlfriend where you were going?" I fixed him with a hard look, letting him know evasiveness wouldn't fly.

Lothian scratched the back of his neck, avoiding my probing stare. "Look, it was business stuff. I didn't want to get into it during the festival." He met my eyes. "And I still don't want to get into it. It has nothing to do with you." He glanced at Emma. "Either of you."

"There's the old Lothian I remember." I stepped closer, eyes flashing. "This reeks of bull. You've said nothing more about the April thing, and you're avoiding me, so I have to assume you're avoiding our talk about it. You jumped off the bench like it was on fire when I mentioned smelling gardenias."

Panic flashed across Lothian's face. "I said I don't want to talk about it."

"Yes. Well, I do. Now talk."

Emma looked at the werewolf, her brow furrowing. She remained silent, but I could see the concern in her eyes as they flicked between me and Lothian.

Lothian looked trapped.

He opened his mouth, then closed it and shook his head sharply. "You know what? No. My business is still just that—my business. And as I said repeatedly now, it has nothing to do with the two of you. Can't we just try to enjoy the rest of the festival?"

He reached for my hand, but I pulled away.

"You will tell me what's going on right now."

"I can't, Astra." Lothian tousled his hair irritably. "Just trust me, please."

I threw my hands up, exasperated. "How can I trust you if you won't be honest with me?"

"I'm not lying to you. I'm just not telling you everything."

I shook my head bitterly. "Secrets don't exactly breed trust, Lothian. Just ask my mother."

Emma held up her hands in a calming gesture. "Okay, you two, let's take a breath here. Getting worked up will not help, and I think once we bring your mother into it, Astra, we're heading toward unrecoverable territory." She looked between me and Lothian, her expression gentle but firm. "Astra, I know you're upset, but it's not fair to demand Lothian tell you absolutely everything going on in his life. He's allowed to have privacy, just like you."

I crossed my arms, scowling. "Sure. I agree with that. Except when he's acting shady. And right now he's acting shady."

Emma turned to Lothian. "She has a point. You being all vague and avoidant makes it seem like you're hiding something bad. Can you share anything to reassure Astra that's not the case?"

Lothian shifted his weight, looking conflicted. "I wish I could tell you both everything, but I can't. Not yet." He met my gaze. "You're just going to have to trust that I'm not keeping secrets to hurt you. When the time is right, I'll explain. But for now, please believe I'm doing this to protect you, Astra."

I jerked back like I'd been slapped. "Do I seem like I need protection to you? Protect me? From what?" Fear and anger warred within me. "Just tell me the truth!"

Lothian reached for me again, but I dodged his touch.

Hurt flashed in his eyes. "I'm sorry, but I can't. Not yet. Please Astra, try to understand."

But I was done trying to understand.

"No." After everything my family lost thanks to my mother's lies, I wouldn't ignore the warning signs again. "If you can't be honest with me, then I can't do this."

The pulsing lights and sounds of the festival faded behind me as I stormed off alone into the night, my heart aching with each step—but I refused to shed tears over someone who couldn't even tell me the truth.

CHAPTER SIXTEEN

I sat in my Jeep, hands clenched, white-knuckled around the steering wheel. The sounds of the festival faded into the distance, but the pounding in my head from Lothian's latest stunt remained loud and clear. The weight of the impasse pressed down like a vise around my chest.

How could Lothian betray my trust like that? Keeping secrets, avoiding my questions, claiming it was to "protect" me? I already had a lifetime's worth of experience with that line thanks to my dear mother's web of lies that started weaving long before I took my first breath.

I swore I wouldn't make that mistake again.

Yet here I was, once again, betrayed by someone's "good intentions."

Hot, furious tears stung my eyes, but I blinked them back, refusing to let them fall. I would not cry over this.

Over him.

With a shuddering sigh, I leaned my head back against the seat.

Why did I ignore all the neon warning signs and let down my guard with Lothian?

Somehow I convinced myself that despite his reputation as an arrogant playboy who smirked and cocked his eyebrow more than actual words came out of his mouth, he was trustworthy. Like a few tender moments and feigned sincerity made up for the smarmy sarcastic jerk I first thought he was.

Silly me for pushing aside my reasonable suspicions he was not only capable of deceit, but probably had a PhD in it.

"I am such an idiot," I said to the empty interior.

A flash of golden light suddenly lit up the inside of the Jeep like a cheesy special effect from a low-budget sci-fi movie, and I turned to see none other than my dear old dad Apollo chilling in the passenger seat next to me. Apparently, the god of the sun has nothing better to do than spontaneously appear in his daughter's car to catch up.

"You know, I'm understanding why the world is such a mess if the gods just spend their time popping into random cars and meddling in relationships," I said, wiping my eyes before the tears could spill over. "Don't you have anything better to do? Like maybe fixing some global problems instead of trying to micromanage my love life?"

I gave him a pointed look, channeling all my simmering anger and hurt into an icy glare. If he was here to defend Lothian with some divine excuse, I was so not in the mood. The gods could take their interference and vanish right back into the ether. I'd had enough of their meddling to last a lifetime.

"After that epic take down you laid on Hermes for being an absentee dad, did you really expect me to just turn a blind eye to your angst tornado over here?" Apollo said, turning to give me a somber yet dramatic look, his golden hair gleaming in the streetlights filtering through the Jeep's windows.

"How generous." I gave him a slow, sarcastic

golf clap. "Father of the Year award is coming your way."

"You can be as stubborn as your mother sometimes, Astra," Apollo replied, still serene. "Did you know that?"

I clenched my jaw, gripping the steering wheel. "Oh, gods, please just go away, will you?"

Having Apollo here lecturing me only added gasoline to the simmering rage I'd been carrying all evening. As he droned on about how he could help fix things, how I was carrying my mother's mistrust into new relationships, I dug my fingernails into my palms, jaw clenching.

Just another arrogant man thinking he knew what was best for me. That my problems could be neatly solved if I just listened to his sage advice.

Apollo pressed on, undeterred. "Your anger arises from deep wounds still needing care, Astra. If you think on it, what Lothian has done tonight did not rise to the level of anger you had for him. Perhaps he knew you would have an unreasonable reaction, and that's why he shielded you from what he knows."

I seethed at him with a scorching glower that could've melted iron. It was all I could do not to backhand that patronizing expression off his infuriatingly angelic face.

"Are you done?" I asked pointedly.

His eyebrows shot up, but he wisely took the hint and gave a terse nod.

"Don't you dare lecture me about my love life," I said, staring down Apollo with a fiery glare. "In case you've forgotten, I'm not a child anymore. I'm a grown woman in my thirties. I don't need romantic advice from someone who changes partners more often than the seasons." Ancient being or not, I would not tolerate paternalistic condescension from my absentee father.

Apollo opened his mouth to respond, but I barreled on, refusing to give him the chance.

"You have no concept of what it's like to be mortal," I said. "To know that your time is finite, that death awaits you no matter what. To have to cram love, meaning, everything into a handful of decades after having been the product of an affair meant only to increase my mother's standing with you people. I have trust issues you likely have no conception of since you gods so often use mortals and then discard them."

"Astra—"

"So no, you don't get to waltz in here spouting platitudes and advice. You haven't earned that right. On the most fundamental levels, Dad, you have no ability to understand my life. You certainly have no ability to understand my relationship or my need for trust and comfort." I met Apollo's amber-colored eyes, my expression stony. "I demand honesty from those in my life. I have the right to demand safety for myself when I'm with them."

"I know it will come as a surprise to you, but I agree with you," Apollo said as if I hadn't just unloaded on him. He gave an approving nod. "You are wise to guard your heart closely, Daughter. Of course the betrayals in your past have taught you to guard against the untrustworthy. I could never say otherwise, and it's not necessarily a bad thing, unless..." He paused, considering his next words.

"Unless what?"

"Unless your fear of further hurt has blinded you to devotion right before your eyes?"

I bristled at the implied criticism. "What are you talking about?"

"This wolf who captured your heart—what has he really done to break faith with you?" Apollo held up a hand as if to forestall the angry response he knew was coming. "Harboring secrets is not ideal, I grant you. But consider his motivation. Did he not claim protection as the cause?"

"I don't need protection! I need honesty!"

"But maybe he needs to protect," my father said, unruffled by my outburst. "Did you think of that?"

His words gave me pause, my rising temper momentarily checked.

Apollo pressed on gently. "You judge him guilty of deception. But perhaps, Daughter, sheltering you from harm is as imperative to him as your need for honesty is to you?"

As much as I hated to admit it, Apollo made a fair point.

And oh, man, did I hate to admit it.

My shoulders slumped slightly as I considered things from Lothian's perspective. He was a powerful werewolf—the instinct to safeguard his mate would be strong, primal even. And if he felt I was legitimately in danger because of the situation, that drive would be amplified exponentially.

Sensing my softening stance, Apollo continued in an ancient tone that I'd rarely heard from him. "My daughter, you have endured such pain and loss. You fear further sorrow should you leave your heart unguarded." His eyes shone with compassion. "But a fortress without windows is no refuge. It admits no light, no joy, no fellowship."

Damn.

That was poetic.

Apollo reached over, gripping my shoulder. "Have care in judging this wolf too harshly. Flaws he may have, but falsehood toward you does not dwell in his heart. Of that I am certain."

I sat silently in the driver's seat of the Jeep, staring out the window. The night-shrouded scenery barely registered as my mind churned.

After a few silent moments, I slowly placed my hand over my father's. I gave it a gentle squeeze, feeling the unfamiliar divine strength beneath my palm. "I can't read you."

"But you can trust me."

Maybe.

Apollo smiled, his eyes crinkling with relief and pride. "There lies the true heart of wisdom—choosing trust and compassion over fear and doubt." His form began glowing, limning the interior of the Jeep in gold. "Remember, the bonds of care can weather any tempest. You need but have faith."

With those final enigmatic words, my father vanished, leaving only lingering sparkles dancing across the passenger seat.

* * *

I MADE my way back toward the pulsing lights and music of the festival, weaving through the lively crowds. Costumed revelers wandered the fairgrounds, their laughter and shouts mingling with the blaring songs.

I barely noticed the celebrations raging around me.

My thoughts swirled with everything Dad said, hope and uncertainty warring within. His advice had given me a lot to think about when it came to Lothian.

Could Apollo be right?

Was I too quick to condemn Lothian as deceptive?

If he had valid reasons for keeping secrets, I owed it to him—to us—to hear him out before making any rash decisions.

Lost in thought, I rounded a corner and collided straight into a solid body. I stumbled back with a muffled "Oof!"

"Watch where you're going, nitwit!" a shrill, grating voice barked out.

I raised my eyes to find April staring daggers at me, her brassy blond ringlets jiggling as she puffed out her chest.

Great.

Just the person I didn't need to deal with right now.

I could use the chance to dig into why she was here in Forkbridge, but my father's words rang in my mind. I wanted to talk to Lothian again before going behind his back. So I just said "Sorry about that," politely, hoping to avoid a confrontation.

But April's glare only intensified, her heavily mascaraed eyes narrowing.

She looked me up and down with disdain. "Well, if it isn't Lothian's latest toy," she sneered. "Though I overheard the two of you are done. Can't say I'm surprised he came to his senses and took off. You're not his type."

I bit my tongue, resisting the urge to unload on the woman.

Arguing would only delight her.

"Yep, not his type at all," I said. "Enjoy the rest of the festival." I moved to step around April, but she sidestepped to block my path, manicured hands planted on her hips.

"Oh no, I don't think so." She tossed her hair, lips curving into a feline smile. "Lothian may find this whole 'good girl' act charming, but just so you don't get any ideas about getting him back, we both know you were just a passing phase to him. He needs someone fun. Unpredictable." April leaned in, lowering her voice. "Someone willing to get a little wild, if you know what I mean." She winked, relishing my visible irritation.

"Yep. Sounds good." I said, struggling to remain composed. "You've made your point. Good deal. Now, if you'll excuse me—"

April smirked, pressing on in a syrupy voice. "The point, darling, is that you should quit clinging to Lothian before you get yourself hurt." Her smile turned predatory. "That man was never made to be tamed."

My eyes narrowed, static crackling around my fingertips as my control slipped. "And let me guess—you're just the adventurous gal for the job?"

April let out a throaty, grating laugh. "Obviously. We have history, Lothian and me." She leaned in. "The kind that men don't forget." Her gaze turned calculating. "Speaking of history...where did Lothian run off to earlier tonight, anyway?"

I was surprised she was asking me where Lothian went. She must not know. But if April didn't know where he disappeared to, that meant Lothian was checking things out behind her back.

Things she wanted to know so badly that she was asking...me.

I shrugged, feigning nonchalance. "He had something to take care of."

"Uh huh. Thanks for that, Captain Obvious." April wasn't buying it. She watched me for a reaction. "Any idea what that 'something' might be? Or do you not even know what he does?"

"Can't say I do, since it's none of my business," I replied.

With a casual air, she examined her nails. "You sure about that? Because I could swear I caught a certain delicious werewolf's scent earlier, somewhere he shouldn't have been."

"Like I said, Lothian's business is his own."

April's face contorted into a scowl, irritated that her insinuations failed to get a reaction. She clearly wasn't expecting that response, and I hid a satisfied smirk at throwing her off.

"You listen to me," she hissed, all pretense of civility gone. "You don't know Lothian like I do. The right circumstances will bring him back to Palm Beach. He's already bored slumming it with some do-gooder witch that can't give him what he needs."

My own temper flickered to life, but I kept my voice low and steady. "And you think you can?

Face it, April—if you knew Lothian's heart, you wouldn't be stalking him at a festival like a jealous schoolgirl."

April's face flushed an ugly shade of red, but before she could spit out whatever crude retort hovered on her lips, I pressed on.

"I don't know what fantasies or agenda you're clinging to, and I don't care. But Lothian told you that your relationship was over. I suggest you respect that and move on."

April looked thrown by my show of spine. But she regrouped, plastering on a smug smile.

"We'll see who he chooses, won't we? But fair warning—I fight dirty when it comes to getting my man." Her saccharine tone turned mocking. "By the way, how is the werewolf queen doing these days? Still running the pack everyone liked into the ground?"

"Boy, you just hate everything Lothian loves, don't you?"

April's expression darkened, no longer so self-assured.

She leaned closer, and the heavy scent of gardenias flooded my senses, cloying and overwhelming this close. My eyes widened.

Gardenias...

Gardenias was the scent clinging to the

amulet Emma pilfered from Mayor Marchand, and the mere mention of the flower's aroma sent Lothian rushing away earlier that night—a fragrance that made him think of April.

Gardenias seemed to be a significant clue somehow connected to Mayor Marchand and the coins and Lothian—by way of April.

Oblivious to my racing thoughts, April prattled on in a spiteful tone. "Let's face reality—nobody in this backwater town wants Eddie's pack of flea-bitten mutts invading their community. It's enough they have to deal with you weird witches. The sooner you and your loser bestie take off, the happier everyone else will be. So do yourself a favor and get lost before more people get hurt."

More people?

Who'd gotten hurt so far?

Before I could ask, April shouldered past me and disappeared into the crowd, not bothering to wait for my reaction.

* * *

I STOOD FROZEN, pulse pounding in my ears as April's venomous parting words echoed through my mind. The overwhelming scent of gardenias still clung to my senses, raising more questions than ever about what April's ties were to Lothian, Marchand, and possibly even Marcus's murder.

What was Lothian hiding?

How was April connected to the Marchand?

Could she have been involved in Marcus's death?

Shaking off the turbulent vortex of questions swirling through my mind, I continued searching for Lothian with renewed urgency. We needed to have a serious talk about what the heck was going on with him and how all these threads around his employee intertwined through a murder of a councilman in Forkbridge.

Spotting Lothian up ahead, I called out sharply to get his attention.

As he turned, surprise flashing across his unfairly gorgeous face, I steeled myself. No more evasive maneuvers or half-truths from him tonight.

One way or another, I was getting the full tea even if I had to Krazy Glue my hand in his so I could read him to make it happen.

CHAPTER SEVENTEEN

*T*he werewolf's broad shoulders were visible up ahead as he stood beneath a string of colored lights, scanning the surrounding revelry. His handsome face was etched with worry, no doubt looking for me after our earlier fight.

I took a moment to really look at him as I approached.

Lothian was undeniably good-looking—tall and muscular, with chiseled features and intense cyan eyes. He could be so gentle when I needed comfort, wrapping me in those muscular arms and speaking softly to soothe my fears. Yet he was also cunning, keeping secrets from everyone and somehow tangled up in this strange situation.

I remembered how safe I'd felt resting against him—but I also recalled the flash of sly triumph in his cerulean eyes when he thought he'd outmaneuvered me. I wished I could reconcile the sides of him I'd glimpsed—the protector and the deceiver.

But I didn't know if I could.

I paused, breathing deeply to harden my determination, then pressed on, one foot in front of the other.

Answers first, emotions later.

I had to stay focused.

As I moved through the costumed crowd, calling Lothian's name, Detective Briggs suddenly materialized out of the revelers, intercepting me. His police jacket and boots stood out amid the vivid colors and wild costumes surrounding us.

"Astra, hang on a minute," Briggs said, grasping my arm. "I see where you're going, and I have to stop you. I need to have a word with Mr. Pennington here first."

I turned to him in surprise. "Why?"

"Official police business," he replied, his eyes flickering over to where Lothian stood, watching our exchange.

I blinked in surprise. Police business with Lothian?

Before I could question Briggs further, Lothian approached, his piercing cobalt eyes darting between us. "Is there a problem here, Detective?" he inquired, his voice low and dangerous.

Setting his jaw, Briggs stood tall and firm, his stocky shoulders rigid beneath his shirt as he locked eyes with Lothian. "Just need a quick word, that's all." He glanced at me. "Without Astra present."

"Are you kidding me?" I shook my head in frustration. "You asked for my help to look into this murder, Briggs. Not the other way around. If you think you can shut me out now, you have another thing coming."

Around us, the festivities swirled wildly, oblivious to the tense scene unfolding in their midst.

"What do you want to ask me, detective?" Lothian asked, crossing his arms like a moody teen as he sized up the man in front of him. "Anything you want to know, you can say in front of Astra. We don't keep secrets from each other."

I barely suppressed an incredulous laugh at that boldfaced lie.

Unless "not keeping secrets" meant constantly dodging my questions and concealing vital information I deserved to know, then sure—Lothian was being totally upfront and honest here.

I gave him my best "are you freaking kidding me" stare, but the werewolf kept his eyes steady on Detective Briggs and avoided meeting my eyes —because not making eye contact screams open communication and trustworthiness.

Briggs squared his shoulders, meeting Lothian's gaze. "Let's speak in private, shall we?" His voice was authoritative. "I have some questions regarding those occult amulets we keep finding everywhere."

The cheap aluminum amulets—like the ones found in city hall and that Emma pickpocketed off Mayor Marchand earlier.

What did they have to do with Lothian?

Lothian shifted his weight, looking uneasy. "Amulets? Can't say I know anything about those."

But there was a flicker of something in his eyes—uncertainty perhaps—that made me wonder if he was telling the whole truth.

"That's interesting," Briggs countered. He held up a plastic evidence bag containing one of the silver disks engraved with pseudo-magical symbols. "We traced a bulk order of these amulets to a company owned by you, Mr. Pennington. Any idea how they made it all the way from your Palm Beach club to a crime scene in Forkbridge, if you do not know of them?"

Lothian threaded his fingers through his windswept golden waves, letting them cascade back into place. "Look, I'm sure there's a reasonable explanation—"

"I'm sure there is," Briggs cut in. "And you can provide it to me over in the police trailer just on the edge of the festival, Mr. Pennington, where we'll continue this discussion." He turned to me. "You understand now, I assume?"

"Absolutely, Detective," I said. "In fact, why don't I tag along in case I can offer any additional insights?"

Briggs's brow furrowed. "You want me to allow you into the room where I'll be interrogating your boyfriend?" He raised an eyebrow. "And you expect me to believe you're coming along to help me?"

"You won't even know I'm there," I said, linking my arm through Lothian's tense one and giving it a sly squeeze. "I'm great at blending into the background."

Lothian shot me a look that said "what are you

doing?" but I just smiled and fluttered my lashes, then stared Briggs down, daring him to object.

After a moment, he sighed, relenting.

"Fine, you can observe the interview. But don't interfere." Briggs nodded and started off through the crowds.

I met Lothian's gaze as we followed, my expression stern. The werewolf looked uncomfortable having me tag along, but he was trapped. Briggs would get his official answers, but so would I.

* * *

BRIGGS LED us to a small trailer set up on the outer edge of the festival grounds, the cacophony of the central Halloween celebrations muted by the distance. A Forkbridge Police Department sign hung on the flimsy door, fluttering in the crisp fall breeze.

A few rickety tables were crammed inside, piled with paperwork and radio equipment, and the smell of burned coffee and stale donuts assaulted our noses. The dingy fluorescent lights flickered erratically, giving the tight quarters an eerie feeling.

"It's not the Ritz, but at least it's quiet. Have a

seat," Briggs said, gesturing to two folding chairs facing a plain plastic table.

I settled into one chair, Lothian taking the other. The werewolf eyed me as Briggs flipped open a notebook, clicking his pen. The detective's congenial manner from earlier had vanished, replaced by stern professionalism.

"Let's start with Marcus Clinton's murder," Briggs began without preamble. "Did you know the victim at all, Mr. Pennington?"

Lothian shook his head. "No. I mean, I knew who he was since he was on the town council, but we'd never met or interacted."

Briggs made a note. "And did any business you own have matters before the council that Marcus might have influenced?"

"No, nothing comes to mind," Lothian replied after a moment's thought. "I own several businesses, though."

I watched Lothian, searching for any hint of deception in his body language or tone, but his responses seemed forthright so far. He sat straight in the rickety folding chair, maintaining unwavering eye contact with Briggs, who continued rapid fire, questioning him about potential connections to Marcus or motives to want him gone.

With each answer, Lothian appeared increasingly bewildered by the line of inquiry.

Briggs eyed Lothian. "So let me get this straight—you're living with three other men, Detective Sullivan, and a baby?"

Lothian shifted on the chair. "Yeah, it's a bit of an unusual situation."

"Seems like more than a bit unusual if you ask me," Briggs said. "What exactly is going on in that house of yours?"

"Nothing strange. We're just friends looking out for each other."

"Uh huh." Briggs clearly wasn't convinced.

Lothian met Briggs' skeptical gaze. "Not everything is a sinister conspiracy, Detective. What does any of this have to do with those amulet things, anyway?" he asked. "You've asked me about everything except what you claimed you wanted to ask about."

"Have I? I already told you why I wanted to talk to you," Briggs scribbled something in his notebook. "Records show the order of occult-themed amulets was made by one of your companies. You bought them. They showed up at a murder scene. Care to explain?"

Lothian hesitated before responding. "It's...complicated."

"I've got time."

"So do I," I told him.

The werewolf glanced at me, then slid a hand through his disheveled strands. "Look, I run a lot of businesses. Someone on my staff handles merchandizing for novelty shops and event vendors. If occult trinkets were ordered, it was likely for a seasonal pop-up store or something. I honestly don't know the details."

Briggs's expression remained stony. "I see. And do you make a habit of not knowing details about your own companies?"

I could sense Lothian's rising frustration as he repeated he wasn't involved in every single business transaction. His answers came across as truthful, but Briggs pressed on.

After covering Lothian's many enterprises and local political connections, Briggs flipped to a new page in his notebook. "Let's discuss your employees now," he said, scanning over his notes. "Who manages this business in Palm Beach for you? The one that the amulet order was placed through?"

Lothian nodded, his jaw tightening almost imperceptibly. "April Hayes manages my club in Palm Beach. She's been assisting with an expansion plan I'm working on."

My pulse spiked at the mention of April's full name.

Hayes.

April Hayes?

I leaned forward. "Did you say April's last name was Hayes?"

Lothian looked surprised by my sudden intensity. "Yeah, why?"

"Do you know if she's related to Angela Hayes here in Forkbridge?" I asked.

Comprehension lit Lothian's piercing azure eyes. "Actually, yes. I believe she mentioned Angela is her aunt. Her family's from this area, and that's partly why she came up here."

My mind raced, piecing together this new information.

After April's heated confrontation with me tonight, I couldn't dismiss the possibility that this whole thing was a gigantic conspiracy. But what I didn't get was this—what did April Hayes stand to gain from Marcus's death? I racked my brain, trying to make sense of it.

Was it an attempt to bring down Lothian for spurning her affections? No, she didn't sound like she wanted revenge on him—she wanted him back. Back with her, back in Palm Beach, like none of this had ever happened.

What could April and Angela accomplish together that each of them couldn't do solo? There had to be an angle I was missing, some shared goal I hadn't uncovered.

My thoughts chased each other in circles, spinning out scenarios and motives. But I kept coming back to the same baffling questions. April's ties to Lothian, her venom toward me, her aunt's involvement with the mayor and the dethroned councilman...it all showed something sinister brewing beneath the surface.

Just like Athena had claimed.

Briggs scrutinized me closely, picking up on my agitation. "This mean something to you, Astra?" he asked.

"It might. But I need more time to be sure. We need to go. Both of us. Okay?"

"I still have—" Briggs started to protest.

"Do you trust me?" I interrupted, holding his stare.

Briggs went silent, regarding me carefully. He crossed his arms, mouth pressed in a tense line as he considered my words. The pulsing music and raucous laughter of the festival was an oddly muted backdrop around us.

After a long, weighted pause, Briggs finally gave a grunt of acquiescence, though his eyes remained narrowed with lingering suspicion. "Against my better judgment, yes, I do trust you," he admitted. "But I still don't like this, Astra."

"Noted. But I promise, as soon as I know anything for sure, I'll find you."

Briggs scrubbed a hand over his stubble, exhaling through his nose. "What else can I say? No? Tell me everything now?"

"You could."

"Would it make any difference?"

"No."

* * *

WE WALKED to the periphery of the sprawling fairgrounds, leaving only muffled music penetrating the tense silence that surrounded us.

Lothian fidgeted beside me as we moved, posture rigid, looking distinctly uncomfortable. I kept my gaze fixed straight ahead for a long moment, gathering my composure and steeling myself for the conversation ahead.

Finally, I turned to face him directly, eyes burning with conviction. "No more games, Lothian. No more evasions or half-truths." My voice was steady and firm. "It's time for total honesty between us. I want the full story—all of it."

He held my gaze, lips pressed in a grim line. I could see the internal struggle play out on his face as he debated just how much to reveal. But I would not back down or let him off the hook this time.

"Please," I implored, my tone softening slightly. "Don't shut me out anymore. If we're going to move forward, I need to understand everything that's happening and why. No more secrets."

Lothian nodded slowly. "You're right. I know you're right." He grimaced. "It bothered me, the idea my past would cause you grief."

Taking a deep breath, he launched into an account of his history and association with April Hayes. They first met years ago when April started working at one of his clubs. They had a brief fling that fizzled out quickly. While it was over romantically, she stayed on as manager of multiple establishments he owned and they'd maintained a flirty relationship. "And she's human, but she knows my true nature. I wasn't always a model of discretion."

"Okay. Why all the surrounding secrecy?" I asked once he finished the back story.

Lothian raked a hand through his hair, unease playing across his chiseled features. "It's not really secrecy. When she dragged me off that first day at the festival, she told me she thought we'd made a mistake ending things. That we belonged together. And..." He trailed off, looking pained.

"Go on," I prompted gently.

"She said my devotion to Eddie's pack had screwed my life up. That I was wasting my potential tying myself to them," he confessed quietly. "She knows what I am. She doesn't really understand what a pack means to us, though. What Emma means to me, what Hunter means to me. She thinks I changed who I am for Eddie's choices, and she didn't like it. So I said nothing—I just didn't want Emma or Eddie to hear what she was saying." He looked at me. "I didn't want you to hear it, either. It's embarrassing."

This was a vulnerable admission for Lothian, and I could understand—but that wasn't everything. "I get how you would feel that way. I do. But there's more to it. The way you rushed off when I mentioned gardenias earlier? What aren't you telling me?"

When Lothian hesitated, I laid my cards on the table.

"Look, Lothian, I spoke with April tonight.

She made it abundantly clear how she feels, and that you two have unfinished business in her eyes."

Lothian looked stunned. "You talked to her? What did she say?"

I relayed the spiteful exchange in blunt detail, sparing no part of April's toxicity. By the time I finished, Lothian was rigid with outrage.

"How dare she speak to you that way?" he growled. "Just her showing up here is completely inappropriate. There's no reason for her to be here, and I told April repeatedly there's no chance of us rekindling anything romantic. She needs to move on."

He grasped my hands, blue eyes boring intensely into mine. "Believe me, Astra. She is not a threat to you and me. My only desire is to be with you."

He was telling the truth.

But there was more...I could feel it in his hands.

"What are you protecting me from?" I asked pointedly. "You're still hiding something. What are you hiding?"

Lothian looked caught off guard.

"Uncomplicate this," I added. "Just be straight with me for once."

Lothian wavered as if at war with himself.

Finally, he exhaled sharply.

"Okay, look. When you mentioned something about the smelling gardenias, I got concerned." His jaw tightened. "April wears a very distinctive perfume I got her from a visit to Paranormopolis"—the paranormal capital city that humans can't visit—"and she only wore it with me. It was a perfume crafted by the capital apothecary to attract pleasure and romance."

I chuckled. "I wonder if she shared some with her aunt. That woman's having an affair with the mayor and Gordon Schmidt."

"When I heard that? I was just worried April would somehow be implicated in a situation she had nothing to do with. But now?" Lothian gripped my hands. "Don't you see? If there was a murder with witchy elements around it, like those coins, who would everyone automatically blame?" His eyes were intense, willing me to follow his logic.

Comprehension hit me like a lightning bolt. "Witches."

Lothian nodded grimly. "April knows I care about you and your family. She knows you and Emma are close. What if she killed Marcus just to blame you and get you and your sisters thrown in jail?"

Could April truly hate me enough to conceive something so diabolical?

Yeah.

Probably.

But then I remembered the amulet Emma lifted from Marchand's pocket.

"Marchand had one of the coins though," I said. "Maybe April is involved somehow, but she can't be the only one behind this."

Lothian looked slightly relieved at my rebuttal. "You're right, there must be more to it than just April." He dragged a weary hand over his haphazard hairstyle, the frantic motion only mussing the chaotic cream-colored tufts further as they stuck out every which way. "I should have told you about her when things began not adding up. I didn't want anyone else to have to deal with my problems."

I wrapped my fingers around his, hoping my touch could banish the regret behind his eyes.

He smiled at me. "Forgive me?"

"Yeah, I forgive you. Look, this relationship thing is going to challenge both of us. It could have just as easily been me with the crazy ex," I told him. "You've been super cool about my undead ex-boyfriend haunting mirrors, so I guess I can overlook your Palm Beach Fatal Attraction situation."

With a delicate touch, he pressed his mouth to my own. It was a kiss as light as a butterfly's wing. "Thank you."

"What can I say? I'm a giver," I replied, patting his cheek. "You're welcome."

"Let's go find my psycho ex."

"You really know how to make a date feel special, Pennington."

CHAPTER EIGHTEEN

*L*othian and I wove our way through the raucous festival crowds, scanning for any sign of April's distinctive platinum curls or the cloying cloud of gardenia perfume she seemed to travel in. Revelers in colorful costumes and glittering masks laughed and swayed around us to the pulsing music.

The longer we looked, the more I felt frustration mounting. Were we going in circles? Just as I was about to suggest we split up to cover more ground, a familiar voice called out, "Astra! Over here!"

I turned to see Emma waving us over, flanked by Ayla, Althea, Melvin, Rex, and Tara.

"Hey, Em. You would not believe the crazy

night we've just had," I said as Lothian and I hurried over to join her group.

Emma's eyebrows shot up, eyes glinting with curiosity. "Oh really? Do tell."

I quickly summarized everything that had transpired: the tense interrogation with Briggs about those odd occult amulets, learning of Lothian's connection to them through his employee, April. "The amulets were ordered in bulk by one of Lothian's companies down in Palm Beach. The one April works at? Yep, that one. And April's related to Angela—she's her niece."

Ayla stepped forward, expression serious. "Well, that's a decent segue into this. I have fairly big news, too."

"Oh?" I asked.

"Aunt Gertie came by earlier," Ayla said, referring to our resident ghost aunt. "She told me she was chatting with some spirits from Cassandra, and they were worried about the tension between Forkbridge and Cassandra this Halloween. She says one of them accidentally let something slip that she was sure was significant, because the ghost took off almost immediately."

I leaned in, intrigued. "What did they tell her?"

"Aunt Gertie said, they told her Angela grew

up in Cassandra. She's originally from there, but left years ago."

My brows shot up in surprise as I absorbed this unexpected twist. "Angela is from Cassandra? Are you absolutely sure?" I asked.

"Well, I'm as sure as I can be under the circumstances." Ayla nodded. "That's what Aunt Gertie heard from the spirits, and that's what she told me, but since they freaked out when they realized what they told her, I'm going to bet it's true. They don't forget former residents."

"Whoa. Plot twist," Emma muttered.

"Is this what Serena was talking about when she want on her rant about us canceling the Halloween festival?" I wondered.

My sister shrugged. "There's more," Ayla continued. "Melvin has something to add, too."

All eyes turned to Melvin, Ayla's lanky teenage boyfriend. He shifted his weight, looking nervous at the sudden attention.

"Yeah, uh, I don't really remember Angela myself since she would have been gone well before I was born," Melvin explained. "But my dad mentioned once there's an old lady named Rutana Hayes who still lives right on the outskirts of Cassandra. Keeps to herself, never comes into town. She's not one of the mediums or psychics, though, and she's got no business and no job in town—which is odd for anyone still living there."

My curiosity found a match in Emma's expression, our wordless exchange alive with unspoken questions. Why would a former Cassandra resident with the last name Hayes end up in Forkbridge—and working in the Forkbridge government?

"I feel like I should point out it's not unheard of for people from Cassandra to work in Forkbridge," I said. "Cassie Blackwood works at the police department and has been for years. Jason was a teacher here. Sure, it could mean something, but it could also mean nothing at all."

"What did Serena say when she came to visit you?" Emma asked.

"She came in all desperate and distraught, begging us to cancel Forkbridge's entire Halloween festival," Althea explained, shaking her head. "She went on about how having competing festivals was going to devastate Cassandra's economy and livelihoods if tourists only came here instead."

Althea crossed her arms, recalling the tense interaction. "Serena was nearly in tears describing how Cassandra depends on their huge

Halloween spiritualist fair for income since most people there don't work regular jobs. She kept saying that without those revenues, businesses might go under and people would suffer."

"I felt so awful about how distressed she was," Ami chimed in, her kind eyes full of sympathy. "She was clearly very scared for her town."

Nodding, Althea continued. "Well, yeah, I felt awful until Serena started getting kind of imperious and lecturing when we said there wasn't anything we could do. She lectured us on 'lacking compassion' and said we should 'reconsider our selfish actions' or something like that."

"Or else?" Emma asked, raising her eyebrow.

"I don't know." I quickly updated Emma on what Lothian had shared regarding his history with April and her potential vendetta against me. "So maybe it was just April trying to get me arrested so she could get her boyfriend back."

Althea shook her head when I finished. "This is crazy. You really think she'd try to frame you for murder just because she's jealous?"

"I don't know," I admitted. "But at this point, we can't rule anything out."

"I don't think April would kill anyone, but finding her is our top priority," Lothian said.

"She's clearly unstable, and she needs to field a few inquiries about what she's really doing in Forkbridge." His jaw clenched, eyes flashing. "And why she felt justified harassing Astra."

Rex nodded. "We'll help look for her. Can you describe what she looks like?"

I gave him a quick rundown of April's appearance. "But for you and your super nose, you might be able to find her better by smell. She smells like gardenias."

"All right, we're on it," Rex said. "Tara and I can cover the whole festival quickly with our enhanced senses. We'll let you know as soon as we pick up her trail."

"Althea, Melvin, and I will go check around the food stalls and picnic tables over there," Ayla said decisively, pointing toward a row of vendors with twinkling lights strung overhead. The aroma of frying oil, grilled meat, and sweet treats wafted from that direction.

"We'll find her," Althea said. "Either way, let's meet back here in an hour."

"Sounds good. Be careful."

Lothian, Emma, and I continued searching the lively festival grounds, weaving through costumed revelers caught up in the festivities.

The air was filled with laughter, music, and delicious scents from the crowded food stalls.

But no scent of gardenias.

I blew out a frustrated breath after twenty more minutes of fruitless hunting through the costumed crowds. "This is impossible. It's like trying to spot a single leaf in a pile of fall foliage."

"You're telling me," Emma agreed. "I feel like we're just going in circles at this point."

Lothian craned his neck, gazing over the sea of heads surrounding us. "She has to be here somewhere."

"Maybe Rex or Tara will find her," Emma said confidently. "In the meantime, we should—"

Lothian tensed abruptly, his head swiveling around as his wolfish senses detected something amiss. Emma cut off mid-sentence, immediately alert. She turned with him to peer toward the bright flashing lights and garish game booths of the midway, eyes narrowing intently.

"What is it?" I asked, instantly on alert.

Lothian didn't answer right away, his gaze fixed unerringly on a spot lost in the chaotic sea of colors and sounds.

"Blood," Lothian said. "I smell blood."

Without another word, Lothian took off

toward the amusement park rides, Emma and I hot on his heels.

* * *

UP AHEAD, a circle of darkened canvas tents stood still and silent, a stark contrast to the flashing lights and excitement of the rides and games behind us. The brightly colored cloth back walls fluttered slightly in the night breeze.

"Do you hear anything?" I whispered.

Emma shook her head no and held a finger to her lips.

A wooden sign hung at the roped off entrance to the ten or so tents that made up a kind of open-air pavilion, announcing in a bubbly font that the face painting and costume stations were closed for the night and would reopen tomorrow. I could see almost ghostly shapes of mannequins just inside.

This section of the fairgrounds had been closed for the evening, making it an ideal spot for clandestine meetings—or, I supposed, violent confrontations.

We stopped at the perimeter of the circle of tents and slipped inside the first booth through a lifted back canvas wall. Ducking down, we took cover behind the pop-up shop's counter, paint bottles, and face painting supplies scattered around us.

"Get your hands off me!"

Carefully peering around the corner, I spotted two familiar figures engaged in a blazing shouting match in the middle of the open space—even at a distance in the dark, Gordon Schmidt and Mayor Paul Marchand were instantly recognizable.

Schmidt had the mayor by the collar, shaking him roughly. Marchand knocked his rival's hands away, jabbing a finger toward Schmidt's chest as he spat his own heated retort.

This was no amicable discussion.

I leaned closer, straining to pick up the enraged argument unfolding across the park. Schmidt's face was mottled with rage, nostrils flaring as he jabbed a finger toward Marchand's chest.

"You lying snake!" Schmidt roared. "How long have you been screwing my girlfriend behind my back?"

Marchand's mouth twisted into a scornful grimace. "Your girlfriend? That's rich, considering Angela was with me long before you swooped in thinking you could steal her away."

"Yeah, because you didn't worship her like she deserved!" Schmidt shot back. He gave Marchand a rough shove. "But I showed Angela what genuine passion looks like."

Marchand barked out a scornful laugh. "Oh please, you were just a temporary distraction for her. A mere amusement." His eyes narrowed cruelly. "Angela and I share something profound you could never touch."

"Angela Hayes and profound don't exactly go together like peanut butter and jelly," I whispered to Emma.

She whacked and hushed me.

With an anguished wail like a toddler denied ice cream, Schmidt grabbed Marchand by the lapels and slammed him against a plywood sign, nearly knocking it over. Marchand let out a pained "oof" but quickly kneed Schmidt in the stomach, breaking his hold.

"Should we break this up?" Lothian asked Emma.

"No one seems in danger. No knives, no guns, and these two couldn't properly fight their way out of a wet paper bag with GPS. I want to hear what else they have to say to each other. They might let something important slip."

The two men descended into a frenzy of wild

blows, cursing, and grappling with the ferocity of grandpas fighting over the last prune danish. Marchand's nose and Schmidt's eye both rapidly swelled up like an allergic reaction to shellfish.

It was less action movie brawl and more like watching two cranky Muppets flail around—but neither seemed ready to throw in the towel and call it a draw.

I winced as Schmidt landed a nasty right hook to Marchand's jaw, sending the mayor reeling.

"Come on. We should break this up before they actually hurt each other," I said to Emma. "Accidents can happen."

But Emma shook her head, green eyes hard.

"Not yet," she said. "They clearly both know more about Angela's schemes than they've let on. We might learn something useful if we let this play out a minute."

The detective in Emma was in full force, willing to allow the brawl to continue if someone's broken nose brought us closer to the truth.

"I treated her like royalty!" Schmidt said, wiping a smear of blood from his mouth. "But it was never enough for that insatiable witch."

My ears perked up at the insult.

Witch?

Just a figure of speech...right?

Marchand dragged himself to his feet, chest heaving. "You foolishly thought you could satisfy her," he shot back. "But Angela craves power, not pathetic shows of devotion." The mayor dabbed gingerly at his rapidly swelling nose, wincing. "And you don't have any power. You're a washed up has been."

Their animosity seemed to arise from a toxic cocktail of political rivalry and romantic jealousy, years of tension brought to a boiling point by the Scarlett O'Hara-like Ms. Hayes and her simultaneously pursued relationships.

But what ambitions had she been pursuing, using both men as pawns?

My gaze snapped to Emma.

"You thinking what I'm thinking?" I murmured.

Emma nodded. "This might be about more than just a sordid love triangle."

Before we could whisper further, heavy footsteps approached the enclosed field. Mayor Marchand whirled, expression morphing to outrage as Vince Briggs marched up to the disheveled pair.

"What on earth are the two of you doing back

here?" Briggs demanded. Taking in their battered, bloodied appearances, he shook his head in disgust. "Assaulting each other in public like a couple of heathens? You're the mayor! You're a former councilman! You both should be ashamed."

The two rivals exchanged a surly, defiant look, but offered no response.

Briggs crossed his arms. "Mayor Marchand, Mr. Schmidt—you're both coming with me to answer some questions. And get those wounds looked at," he tacked on with a frown at their split lips and bruising.

Before Briggs could haul off the disgraced politicians, a woman's biting voice cut through the tense nighter air.

* * *

"Oʜ, I don't think anyone's going anywhere just yet."

We all spun to see none other than Angela Hayes strolling through the entrance and heading straight toward the group. With her tight Elvira costume retired, her blond curls—along with other things—were back to bouncing wildly with each furious step.

At her side strode April, smirking at the unfolding drama.

My fists clenched at the sight of Lothian's toxic ex. April's cruel words still rang in my ears, fueling my frustration with this increasingly convoluted situation.

Angela bore down on Marchand and Schmidt, hands planted on her wide hips. "Would either of you fools care to explain yourselves?" she demanded shrilly.

Both men shifted under her withering glare, wearing matching expressions of dread. Their battered faces evidenced just how dangerously scorned she was by their two-timing betrayal.

Briggs stepped forward, puffing out his chest officiously. "Ms. Hayes, this is a police matter. I need to insist you move along and allow me to—"

He didn't get any further before April—who had been standing slightly behind the detective—pulled a perfume bottle from her pocket and sprayed Detective Briggs.

Briggs's eyes went wide as he inhaled the vapor. He reeled back, stifling a violent sneeze. For a moment, he staggered on his feet. Then his eyes rolled back, and he collapsed like a sack of bricks, out cold before he even hit the ground.

"Briggs!" I gasped, hand flying to my mouth as

I jumped out into the clearing. "What the hell did you do to him?" Beside me, Emma and Lothian flanked me, tensed, ready to spring into action.

April stood over Briggs's limp form and chuckled when she saw me. "Don't even think about interfering. He's fine. He'll wake up with a headache, but that's all." Her gaze slid to her aunt. "Get his gun and grab anything else useful."

With a sly smile, Angela kneeled and efficiently disarmed Briggs as Emma gripped my hand tightly.

I saw through Emma's eyes as she calmly confronted a raging gunman holding a hostage. She spoke gently but firmly, keeping him talking and slowly wearing him down. Buying time until the right moment presented itself.

The memory faded, and I opened my eyes to meet Emma's resolute gaze. Her intent was clear —we would wait for the best opportunity to act. No reckless bravado.

I took a deep breath and gave a small nod of understanding.

I turned to see how we could communicate the plan to Lothian, only to find his gaze fixed intensely on the two of us, his body coiled tight as a spring, muscles bunched in readiness.

It hit me then—Lothian's only concern was

protecting me and Emma. The familial werewolf bond, the need to protect? It overrode everything else for him.

"You realize you just attacked a police officer, right?" Emma asked April.

"I did nothing of the sort. He's sleeping. And he won't remember a thing."

"I will," Emma said. "He will. She will. They will. I know the two of them are pretty corrupt, but they're not that corrupt."

Marchand straightened his rumpled suit jacket. "I'm not corrupt at all." The mayor turned toward Angela Hayes. "He attacked me, Angela. I was just defending myself."

But she silenced him with one sharp look.

"Spare me your excuses." Angela's eyes flashed behind her cat-eye glasses. "I know exactly what's going on here. Did you fools really think I wouldn't uncover your murder of Marcus?" Her lip curled in a sneer.

Both men rushed to deny being involved in any murder, tripping over each other's words in their haste to placate her wrath.

Angela cut them off with a slash of her hand. "Enough! Your deceit ends tonight." Eyes blazing behind her glasses, she turned on Schmidt. "Let's discuss why you really killed Marcus."

My eyes widened. Schmidt had killed Marcus? For certain?

Schmidt recoiled as if she'd struck him.

"W-what? No! Why would you accuse me of that in front of these people?" he spluttered. "Why are you doing this?"

"Okay, wait a second," Emma said, brow furrowed as she scratched her chin in thought. "I'm confused—who's the good guy here and who's the bad guy?"

I let out a long breath, mind spinning. "Honestly? I'm not entirely sure anymore."

Angela barked out a harsh laugh. "Gordon. Did you really think I wouldn't piece together that it was you who bashed Marcus's skull in when he refused to approve your building project?"

Marchand's mouth parted in shock as he swung his stare toward his rival. "It was you? You killed Marcus?"

Grim satisfaction played across Angela's face as Schmidt crumbled under her accusations. "Yes, all right!" he shouted, raking both hands through his receding hairline. "But she told me to! I did it for us, Angela. For our future! You told me that if I did it, you would be the mayor! We were going to blame it on him! I thought that's what you wanted."

"Oh, I do want that, darling." Angela smiled coldly, all traces of warmth gone. "What I don't want is a sloppy loose end like you flapping your gums. You've become a liability."

With lightning speed, April sprayed a cloud of purple at Schmidt, followed by his howl of protest as he collapsed to the ground next to Detective Briggs.

Marchand stumbled back, stunned disbelief etched across his face. "Angela! What are you doing? What is that stuff?"

April winked at Lothian. "This is all thanks to you, you know. You were the one that told me about Paranormopolis and the magic perfumes they have there. You know, it's not that hard to find a witch that can run in and get some for me —especially when I have access to all your money."

"April, what did you do?" Lothian demanded.

I gave Lothian an exasperated look. "Did you ever wonder why we're supposed to keep paranormal stuff secret? This. This is why." I patted his shoulder sarcastically. "Maybe rethink telling humans you're sleeping with about all our top secret info. I'm just saying—it rarely ends well."

Lothian flushed, clearly regretting his past indiscretion. But the damage was done now thanks to his big mouth. At least I could say "I told you so" later.

If we survived, anyway.

Ignoring April and Lothian, Angela Hayes circled Schmidt's prone form like a vulture homing in on carrion. "You are a pathetic excuse for a man," she sneered down at him. "Couldn't keep your mouth shut, couldn't stay away from Marchand until the end of the festival. Couldn't trust me to do what needs to be done."

"What is that perfume?" I asked April with one eye on her aunt.

"You witches have so many! That perfume makes you forget everything about anyone in my bloodline. I gave the witch a drop of my blood and she had someone in Paranormopolis make a batch so I could come back and take what's mine"—she glanced at Lothian—"and my Aunt Angela could take what's hers. That'll show those idiots over in Cassandra that just because you can't talk to ghosts doesn't mean you're useless!"

"No, you're useless because you can't keep your mouth shut!" Angela told her niece. "Do you want to just hand them an outline of the plan?"

"What does it matter? We're just going to spray them with the magic spray."

"Yeah, that might be harder than you think," Emma told her.

"Step away from the two men on the ground," I said as I sent a concentrated bolt of energy arcing from my palm. "Now."

"Oh, isn't that cute," the woman sneered.

Yep.

I'm adorable.

The sizzling blast struck Angela squarely in the chest. She went rigid as the electricity coursed through her. Finally, it ceased, and she collapsed to her knees, gasping.

I hurried to check on Briggs and Gordon Schmidt, forgetting—for a moment—about April Hayes and the detective's gun. The former councilman/current murderer and the fallen detective remained unconscious, but breathing steadily. I exhaled in relief.

"Astra, look out!" Emma yelled.

I whirled just in time to see Lothian's ex leveling a pistol at me, her eyes crazed.

"You shouldn't have interfered, witch!"

A gunshot cracked the air.

CHAPTER NINETEEN

*V*ampires are fast.

Well, they're more than fast.

They're lightning-quick. Faster than a cat on catnip, quicker than a sneeze, speedier than a teenager late for curfew, hastier than a kid dashing to the ice cream truck, lickety-split like Roadrunner from Looney Tunes. Blink and you'll miss their velocity.

I had a healthy respect for the formidable powers possessed by vampires. Far more than just blood-drinking creatures of the night, vampires had an arsenal of supernatural abilities, giving them a lethal edge over mortals.

There was the hypnotic allure, allowing them to mesmerize and twist mortal minds with a concentrated glance. Their herculean strength could easily lift cars and shred metal—even Tara's deceptively slight frame housed that power.

But their speed? It was astonishing. It's a preternatural, supernatural, unearthly speed that makes race cars look like golf carts. They could cross a mile of fairground in the blink of an eye once their vampire hearing detected a conversation clear on the other side of the park that hinted their friends might be in trouble.

One moment, April had the gun pointed directly at my chest, her finger tensing on the trigger as her eyes glinted with malice. Time seemed to slow, the imminent gunshot flashing before my eyes as I mentally kicked myself for getting distracted. I could feel Lothian's terror as he pulled me—as if he could jerk me clear of the bullet's trail.

Which he couldn't.

He wasn't fast enough.

Vampires, on the other hand?

I saw nothing more than a pale streak knock April violently to the ground as the gun shot upward into the air. Like a materialized apparition, Tara wrenched the weapon from her grasp with one sharp twist of her slender fingers and sent it spinning uselessly away, landing so deep in the shadows no one but the werewolves or vampires could find it easily.

I barely had time to thank her before Rex, too, appeared like magic at Angela's back. His powerful arms wrapped around her like a vise and she let out a startled gasp as he pulled her tight against his broad chest.

"It's easier if you don't pull away," he told her politely. "My arms are quite solid, and you wouldn't want to hurt yourself."

"We overheard what was happening and thought we could be of some help," Tara said as she hauled a struggling April to her feet. "It sounded like the situation was getting a bit out of hand."

Before I opened my mouth, Gordon Schmidt bolted toward the exit, eyes wide with panic.

"Hey, stop!" I yelled after him.

"Isn't that man the actual murderer?" Tara asked.

"I think so," Emma said with an exasperated eye roll. "But honestly, I'm going to have to sit down with a pen and paper to connect the dots on this one." She looked at Lothian. "Could you drag the former councilman back here, please?"

Lothian nodded once and caught the out of shape former councilman in seconds.

"Get off me, you psycho!" Schmidt wheezed.

Lothian's expression was stony as he marched the murderer back to the thick of the impromptu meeting. Once the two reached us, Lothian shoved him down next to the still-unconscious Briggs. "Stay," he said.

Schmidt's eyes went wide in terror, and he scuttled back and huddled against Briggs like a frightened crab.

I looked around the clearing to make sure I wasn't missing anything.

Angela Hayes refused to stop writhing in Rex's inflexible grasp, swearing blue enough to make a sailor proud. The vampire seemed unbothered and kept the enraged woman contained as easily as if she were a fussy toddler.

April wilted into Tara's embrace, her arms pinned without resistance. It seemed the fight had gone out of Lothian's volatile ex-lover once she realized her aunt's scheme had failed.

I studied the four in turn: the bitter, discarded girlfriend; the power-hungry civil servant; the corrupt mayor; the murderous, spurned councilman.

What a quartet of chaos these four made.

Emma looked at the captured criminals with

satisfaction. "Well, I'd say we've wrapped up this case, wouldn't you?"

Just then, Briggs let out a low groan, stirring back to consciousness. He took a few heavy breaths, his chest heaving beneath his rumpled jacket as he tried to get his bearings. "What happened?" he mumbled, blinking groggily.

I hurried over and helped him sit up. "You were attacked by Angela Hayes," I said, instinctively not fully describing what took place. "But we've got them under control now."

The detective swayed unsteadily, blinking in confusion as his eyes struggled to focus. "Angela Hayes?" He met my worried gaze, his own eyes still cloudy and dazed from the perfume that had rendered him unconscious just moments before.

"Yep. Can you stand?"

Lothian frowned. "Maybe he shouldn't."

Comprehension slowly dawned on Briggs's face as he took in the scene—Schmidt sitting next to him terrified, the elder Hayes struggling against Rex, April's hands now held by Tara behind her back. "Looks like you cracked this one wide open," Briggs said. He accepted my outstretched hand, and I pulled him to his feet, catching him as he wavered for a moment. "Did I help at all? I can't remember."

"Absolutely," I said.

"Help at all?" Emma said. "This was all you, Briggs!"

Briggs shot her an irritated look. "I guess I should arrest them all immediately."

"Maybe. They're all terrible people, but I honestly don't know that everyone broke the law here." I looked at Emma. "You're better at this than we are—"

"Thanks," Briggs said, crossing his arms over his chest.

"No problem."

Briggs just shook his head, but I could detect a hint of amusement behind his gruff exterior.

"I feel like a prosecutor worth his salt could find something for everyone. April pointed a gun at Astra and made it pretty clear she intended to shoot her—that's an aggravated assault. Gordon is Marcus's murder, obviously. If I were the detective on the case, I'd arrest both Angela Hayes and Mayor Marchand for conspiracy to commit murder—we've all overheard enough shady conversations to suspect they did something shady."

Mayor Marchand straightened his rumpled suit jacket indignantly. "Now see here, I've done nothing wrong!" he insisted, jowls quivering.

"Well, obviously, I had an affair and my wife won't be very pleased about that, but Marcus's murder? That's ridiculous. I knew nothing about that!"

Emma cocked an eyebrow. "Oh, really? So Gordon Schmidt killed Marcus Clinton completely on his own, with no involvement from you or Ms. Hayes?"

"I don't have a clue what that woman knows and what she doesn't. But I knew nothing," Marchand insisted. "Why would I stoop to murder?"

"To get a council seat that will vote with you? To stop his affordable housing proposal? Because he was sleeping with your mistress?" I said, then turned toward Angela. "Wait. I'm losing track. Were you sleeping with Marcus, too, or just these two?"

"I was not! And none of those are reasons for us to kill him!" Angela huffed at me, blond curls bouncing. "Neither of us had anything to do with Marcus's tragic demise." Her lips pressed in a prim line. "We're innocent victims in all this. Victims of circumstance and Gordon Schmidt's vengeful plot."

"I planned nothing!" Gordon said. "It was you! All you!"

"You do realize we literally heard you threaten to kill someone a few minutes ago, right?" Emma asked Angela.

"I don't know what you're talking about," she responded coldly.

"Maybe she got a snootful of April's magic perfume and forgot," I said.

"I had nothing to do with any of—"

"Oh, stow it," Emma said. "You two are about as innocent as Bonnie and Clyde."

Angela gasped dramatically. "How dare you! We were set up, I tell you. Gordon's clearly lost his mind. Isn't that right, Paul, dear?"

She shot a pointed look at the sweating mayor. Marchand swallowed hard, his prominent Adam's apple bobbing nervously, but gave a jerky nod of agreement.

With a swivel of her slender neck, Emma's piercing green stare ricocheted around the circle —Gordon slumped on the ground, the mayor smoothing his disheveled tie with a shaky hand, Angela's ruby lips pursed in defiant indignation, April's icy blue glare burning back. "You know, I still don't completely get what happened here."

"I do."

* * *

SERENA BLISS APPEARED at the edge of the tent enclosure, her flowing white-blond hair and diaphanous rainbow skirt rustling as she strode forward. Tiny glittering crystals adorned her wrists, catching the moonlight with each graceful movement, and they chimed ever so softly as she raised a slender hand to gesture toward us. Her normally serene face was etched with concern, ice blue eyes sharp and assessing.

"Uh oh," Emma whispered, pointing. "Look."

On Serena's heels strode an imperious white-haired woman in an elegant burgundy pantsuit—Mayor Lillian Thornton of Cassandra. The mayor's keen gaze scanned the strange scene, lips pursed in a tight line.

"Fantastic," I muttered.

"You people are making the ghosts nervous," Lillian said, fixing her steely stare on Angela Hayes. The blond shrank back slightly under that piercing look. "What is wrong with all of you?"

"Mayor, please." Serena arrived at the core of the tense gathering, holding up a slender hand for quiet. "The spirits have made everything clear to us," she said, her melodic voice ringing out. "They told us—finally—that Angela Hayes was the mastermind behind a plot to pit Forkbridge and Cassandra against one another."

Angela sputtered indignantly, but Serena silenced her with an icy look.

"Hear me now," Serena continued, sweeping her gaze over the assembled group. "No deceit can hide from the eyes of the dead. We know what Angela has done, and why she has done it. We have come to address not only the crime, but to mend that which allowed the crime to get so close to success."

"What do you mean?" Detective Briggs asked.

"The fault is ours." Serena turned her attention to Mayor Thornton then. "While Angela's actions were driven by bitterness and envy—seeking to deprive Cassandra of prosperity out of spite—her efforts to sow division could not have gone as far as they did if the bonds between our communities had not frayed. And they frayed due to your unwarranted anger toward Astra Arden and her sisters."

I swallowed and watched, unsure of what to say.

And I wasn't the only one.

The entire motley circle of paranormals and suspected criminals seemed mesmerized by Serena and her speech.

"The spirits see all, and they have shared troubling revelations about the darkness infecting this place." Serena's pale blue eyes moved between Angela and Mayor Marchand as if seeing into their souls. "You sought to sow discord between two allied towns. To set neighbor against neighbor."

Angela scoffed, but Serena pressed on, undaunted.

"But the ties binding Forkbridge and Cassandra are ancient and deep." Serena's melodic voice took on a commanding tone. "Forkbridge is a haven where vampires move unseen through moonlit nights, where werewolves roam beneath the full moon's pull. Where witches walk freely, unafraid of pyres. Cassandra is a place where ghosts find solace and comfort among the living until they are ready to move on.

"For generations, an unspoken vow has held these lands sacred. A covenant forged between our ancestors and the Ardens, whose divine magic breathes life into the ancient pacts." Her eyes flashed with conviction. "I say to you all, now—our towns must mend ties sundered by mistrust. Together, we are strong. Divided, darkness prevails. Forkbridge and Cassandra must have leaders worthy of it." She turned her piercing gaze on Mayor Thornton. "And to you alone I say this once more—for you to be that leader, you must forgive Astra for Jason's death. You must forgive, or you must step down."

A charged silence followed Serena's demand.

Mayor Thornton looked at Serena, confliction clear on her face. Her lips pressed into a thin line and her brows knitted together as she seemed to wrestle internally with the demand.

After a long tense moment, the mayor sighed heavily.

Though her eyes still held hints of defiance, it was clear Serena had backed her into a corner she couldn't escape from.

"Very well. You've made your point, Ms. Bliss," Mayor Thornton said. She straightened, smoothing out her blazer. "Serena speaks wisdom. Our towns share a proud legacy." Her expression was wary as she looked at me. "Perhaps it is time to put old grudges aside for the greater good."

I could sense the mayor's displeasure at being forced into this position.

Mayor Marchand looked around wildly, his expression as confused as Cerberus trying to open the dog treats canister. "What the heck are you people talking about?" he sputtered. "Is this some kind of cult initiation?"

Angela's eyes flashed with impatience. "How did you become mayor of a town you knew so little about?" she asked him. "They're discussing matters beyond your comprehension, obviously —mystical forces that have influenced these lands for centuries and which you know nothing about."

Marchand paled, staring between us in disbelief.

"Okay, I think it's time the grownups talked," Emma said sternly, green eyes flashing. With April restrained in Tara's unbreakable grip, she strode over and began roughly searching April's pockets.

April struggled violently, spewing vicious curses, but Emma's face remained stony with determination as she patted her down. After a moment, she extracted a small purple glass perfume bottle.

"Gotcha," Emma said triumphantly, holding up the bottle.

Popping the lid open, Emma waved the bottle under April's nose and squeezed the nozzle. A fine mist of lavender-scented liquid sprayed directly into April's contorted face. Almost instantly, April's protests died away and her body went limp in Tara's arms as she slipped into unconsciousness, head lolling forward.

Emma turned swiftly, aiming the perfume at Angela next. Before Rex could react, Emma misted the concoction into Angela's face. Angela's green eyes fluttered closed as she sagged in Rex's embrace, his arms the only thing keeping the sleeping woman on her feet.

Mayor Marchand had time for a bewildered "What the hell?" before getting a face full of the sleeping-draft-laced perfume, too. He immediately crumpled to the ground, soft snores emanating from his unconscious form.

Emma finally strode over to the cringing, trembling Gordon Schmidt. His pleas turned to muffled coughs as the perfume hit his face at close range, sending him into a deep slumber alongside the others.

Tara and Rex lowered the sleeping bodies to the ground.

* * *

EMMA TOOK charge of the chaotic scene, her authoritative voice cutting through the tense night air. "Okay, let's go over what happened here from the beginning." She looked at Serena. "You speak beautifully, but I'm just a simple girl. I need the plain facts to understand."

Serena nodded. "My apologies."

Emma crossed her arms, gazing around the circle. "Gordon Schmidt killed Marcus Clinton, correct?"

Gordon Schmidt remained unconscious on the ground, unable to respond.

"Yes. He took Marcus's life in a fit of petty jealousy and ambition," Serena confirmed. She shot Schmidt's sleeping form a stern, reproachful look. "Marcus's spirit stopped by on his way to the next plane of existence and let us know."

"And what was the deal with those weird occult coins they kept finding all over city hall?" Emma asked. "Anyone know?"

Lothian spoke up hesitantly. "April ordered them in bulk through one of my companies. But I have no idea why."

I moved over to where April Hayes lay passed out in the dirt and grabbed her limp hand, concentrating on awakening any memories of her ordering the amulets. After a moment, I straightened, annoyed but unsurprised by what I'd glimpsed.

"April scattered those coins around hoping to frame my sisters and me for Marcus's murderer," I told the group, my voice hard. "She thought it would help her aunt and convince Lothian to return to Palm Beach with her. And Angela hoped it would weaken any magical protections on Forkbridge."

"Would that have worked?" Rex asked.

"Honestly, I don't know. There's a lot about what my mother did here that I apparently don't know." I met Serena's troubled gaze. "Why were these two so focused on creating bad blood between our towns?"

A flush of pink colored Serena's cheeks as she averted her gaze, discomfort playing at the edges of her mouth. "There is bitterness in some families without psychic gifts toward those who possess such talents. The Hayes clan has resented their inability to hold leadership positions in Cassandra for generations."

Comprehension lit Emma's face. "So they took over Forkbridge instead?"

"Well, Angela did, at least," I said. "Wow." I looked at the four at our feet. "Well, what now?"

Mayor Thornton turned to me, her piercing gaze steady. "Forkbridge now finds itself without a mayor. Your mother served faithfully on the city council for many years. She understood the need to protect the unseen forces that live here.

We are all vulnerable now that her protection is gone.

"Places like Cassandra only exist because the government allows it, for now. But Forkbridge could attempt to annex Cassandra and consolidate control over it at any time. Our fire protection, police force, education—it is all non-traditional," Mayor Thornton continued. "Cassandra needs allies here in Forkbridge, as this debacle with the competing Halloween festival proved."

The mayor wasn't wrong. Angela's petty scheme could have done actual damage to the allied sister towns.

Mayor Thornton stepped closer, her expression solemn. "Your mother kept watch as a representative of the old ways—whether anyone knew it or not. She oversaw the pacts binding our communities in trust. With her gone, darkness crept in. Forkbridge needs a new leader to bring light once more. One who will honor our legacies and protect our future."

I blinked, momentarily stunned—was she suggesting that I step up as mayor? The possibility winded me like a blow, momentarily robbing me of breath.

"Me?" I finally managed. "But I'm no politician."

A smile broke across her tired face. "No, Astra. You're a guardian sworn to protect—despite Jason's death being evidence to the contrary—"

"Mayor," Serena warned.

"Yes, yes, I know my duty, Serena. I don't mean you, Astra." She glanced meaningfully around the clearing. "One of your paranormal pals here needs to step up. Or your sisters. It doesn't matter who it is, but someone must protect us."

I let her words sink in, turning over the possibility in my mind.

With my mother gone, Forkbridge had lost its ruthless magical Machiavellian secret monarch. The town needed a new supernaturally savvy leader to put its paranormal residents on equal ground with the humans that called this place home.

I met Mayor Thornton's gaze and gave a single resolute nod. "We'll figure it out," I said. "For the good of both towns."

CHAPTER TWENTY

I collapsed into bed, exhausted after the chaotic events of the night. Despite the swirling questions still lingering, my frantic thoughts soon slowed to a lull as sheer tiredness took over. The tension eased from my body and I quickly slipped into a deep, dreamless sleep, worries fading away.

But it wasn't long before a familiar presence stirred me.

I opened my eyes (or so it seemed) to find Athena standing at the foot of my bed, the room awash in soft golden light emanating from the goddess.

"You have done well," she pronounced, eyes glinting with approval. "Bringing together

Forkbridge and Cassandra was a noble act. The bonds between your communities must remain strong."

I sat up. "Yeah, it was definitely eventful. But I'm not sure how much credit I can take."

Athena waved a dismissive hand, the silver cuffs adorning her wrists catching the light. Her expression remained impassive, as if swatting away an irksome fly rather than brushing off a serious accusation. "You give yourself too little credit. You set aside old grudges and forged an alternative path of unity. My gifts chose well when bestowed upon you. Speaking of old grudges, will you speak to your mother now?"

I grimaced, shifting against the pillows. "No."

The goddess' smooth brow furrowed, her radiant features clouding over with a troubled expression. With a soft sigh, she lowered her head. "I understand your lingering anger toward Minerva. But she is still your mother. Will you not seek reconciliation?"

I let out a harsh laugh. "Reconcile? After she lied to us our whole lives, then sacrificed Jason for more power? Fat chance." I fixed the goddess with a challenging stare. "I don't owe her a thing. Not after what she did."

Drawing herself up, the immortal aura of

power and command returned even as her ageless eyes seemed to soften with sympathy. "The bonds between mother and child run deeper than any rift or betrayal. I have faith you will find your way there when the pain lessens." Her form began glowing brighter, limning my bedroom in searing radiance. "The path of forgiveness can be trying, but it leads to peace. Your destiny still awaits, Astra of the Stars."

"What destiny would that be?"

"Until we meet again."

With those last words, the goddess vanished in a flash of divine light, leaving me sitting upright in the dark bedroom once more.

I awoke slowly, clinging to the last wisps of the strange dream. As my eyes fluttered open, I was met with the sight of Archie's face mere inches from my own, his enormous amber eyes unblinkingly fixed on me.

"Gah!" I exclaimed, jolting up in bed in surprise.

"Aw, is someone past their prime?" Archie taunted. "Don't feel bad. All reflexes slow down with old age."

I shot the cheeky owl a wry look as I sat up in bed, rubbing the sleep from my eyes. "Keep it up, wise guy, this 'old lady' can still whip your tail feathers into shape," I retorted through a yawn. "I really missed you this weekend."

Swinging my legs out of the warm blankets, I stretched and shuffled sleepily to the open bay window. Archie glided over to perch on my shoulder, nuzzling against my neck affectionately despite his earlier teasing. "I was worried a couple of times," he said. "For me, you understand. If something happens to you people, I'll have a real problem trying to cook my own bacon."

"Yeah, love you, too, brat," I murmured, scratching his downy head. He leaned into the touch, letting out a contented coo.

I let out a long breath, thoughts churning with everything Athena said.

Maybe one day I would find it in me to reconcile with my mother. To face her and sort through the tangled hurt and betrayal her choices had caused.

But not yet. The wounds still felt too raw. For now, keeping my distance remained the healthier path forward. With time, perhaps forgiveness would come easier. But it would have to happen on my terms when I was ready.

The sunrise was just cresting over the treetops, washing the sky in hues of orange and pink. "Athena was in my dream last night," I said, stroking Archie's speckled back as he perched on my arm. "She's not very direct, is she?"

Hopping onto the windowsill, Archie gazed out at the dawn sky in thought. "The gods don't fret over trifles, Astra. I'm sure if Athena thinks you should speak with mother dearest, it's for a profound cause and not just because the eternal beings crave distraction from the tedium of immortality."

I looked at Archie.

"Well, I mean, it could be some cosmic need for drama, too," he said. "But probably not. I mean, I'm pretty sure it's not." In a startling contortion, Archie craned his neck backward, rotating his head just shy of a perfect right angle. "It's because of some deep cosmic significance, and not just run-of-the-mill meddling." His head cocked skeptically to one side. "I think."

I zombie-shuffled toward the welcoming softness of the quilted bed covers, craving more sleep. "I'm going back to bed."

"Sounds good," said Archie, an obvious note of sarcasm in his voice. "Wouldn't want you to overexert yourself with crazy notions like taking charge of your destiny."

I froze mid-step, looking over my shoulder at the owl perched behind me.

"What?" He blinked his wide, golden eyes slowly. "What did I say?"

* * *

THE NEXT MORNING I came down the stairs just as the electronic doorbell blared its tinny tune. Pulling the door open, I blinked in surprise at the sight of the detective and police chief standing on the front porch.

"Morning, gentlemen," I greeted them. "What brings you by so early?"

"We wanted to give you an update on the suspects from last night's situation," Chief Harmon said.

Detective Briggs nodded. "As soon as they saw the inside of an interrogation room, they folded quicker than a house of cards in a hurricane. Pointing fingers everywhere, just like that meme with the cartoon spider guy my niece showed me on her phone."

"You already knew that Gordon Schmidt was the murderer. Well, he had a recording of Angela Hayes confessing that she orchestrated the whole thing on his phone," Chief Harmon continued.

"Once confronted with that, she admitted pushing Gordon Schmidt to kill Marcus Clinton and to providing the murder weapon."

"When Schmidt did it, she set about making sure the finger would be pointed at you guys," Briggs added. "But she kept enough evidence to pin the murder on him if her frame up job didn't work."

I shook my head. "What a piece of work. I'm glad you have it all on record now."

Chief Harmon grunted in agreement. "Yep. She sang like a canary once we had her in custody. Practically trampled over Schmidt trying to cut a deal first."

"Of course, Schmidt immediately threw himself at our feet, confessing everything and begging for mercy," Briggs said wryly. "He admitted killing Marcus in a rage and claimed he was manipulated by Angela the whole time."

"Crocodile tears if you ask me," Chief Harmon snorted. "The man bashed in another's skull in cold blood. His sniveling doesn't earn him any sympathy from me."

I nodded. "I'm just relieved you have solid confessions. What about April and the Mayor?"

"Prosecutor is going to try to get them both on conspiracy just based on the two of them buying and having those coins, but he's not that optimistic anything's going to stick on either of them," Briggs agreed. "Told us he might use the charges to flip them and make sure Angela and Gordon go away for a long while. We never would have cracked this case so quickly without your help, Astra. And Emma's too, of course," he added. "You two make a good team."

Chief Harmon gave a gruff nod of agreement. "As much as I hate to admit it, we needed your...unique skills on this one."

I smiled. "I'm happy I could assist however I could, Chief. Hopefully, this will close the book on recent tensions plaguing Forkbridge and Cassandra."

"Here's hoping," Briggs replied.

After exchanging a few more details about the case, the two men took their leave. I watched them go, satisfied that justice had finally been mostly served in this convoluted murder plot.

Perhaps now both towns could begin healing and move forward in unity.

* * *

LATER THAT AFTERNOON, as I was tidying up the living room, the doorbell rang once more. I opened the door to find Lothian standing on the porch.

"Hey," he said. "Do you have a minute? I was hoping we could talk."

I gave a wordless nod, stepping back and letting the stained oak door swing wide.

We moved toward the patio door in silence, his leather boots scuffing against the floor until we emerged into the sunshine-bathed patio. I sank into the cushioned seat as he did the same across from me.

For a moment, we just sat in awkward silence. Finally, Lothian spoke up.

"Look, I just wanted to say I'm sorry for how I handled everything with April," he began earnestly. "You were right—I should have been more upfront instead of avoiding your questions. You deserve honesty from me."

I nodded slowly. "I appreciate you saying that. We both have stuff to work on, I think. I know I get defensive about trust pretty quickly, and I probably overreacted without letting you explain or giving you a chance." I gave him a sheepish look. "Past relationships left some scars, you know?"

Lothian's broad shoulders rose and fell as he heaved a heavy sigh, his blue eyes relieved. "Tell me about it. I'm no expert at intimacy and being vulnerable. Keeping things light and uncomplicated was always easier for me." He met my gaze. "But you make me want to try doing this a different way. The right way."

"Whatever that is," I chuckled, reaching over to give his hand a gentle squeeze. "I want that too. I think we both just need to remember to communicate better. And maybe have a little more faith that the other person has good intentions, even if we don't always understand their actions."

Lothian nodded, twining his fingers through mine. "You've got yourself a deal. I promise to be more open from here on out. No more holding back things you deserve to know." Those clear blue eyes regarded me without pretense or guile.

"And I'll try not to jump to conclusions or assume the worst," I told him. A playful smile tugged at my lips. "We'll probably both mess up sometimes. But as long as we're committed to working through it together, I think we'll be okay."

Lothian smiled back, the warmth reaching his eyes. "Together sounds perfect."

He leaned in and kissed me softly.

I knew our relationship still had challenges ahead.

But in the warm cocoon of his embrace, the worries and obstacles facing us melted away, leaving only a glowing kernel of hope in my chest that we had the strength to endure.

CHAPTER TWENTY-ONE

I sat on the back porch, watching the last embers of sunset fade along the horizon as evening crept in. The air held a subtle cool, signaling winter's gradual approach despite the mild Florida climate. Archie perched on the railing beside me, his soft hoots a soothing backdrop to my pensive thoughts. I absently stroked his feathers as I pondered my complicated feelings about my mother.

Minerva's overly harsh protective wards had been intolerant, even paranormally racist in a way. But maybe there was a rationale behind them that the rest of us couldn't fully comprehend. Perhaps she sensed looming threats

I remained blind to, dangers requiring such uncompromising defenses.

Her methods were flawed, but...

I sighed deeply, emotions churning within me like the darkening waves along the shore. There were still more questions than answers when it came to understanding my complex mother and her motivations. But perhaps with time and wisdom gained from my own experiences, I could unravel the reasoning that drove her questionable choices.

For now, I could only hope I'd inherited some of her fierce protective instincts, even if they manifested in less ruthless ways.

The creak of the screen door drew my attention. Emma stepped out with two mugs of steaming tea.

"Thought you could use this," Emma said, handing me a mug as she settled into the vacant chair.

"Thanks. You read my mind." I cradled the warm ceramic, letting the minty aroma soothe my senses.

"Ha! I wish."

For a few moments, we sat in a comfortable silence. The first twinkling stars emerged overhead as dusk settled around us in hues of indigo and violet. A tranquil energy seemed to enfold the pair of us.

Finally, Emma spoke up. "Quite the weekend, huh? You okay after everything?"

I took a sip of tea before responding. "I'm doing all right. Still processing, honestly."

Emma nodded. "Understandable. It's been a rollercoaster few days." She smiled wryly. "At least the murderers are behind bars now."

"There's that," I agreed with a small chuckle. "Hopefully, things will calm down now."

Just then, the screen door creaked open again, and Ami stepped out onto the porch. "Mind if I join you guys?"

"Not at all! Pull up a seat," Emma said, patting the chair next to her.

Ami settled in with a tired sigh, tucking a loose strand of hair behind her ear. "I'm exhausted. The shop was packed all day with people stocking up on potions before leaving town."

Archie ruffled his feathers, turning his sharp golden gaze on Ami. "Yes, we've established it was a busy day. Now, don't you have something more interesting to share?" He angled his head meaningfully toward the house. "Perhaps regarding a certain divine paternal figure?"

Ami's cheeks flushed pink. "Oh, right. Well...Hermes and I had a long talk earlier. I know he can't undo years of absence, but I'm choosing to give him a chance." She met my gaze. Her shoulders tensed, brow furrowing as if bracing for a verbal blow, certain I'd chastise her for extending an olive branch to someone so undeserving. "He seems genuinely remorseful and committed to building a relationship now."

Seeing her tense anticipation, I reached out to lay my palm over her balled-up hand, hoping the supportive squeeze eased the fight-or-flight tension coiled within her. "I'm proud of you, Ames. I know that couldn't have been easy."

"It wasn't," Ami acknowledged, relieved. "But I'm hopeful we can find a way forward together."

Just then, the door groaned open a second time and Althea stepped out holding a bucket containing bottles of homemade ginger ale. "Aunt Gertie's ginger ale is ready. She said she gave it a bit of an extra protective punch. Anyone want one?"

She passed the drinks around before settling cross-legged in one of the empty chairs.

"So, Thea, I heard you and Tara really hit it off," Emma said, a playful smile dancing on her lips.

Even in the dimming light, I could see Althea's cheeks flush. But she held Emma's teasing gaze evenly. "We did. She's incredible—so smart, worldly, confident..." A dreamy smile crossed Althea's face. "I know it seems fast, but I feel like we really connect, you know?"

Ami smiled warmly. "That's so wonderful, Thea. We're happy for you."

"Thanks," Althea replied softly. "It feels good to be open about it all, finally. I just don't know how we're going to make it work, though. She sleeps all day, and I have to work at the shop during the day. It's hard."

I reached down and gave Althea's shoulder an affectionate squeeze. "You'll figure it out. And we're all here to help."

A creak of the porch heralded Ayla's arrival, followed by an enthusiastic Cerberus. "Hey guys," Ayla greeted us, plopping down beside Althea and giving her big dog a scratch. "So Melvin just left, and you'll never guess what he told me..."

As Ayla regaled us with the latest happening in Cassandra, I leaned back contentedly in my chair. After the tumult of the last few days, it felt good to unwind with my sisters and best friend, sharing laughter and comfort.

When Ayla finished her story, a comfortable

silence settled over the group. Archie resumed his soft hooting from his perch. The evening stars glittered overhead like scattered diamonds against velvet.

Emma turned to me, green eyes thoughtful. "So, I have to ask. Have you spoken with your mom at all since Athena said you should?" she asked.

Ami and Althea exchanged a loaded glance at the delicate question.

I stiffened, the ease of moments before evaporating.

I knew I shouldn't have told them about the nocturnal visits.

I busied my hands stroking Archie's feathers. "No," I said after a taut pause. "And for the moment, I'm not going to."

Sensing my defenses going up, Emma hesitated before responding. "I understand she hurt you all deeply. But holding on to anger can be exhausting." She touched my arm. "Maybe talking could help heal things between you two?"

I shook my head sharply, dislodging Emma's hand. "What's there to talk about? She wasn't truthful at any point, but Jason's the one that got shafted because of her actions." My voice hardened. "I don't follow Athena. No matter what the goddess said, no matter what she wants from me, who I forgive is still my choice. And right now, I just can't."

A heavy silence followed my biting words. The others exchanged worried looks, but no one seemed inclined to argue further.

After a long moment, my shoulders slumped. I gazed out into the darkening backyard, regret softening my expression. "Sorry," I told Emma. "None of that is your fault, and I didn't mean to snap at you."

Ami slid over and wrapped an arm around me. "It's okay. We understand."

Althea reached up and laid a comforting hand on my knee. "Whenever you're ready, we're here."

Emma gave me an affectionate shoulder bump. "You know I've got your back, no matter what."

With a small, tired smile, I met Emma's compassionate gaze. "I know. Thank you, Em."

Together, we sat in companionable silence as the stars above shone ever brighter. For now, it was enough to be here, unified by bonds of family and friendship that I truly believed could weather any storm.

* * *

THANK YOU FOR READING!

I hope you enjoyed **Owl Out of Magic**. Please think about leaving a review! Astra, Archie and the whole Arden family continue their adventures in Book 15, A Hoot and A Hex.

KEEP UP WITH LEANNE LEEDS

Thanks so much for reading! I hope you liked it! Want to keep up with me?

Visit leanneleeds.com to:

Find all my books…

Sign up for my newsletter…

Like me on Facebook…

Follow me on Twitter…

Follow me on Instagram…

Thanks again for reading!

Leanne Leeds

FIND A TYPO? LET US KNOW!

Typos happen. It's sad, but true.

Though we go over the manuscript multiple times, have editors, have beta readers, and advance readers it's inevitable that determined typos and mistakes sometimes find their way into a published book.

Did you find one? If you did, think about reporting it on leanneleeds.com so we can get it corrected.

ARTIFICIAL INTELLIGENCE STATEMENT

Portions of this book were created with the assistance of AI tools used for editing, proofreading, and refining the text. However, the ideas, storyline, characters, and overall creative vision remain my own original work.

While some aspects of the cover image were generated using AI tools, it was done so under my creative direction and curation.

I want to acknowledge the use of these technologies as part of my creative process, while affirming that the essence of this work comes from my own imagination and effort.

Leanne Leeds

www.ingramcontent.com/pod-product-compliance
Lightning Source LLC
Chambersburg PA
CBHW021431240626
47153CB00001B/103